WILKENSON Cole

SBL 2-89

TRAPP AND WORLD WAR THREE

Having exploited the Royal Navy as a profit-making enterprise in *Trapp's War* and instigated a lunatic clash with Arab and Chinese gangsters in *Trapp's Peace*, Trapp is back – as unrepentantly devious and self-interested as ever. In his latest hulk, *Charon II*, he commands an equally undisciplined and cowardly gang including those very few survivors of his previous escapades, the awful Gorbals Wullie, blind Second Officer Spew and the psychopathic Bosun Bligh. He's even succeeded in conning the eminently sane Chief Officer Miller, who detests Trapp of old, into joining his appalling ship as her unfortunate second-in-command.

On this occasion they are lured by a two-million-dollar bait into sailing a curiously well-armed team of 'mercenaries' to Libya, for what Trapp believes will be a glorified bank heist. Of course it doesn't quite turn out that way, whereupon Trapp and his moronic shipmates find themselves the focus of a Serious International Incident. Even the Captain's irrepressible optimism is dented when *Charon II* finds herself on a collision course with some ominously unidentifiable torpedoes in the Gulf of Sirte . . .

Brian Callison provides hilarious adventure as his misbegotten hero once again precipitates major hostilities in the Med. The Superpowers are completely baffled by who is firing at whom, and why. In fact the only absolute certainty is that it was all Trapp's fault.

By the same author

A FLOCK OF SHIPS
A PLAGUE OF SAILORS
THE DAWN ATTACK
A WEB OF SALVAGE
TRAPP'S WAR
A SHIP IS DYING
A FRENZY OF MERCHANTMEN
THE JUDAS SHIP
TRAPP'S PEACE
THE AURIGA MADNESS
THE SEXTANT
SPEARFISH
THE BONE COLLECTORS
A THUNDER OF CRUDE

BRIAN CALLISON

Trapp and World War Three

COLLINS
8 Grafton Street, London W1
1988

William Collins Sons & Co. Ltd
London · Glasgow · Sydney · Auckland
Toronto · Johannesburg

First published 1988
Copyright © Brian Callison 1988

BRITISH LIBRARY CATALOGUING IN PUBLICATION DATA

Callison, Brian, 1934–
Trapp and world war three.
I. Title
823'.914[F]   PR6053.A39

ISBN 0 00 222887 4

Photoset in Linotron Trump Medieval by
Rowland Phototypesetting Ltd
Bury St Edmunds, Suffolk
Printed and bound in Great Britain by
William Collins Sons & Co. Ltd, Glasgow

Prologue

It has to be conceded that Trapp really didn't mean to do it on purpose.

That in the final analysis he caused World War Three to break out in much the same manner that he'd achieved most things – by sheer accident. Or, more accurately perhaps, by accident precipitated by that obsessive greed of his, the factor common to all other such seamarks of maritime perfidy trailing in the wake of the bloody-minded Captain's haphazard voyage through life.

Come to that, he would have proved quite capable of having started the Second World War as well – and more than likely by pure mischance then too – only Hitler thought of it first. All Trapp could contrive in the end was to turn what threatened to be an unsettlingly profitless situation to his advantage when he chartered his utterly appalling coffin ship and even more revolting crew to the Royal *Navy*, for God's sake! Only to steam forth on that occasion sporting the White Ensign, His Britannic Majesty's weaponry and an RN Commission, yet still finish up doing battle with the *Kriegsmarine*, the *Luftwaffe* and most of Rommel's *Afrika Korps* strictly on his own account . . .

However, *Trapp's War* is another story which, despite its having been hastily expunged from all Admiralty records on the very first day of peace, nevertheless remains embarrassingly documented in the more lunatic annals of infamy.

To say nothing of being constantly and excruciatingly

5

recalled twice nightly during my own tormented hours of sleep, notwithstanding its having taken place half a lifetime ago and me now a master mariner in my own right.

So, to be grudgingly fair to Trapp, he probably didn't mean to this time. Not actually to cause a whole shooting war to break out between the Superpowers, that is. His view had always been that global hostilities, with or without the added nuisance of nuclear exchanges, do tend to act as irritants disturbing the free flow of international trade – or at least that euphemism would broadly reflect Trapp's own shameless portrayal of his one-man crusade in search of the god Profit; in reality the Captain's tunnel-visioned determination to exploit every avenue of seagoing villainy from common smuggling, illegal immigration and sanctions-busting, through the finer nuances of maritime fraud, barratry, arms dealing, Collusion With An Enemy and strictly non-aligned freelance spying to, last but by no means least, the good traditional swarm-aboard-an'-spittem-lads craft of piracy.

So perhaps it was as well that Edward Trapp cherished slightly more laudable views on the actual ethics of the skulduggery trade; on the contractual responsibilities incumbent upon those jointly engaged in such entrepreneurial fields of commercial endeavour.

Well, if he hadn't evinced *some* principles, any chap who unwittingly became involved with him might otherwise have presumed the Captain simply to be an overbearing, conceited, illogically dogmatic, utterly amoral bastard altogether. A thoroughly anti-social pariah without any redeeming features at all.

Oh, not that *I* ever imagined Trapp to be quite as awful as that, mind you.

. . . I mean, after having barely survived that Second World War lunacy as First Lieutenant of Trapp's supposed 'Q'-ship *Charon* and her predominantly moronic ship's company, followed by a brief but equally traumatic association with him and his ocean-roving band of neanderthal troglodytes during the subsequent peace – well, after that experience I knew for *certain* that he was!

Seemingly it all began – Trapp's involvement with World War Three, that is – in the dim-lit Alley of the Tasselmakers, better known to Ottoman locals as Püskülcüler Sokak, just before the point where it links with Keseçilar Caddesi, that noxious Street of the Sheath-makers within the Great Covered Bazaar of downtown Istanbul.

Mercifully I hadn't become embroiled in this latest manifestation of Trapp's kamikaze penchant for international intrigue at that juncture, but the locus of its spawning doesn't surprise me. Because the subject of money invariably dominates any Bazaar conversation within eavesdropping range of the Beyazit and Nurusmaniye Mosques, it was precisely the sort of area to which Trapp naturally gravitated on arrival in every port – or as soon as he'd satisfied himself that his corroded command wasn't likely to sink at its berth while he nipped ashore anyway. A bit like an opportunist flea that finds itself drawn irresistibly to the nearest warm flesh in the hope of bleeding it dry.

And equally predictably, talking of insects, Trapp was accompanied as ever by the sub-humanoid figure of one Gorbals Wullie, a creature of vaguely Celtic public house origins who undoubtedly represented a quality-control reject from the mould for the original Cretin. I retain an indelible memory of the first time I ever set eyes on Gorbals Wullie – and on Lieutenant Commander Edward bloody Trapp RN as he then was, too, for that matter. July 1942 it had been, during the blackest days of the Mediterranean war. In Valletta's bomb-torn Grand Harbour, with the slipstreams of departing Stukas still ripping the billowing sandstone clouds of Maltese debris to

7

tatters and the so-gallant survivors of *Operation Pedestal* still fighting the crippled tanker *Ohio* through to relieve the besieged island.

Me a disillusioned young Naval Reserve Lieutenant at that time, and Wullie a typical member of the loathsome ship's company which wartime expediency and a particularly sadistic admiral had decreed I should join. It was to prove an unnerving precursor of the shape of nightmares to come – the spiteful, undernourished apparition of a cloth-capped Gorbals Wullie prancing and waving two fingers while challenging hysterically, 'Poofy officer . . . Poofy officer! Hey youse – Jesse lad wi' the fancy uniform. C'mon ower an' gie's a square go at ye, Nancy boy!'

Certainly it had been an imaginative way for a newly drafted Royal Naval rating to welcome his First Lieutenant aboard, though to be absolutely impartial about the revolting little wimp I soon discovered that Wullie never was able to express himself in other than manic-aggressive or whining-cowardly terms. In more ordered social circles the moronic little matelot couldn't have held his own in a conversation with an Action Man doll.

. . . which brings me neatly back to Trapp, and to Istanbul in much more recent times, and the globe-threatening events which began to gather momentum following that most curious happening on Puskülcüler Sokak.

It seemed that the Captain, volatile as a negotiator at the best of times, particularly when it came to laying his own private funds on the line, had positively been approaching lift-off temperature during a particularly stubborn haggle with a commercial adversary of long standing, the venerable merchant Korkut Tokoglu the Fifteenth. On this occasion their barney was over a prayer carpet – or rather, a couple of hundred carpets.

Trapp had set his heart on screwing the old Ottoman

miser to a rock-bottom price. He felt compelled to, in order to get any satisfaction at all from the deal. Prayer-carpet running didn't offer much *cachet* in international crime terms, being more or less legitimate for a start, so it was mainly as a small side cargo he had Korky's gear in mind; a bit of extra ballast to help defray the overheads of yet another of the Captain's bread-and-butter forays into the esoteric field of Middle Eastern contraband running.

But periodically, when the market for entrepreneurial villainy was at a temporary ebb, Trapp had a penchant for returning to the south-eastern Mediterranean waters which he knew so intimately, in which a profit could be turned simply by dodging either the Egyptian Navy, the Israeli Coastal Forces, Qaddafi's gunboats and/or the entire US Sixth Fleet, depending on his destination at the time.

It so happened that Trapp had the Lebanon in mind as the beneficiary of his free trade enterprise on this occasion. Everything was arranged – Charlie Franjieh's only slightly bullet-riddled ex-Syrian Army transport column, fresh from ambush and with replacement healthy drivers, would be anticipating his arrival six nights hence, off a discreet beach situated just outwith Christian Militia artillery range to the north of Beirut. Trapp's contract with Charlie was to deliver two thousand cases of Bulgarian whisky substitute, covertly distilled by leading Serbo-Croat scientists in a wooden shed at the back of the State petrochemical plant in Burgos before being tarted-up most convincingly by a pure artist seconded from the Stara Zagora Police Department's fraud squad.

As a consequence of this technology-based Balkan beavering, the final product bore the sort of Gaelic proprietary labels guaranteed to bring not only a dryness of the throat and a nostalgic mist to every expatriate Scotsman's eye but, more practically for Trapp, a hurried fumbling for convertible currency in an economically favourable civil war situation.

And it wasn't as if the Captain was ripping the luxury-deprived punters off to no advantage at all. Hell, a few really hard-case war correspondents had even been known to live for several days after drinking the stuff – Gorbals Wullie and one or two of Trapp's other lads actually rated it a considerable improvement on their standard shipboard bootpolish and Brasso sundowners ... However, Trapp never did get to rendezvous with Charlie Franjieh at the appointed hour as things turned out. Which was a pity considering the trouble the little Lebanese hood must've gone to in order to become owner-manager of a whole column of Soviet-built trucks in which to move the consignment, plus incidental Syrian military cadavers. But what Charlie later threatened to do to the Captain wasn't unique – he would've had to wait his turn in a multinational queue of villains who coveted Trapp's guts, for a start – and has no place in Trapp's precipitating World War Three anyway.

Which, after all, *is* what this particular story is about.

Chapter One

''OW much each, you robbin' Turkoman coot?' Trapp finally exploded.

Gorbals Wullie sniggered, thoroughly at home in the rancid perpetual gloom of the Great Covered Bazaar. Apart from which he always felt more secure while Trapp's parsimonious vitriol was being directed at someone else.

'Maybe he's gi'ing youse a price f'r all twa hundred carpets, eh Captin?'

'Shut UP!' Trapp snarled automatically. 'You couldn't negotiate your way out o' a rice paper bag, dim brain . . .' The Captain went a deeper shade of choleric. 'Look at 'im. Go on, then – *look* at the bloody old pirate now! Shrugging 'is shoulders, he is. Like he din't even want to do business on an internashnul level.'

'No, no, NO sair!' Tokoglu the Fifteenth's bejewelled hands protested in dramatic denial tinged with just a suggestion of abject surrender, the performance made only slightly less convincing by Trapp's having regularly been treated to much the same routine over the last forty years. 'OK! So I discount these magnificent silk carpets, each superb creation painstakingly fashioned by the crippled fingers of my mother and my twelve sisters mark you, sair, by – and even though Allah will undoubtedly strike me blind that I should place my family in such dire financial jeopardy on uttering such foolishness – by say, one Turkish lira twenty five *kurus* . . . ? But only special for you, Mistair Capitan Trapp sair. Only as a token which, though it will leave me destitute as any pitiful beggar in the Bazaar, reflects the overwhelming respect, consolidated over many years of our association, that I hold for your superiority as a business gentleman.'

'My, but he *can* put things into words,' Trapp said admiringly, forgetting momentarily his negotiating stance in the face of such irresistible flattery. 'You gotter give him that. 'E's a real old pro when it comes to screwin' the prospect.'

Wullie's eyebrows screwed together under the peak of his scrofulous, oil-stained cap – the same one he'd been wearing back in 1942, when I first met him.

'Aye, but who's he kiddin' aboot bein' prostitute?' the little seaman demanded, uneasy lest Trapp's wrath be diverted back to him. 'We seen him oorselves, didn't we? Less than an hour ago. Gettin' out've that fancy white Cadillac driven by yon mulatto bird wi' the big tits an' the false eyelashes, doon by the Galata Bridge, mind?'

'My mother, sair,' the ancient Tokoglu interjected hastily.

'Ah thought *she* wis too busy fashionin' silk carpets wi' her crippled fingers,' Wullie jeered triumphantly. 'And onyway – if your mither's still in the business she must be near on a hundred an' fifty year old if she's a day, grandpaw – *and* we ken fine half o' your twelve sisters is drawin' the pension, while the ither half is a' oot on the game, scorin' wi' the Yankee tourist punters ower by the Tree of Idleness.'

'Apart from which,' Trapp returned to the fray with deceptive mildness, 'not only are them pure silk, dye-fast prayer carpets o' yours artificial, but the colour runs as soon as water touches 'em. *And* they wus manufactured in bloody Taiwan – I know that 'cause it wus me helped you evade the import tax on'em less than three months back, Korky me old matey . . . Now you discount by two twenty-five each an' you're on!'

The white beard of Tokoglu trembled as if palsied. 'May Allah look with grace upon the worthless spirit about to be drawn from my tormented body. Pleese, you are *murdering* me, Mistair Capitan Trapp! You sentence me to a lingering death over the unhappiness I feel at having to deprive you of the joy which your ownership of these carpets would bring. My once strong heart –'

'Now weakened by too much screwin' at yon big mulatto bird you thought f'r a minnit wus your mother?' encouraged Wullie helpfully.

'We are a very close family, sair.'

'A round two lire then,' Trapp proposed, cheerfully unmoved by the prospect of the aged Turkoman's imminent demise. 'Off've each. You deliver to the ship.'

'One fifty! Not one miserable *kuru* more!'

'One eighty!'

'One sixty-five. Cash in my unworthy palm! And may Allah grant me forgiveness by His understanding that I have obviously become stricken with madness.'

'Done!' Trapp suddenly looked anxious at the prospect of parting with actual money. 'You, er – you wouldn't consider takin' American Express, would yer?'

'You *gotta* be joking, pal!' Korkut Tokoglu the Fifteenth jeered forgetfully but Trapp, with uncharacteristic tolerance, pretended not to notice. The old brigand was still an artist and it couldn't have been easy, learning the Grand Covered Bazaar routine after having spent the first half of a long career in the con business as one of Capone's numbers game touts working the Turkistanian reaches of nether-Chicago.

'Course I'll need the usual papers,' Trapp reminded him. 'Certifyin' them as bein' at least two hundred year old, every prayer guaranteed to bring results an' every carpet used personal by the Grand Vizier to Ali Pasha hisself.'

'Naturally. Perhaps you will be so kind as to wait one

minute, Capitan sair? I go to my humble office to prepare the appropriate documentation.'

The ancient salaamed low while ringing down for full astern, withdrawing obsequiously backwards through bead curtains concealing what appeared to be only a black hole even more noxious than the rest of the Turk's cramped place of business.

Trapp preoccupied himself with inspecting the multifarious tourist bargains festooning that mystic eastern emporium of Tokoglu the Fifteenth. Genuine nylon bearskins shot in the Palandoken Mountains; rare Armenian silks manufactured in South Korea; 2,000-year-old solid gold toothpicks from the King of Bithynia's royal table, only recently disinterred by a Birmingham brass founder's sales rep; rare Islamic manuscripts by fourteenth-century Erzurum scribes, every one crafted at least a week before over in Sahaflar Carsisi, the Market of the Second-hand Booksellers down by the Gate of the Spoon-makers . . .

Gorbals Wullie, meanwhile, had fixed his beady eyes on the wad of notes gripped in sad anticipation of their farewell by Trapp's vice-like paw. 'It must be braw,' he said, risking just a tinge of spite, 'to hae money. Is that the crew's wages doon the tubes again, then?'

Trapp automatically batted him on the starboard ear. 'Mind yer own bloody business, Mister! Anyroad, what would that foc's'le full o' beatniks want wi' wages? They daren't go ashore to spend 'em anyway. Most've 'em have to hide out o' sight below all the time we're alongside – on the *Most Wanted* lists of every police force between Murmansk an' Port Swettenham, they are.'

'Aye,' Wullie fawned, hastily trying to curry his Master's favour. 'Ye've signed on a braw bunch o' lads this trip, Captin – every wan a top qualified man an' that's a fact.'

There came a muffled *thud* from the back of the shop,

and a slight scuffle. Trapp pursed his lips critically. 'Dark as a Sudanese stoker's ass through there, an' Korky gettin' blind as a bat. 'E'll have to spend money on rush lamps or 'is gift for forgery'll go all to hell.'

They watched idly as one of the Bazaar *hamals* came by. Bent almost double and protected only by a thickly padded *semer*, the huge Anatolian porter still managed to make carrying a grand piano all by himself look easy.

'Now if I could sign one o' them monsters on ship's articles,' Trapp debated thoughtfully, 'I could save a reglar fortune on repairs to her derricks an' cargo handling gear.'

'You don't *do* ony repairs tae the cargo gear,' Wullie pointed out reasonably. 'That's how Sammy the Acid Man got hissel' squashed by that sling-load of Peter Stuyvesants thon time off Macao. Stubbed oot by bluidy near two ton o' fags, so he wis.'

'He was warned cigarettes could be dangerous to 'is 'ealth,' Trapp retorted unfeeling. 'Said so on every bloody packet that fell on 'im – all seventy-five thousand of – !'

From the dark inner sanctum of Tokoglu the Fifteenth there filtered a bubbling liquid cry. It was just the sort of appeal you'd expect to hear a business associate make when he . . . well, when he gets his throat cut, or something.

Gorbals Wullie, a worldly veteran of many terminal mêlées and thus being not entirely unfamiliar with such plaintive indications of discomfort, immediately froze rigid while the Captain's eyebrows met in a ferocious 'vee' of concentration.

'Ah suspect, Captin,' Wullie diagnosed nervously, 'that you an' me have gone an' got oorsel's in the shit. Again!'

'Shurrup an' lissen!' Trapp hissed, his eyes suddenly very hard.

Because immediately following upon that ghastly alert, and despite the cosmopolitan hubbub from the *sokak* outside, the Captain detected the quite unmistakable slither of Turkish slippers being dragged across a Grand Covered Bazaar floor.

. . . the great misadventure, which was to precipitate the Third World War, had begun.

With measured precision Trapp replaced the wad of currency in the inside pocket of his reefer, then meticulously checked again – just to make certain it really was secure. Then, and only then, having satisfied himself that the most important precaution had been attended to, did he turn his mind to the lesser concern of seeing Gorbals Wullie survive to whine and cringe another day.

That he himself might not was a consideration which never entered the Captain's head. But then, in that egotistical belief lay the whole nub of why Trapp always *did* rush pell-mell into situations which would cause any normal person – even a moderately cautious potential suicide, come to that: one only toying with the general idea of self-destruction – at least to think again . . . the bloody man's sublime faith in his own immortality.

You see, Trapp cherished an absolute conviction that he, himself, was destined to be a natural survivor. He'd maintained it ever since the time, many decades before, when child-sailor and then starry-eyed Midshipman Edward Trapp, Royal Naval Volunteer Reserve, had found himself alone in mid-Atlantic: the only remnant of a four-hundred-man complement who'd fought and died for King and Country aboard his first warship, a very gallant but quite inadequately armed convoy escort.

Oh, he'd had a bit of company for the first few days. Though 'bit' had sadly been the operative word because his companion had only been the top half of a rating who'd come floating by, still clinging to an admittedly very welcome liferaft. But gradually the sea creatures reduced even his part-shipmate until he was no company at all for little Edward, and that had upset the boy too, because possessing even a part of a friend was better than having no friend at all.

Ten days of absolute loneliness and suffering later, while still many hundreds of miles from land, little Edward had grown to resent his country for what it had done to him and to his by then totally disappeared late companion, and to all the other shipmates he had lost. The opinion had begun to form in his young head that patriotism and the principle of giving your life for others left a great deal to be desired, and that selfishness seemed to be a much more practical trait to develop when planning a chap's future.

By the twelfth day Midshipman Trapp had got quite fed up with everything and made up his mind to die. But then a tiny reddish-coloured fish flipped itself clean out of the water and on to his liferaft. Little Edward ate it even while it was still gasping and staring at him with bulbous, reproachful eyes. It was his first lesson that the personal feelings of others are not necessarily paramount, and that greed can be a very satisfying emotion. Certainly it kept him alive for seven more days until he was finally rescued.

By the enemy. A German raider. Which helped him get better, then transshipped him to a prisoner-of-war camp where he starved yet again and learned an even greater hardness, fine-honing his ability to survive for two whole years more.

When Edward Trapp finally became a free man he had developed a pathological hatred for nationalism and for futile ideals, for those who created so-called laws and those who prescribed the rules of a society he considered immoral anyway. He'd proved that he could survive, not by being a jolly decent patriot but by greed and animal cunning. In essence, he'd learned to look after Number One, and sod the rest of the bloody world.

Oh, maybe, when Trapp did emerge from that holo-caust as the only man alive out of a ship's company of four hundred, he'd formed the wrong conclusion regarding his way ahead. It didn't really matter – Trapp, apparent survivor or no, had still become a casualty of war every bit as much as any blinded airman or military amputee.

It was to make him – as many who underestimated him had already discovered to their ultimate cost – a mercilessly unforgiving, indeed a most terrible man to take liberties with.

Having satisfied himself that his cash would survive at least as long as he did, Trapp then fell back on the seaman's oldest and most trusted formula.

'Abandon SHIP, Mister!' the Captain ordered in a bellow which had been known to upstage a typhoon's roar, whereupon he himself immediately set course, not without a certain frayed dignity it has to be conceded, for the exit to Tokoglu's suddenly unwelcoming place of business.

It goes without saying that the urging of his Master's voice proved quite superfluous to Gorbals Wullie, that sneaky wee matelot already racing full ahead as he was for the companionable protection of the crowded *sokak* like a cloth-capped Halley's Comet. But then, Wullie always had observed three strict orders of priority in life when it came to extending his own: Wullie first; then Wullie – and then Gorbals bluidy Wullie! Probably much the same sort of objective approach to self-survival en-ables other organisms of similar station to Wullie, like gastro-enteritis bacilli, to evade everything modern medi-cine can throw at them.

Only this time the usually reliable ploy didn't work.

A large – no, a bloody great MASSIVE! – silhouette materialized before the steaming mini-Scot and simply stood with folded arms, blocking all but a few vagrant chinks of light still filtering weakly around the edges of the doorway. Cannoning head-down into this inflexible Goliath, the unnerved Wullie bounced off with skinny legs still going like a blur, returned for a second go with the determination of a billiard ball projected from the cush then, accepting that the subtle approach had failed, began to pummel the monster's belly while all the time bawling, 'Let me *oot*! Aw Jeeze, let me OOT ye bast . . . !'

Trapp, a true connoisseur of the *fait accompli* if there ever was one, immediately abandoned his current flight plan and ground to a halt. 'Stop HITTIN' 'im!' he bellowed warningly to Wullie. 'Or 'e'll . . .'

The man mountain lifted one fist and ever so gently allowed it to drop upon the bonnet of Gorbals Wullie. Wullie went down like a pole-axed ferret and lay still.

'. . . flatten yer!' Trapp concluded, somewhat unnecessarily.

He didn't turn immediately and attempt to withdraw through the curtains which concealed Tokoglu's inner sanctum, anticipating with bitter certainty that there wouldn't be any point. The earlier indications of the merchant Turk's abrupt demise told him that their one remaining evacuation route would already be occupied.

He didn't have to wait long. Confirmation came in the form of an indisputably American voice from behind. Quite a mild one. Almost conversational really.

'The little guy: now he seems a real fighter, Captain. Real spunky. But you see the big fellow at the door there? That's Hermann . . . And Hermann gets this irresistible inclination to crush a man's skull with one hand when he gets upset. Rather like a ripe melon, sir. In a juice press?'

The spunky little guy tried to sit up, clutching his head.

'I'm still goin' to have a hell of a job,' Trapp warned

bleakly. 'Keepin' my Chief Officer from tearin' your man's throat out.'

Gorbals Wullie surveyed the lower slopes of Mount Hermann through one bleary eye; muttered an awed, 'Och, *Jeeeeeze*!', and promptly lay down again.

'. . . once 'e gets really mad, that is,' Trapp qualified with superhuman aplomb.

He swivelled calmly – and very carefully. There were three of them. The one in the middle, obviously the leader, showed iron-grey hair, appeared to be in his late forties and wore white leather shoes setting off a neat tropical suit. Though he stood quite relaxed, merely watching Trapp with a certain cold amusement, the Captain nevertheless sensed with professional intuition that the amusement factor was liable to prove very short-lived indeed.

Rather as, he bleakly suspected, the now late Korkut Tokoglu the Fifteenth had already discovered. More'n likely within ten seconds of White Shoes and Company having introduced themselves via his back door.

There wasn't a lot to notice about the other two. Other than that they were pointing folding stocked Israeli *Uzi* sub-machine-guns at him, that was; and in a manner which suggested familiarity based on regular usage.

They didn't look at all amused. Just cold. A deadly impassivity.

While there was still Hermann, of course. Looming silently astern and as stolid as a blockading hulk across the doorway. Trapp decided to implement Exfiltration Plan B.

'Me an' him,' he indicated Gorbals Wullie who was still lying discreetly rigid on the floor, 'we're goin' to let you off lightly. We're goin' to walk out of here nice an' quiet, an' without trouble.'

'NO, ah'm not!' Wullie said emphatically. 'Ah'm no' getting *mah* heid squished intae a melon salad, ah'm no'.'

'Damn, but you've called my bluff at that, sir,' the cool American conceded with enormous good humour. 'Obviously there's no way by which Hermann would perpetrate an unfriendly act like that. Not just because you insist on your right to be free men. Hell, no.'

'That's all right,' Trapp afforded generously. 'An' I have to say I don't blame you f'r tryin'.'

'Hell, no – we'll just shoot you both! One shell each. In the belly!'

Trapp turned triumphantly to leave. 'See? Now I know he's bluffing. C'mon, get UP, Mister – 'e woul'n't *dare* let 'em pull triggers in a crowded place like thi – !'

White Shoes jerked his chin. Each flanker placed a six-round burst to port and starboard of the prostrate Gorbals Wullie. The cramped emporium reverberated deafeningly before filling with cordite smoke.

Ever so slowly Trapp's confident expression melted as, from outside, the hubbub of chatter from the bustling *sokak* continued unabated above the background clamour which formed a steady accompaniment to the daily life of the Grand Covered Bazaar.

But that peripheral cacophony *did* sound just like repetitive machine-gun fire when you came to think about it: echoing as it did from the adjacent Street of the Tinsmiths – every last Ottoman mini-industrialist hammering the Istanbul iron like crazy. Until then it hadn't occurred to Trapp that you could fire a bloody field gun along Püskülcüler Sokak an' nobody would notice . . . !

The Captain directed one glare of withering contempt at his Chief Officer, now curled into a terrified fœtal ball with haze still rising lazily from bullet holes either side of him, then caught sight of his watch with feigned surprise.

'Oh, it's only *that* time!' he exclaimed. 'Well, in that case I might just be able to spare a few minutes f'r a chat, after all.'

But give Trapp his due, even then it wasn't so much the prospect of being blown away Chicago-style which was finally to persuade him to extend his chat with White Shoes into – for the Captain, at least – a totally magic conversation.

Lord, no!

No, Trapp being Trapp, and naïve to the point of idiocy when the prospect of gain was dangled before him, it was more the content of his new host's next somewhat dry invitation which did it.

'Splendid! Then tell me, Captain: how would you like to earn yourself and your crew, say – two *million* dollars?'

. . . now *that* was the sort of bait which was guaranteed to keep Edward Trapp hanging around until the waters of the Red Sea parted for a second time!

'Two . . . million . . . *dollars* . . . ?' Trapp muttered faintly and for the tenth time.

'C'n ah get up now?' Gorbals Wullie asked cautiously from the floor.

'Shut up an' lie still,' Trapp snarled dazedly. 'Don't irritate them: I gotter think.'

He took a firm grip on himself. Moral justification to enter into further discussions was what was desperately needed here . . . All right! So maybe the old Turkoman *had* got hisself terminated in a somewhat bloody an' abrupt manner. But on the other hand, Korky always had been a bit o' a philosopher: he must have accepted he'd chosen a dodgy career, ripping people off like he'd been doin' f'r the past seven decades . . . therefore merely acting as the Hand o' Allah in itself, so to speak, din't necessarily mean the suave – and obviously well-funded – American had to be *all* bad, did it?

But there again, there had to be a principle or two involved somewhere along the line. Ethics – plus his

22

basic negotiator's aversion to being seen to be too enthusiastic.

He jury-rigged an especially sour look.

'An' what about my existing commitments then,
Mister? I got a contract already. With Korky an' my
shipping agent in Beirut.'

'Correction, Cap'n,' White Shoes said mildly. 'You *had*
a contract. The carpet business has just . . . ah – gone into
liquidation? The Turkish gentleman back there asked me
to tell you.'

'It must've been difficult f'r 'im,' Trapp muttered
darkly. 'Speakin' through a slot in 'is windpipe . . .'

He brightened as a further mitigating possibility struck
him. 'Hang on! You workin' for the Chicago *Mob*, are
yer? The boys from the Mafia . . . ? Catchin' up with
Korky after all these years.'

'Och, bugger Korky!' Wullie whined plaintively. 'Whit
aboot me, then?'

A slightly confused expression flickered in their new
host's eyes. But there again, anyone confronting Trapp
for the first time tended to finish up looking like that.

'The Chicago Mob?'

'Yeah!' Trapp leered cleverly. Always an incurable ro-
mantic, suddenly it was all falling into place. 'Korky
ripped Al off at the numbers game all them years back,
din't he? An' now you an' your boys – the Sons of Al
Capone – have come to extract the Mafia's bloody due.'

'That wis yon crappy movie we saw las' year in Port
Said,' Wullie jeered, caustically forgetful of his current
predicament. 'Ye'd have tae be off your heid tae imagine
that wis f'r real!'

'*You* thought *The Beast from Twenty Thousand
Fathoms* wus real,' Trapp countered devastatingly. 'You
wouldn't go out on deck on your own f'r a whole voyage,
so shut UP!'

Hermann the Melon Squeezer hadn't budged an inch

23

all this time, but the two gunmen on either side of White Shoes looked distinctly nonplussed. Presumably Murder Most Foul, to say nothing of their *Uzi*-based superiority, had seldom been ignored before: certainly never so blatantly, and in favour of an academic dispute between film critics. Their previously suave leader frowned uncertainly too. Quite incredibly under such circumstances he sensed the situation getting beyond his control.

However, Gorbals Wullie was positively wriggling like a spiteful centipede by this time, heels hammering on the Bazaar floor with long-suppressed frustration. 'Oh, aye . . . ? Ohhh, AYE? So it's gettin' doon tae personalities now, is it? Then whit aboot thon pitcher wi' Gregory Peck innit? When you thought you wis Admiral bluidy Hornblower f'r *months* after . . . !'

'CAN IT, both of you!' the suddenly not-so-quiet American roared. 'Forget your goddam MOVIES . . . !' He regained his disintegrating composure with obvious effort. 'Now you hear me, and you hear me good, Captain! My name is Buck Weston – Colonel Buck Weston! And I came all the way to this goddam oriental grease spot to offer you two million goddam DOLLARS . . . !'

'I din't know you had military ranks,' Trapp persisted. '*Who*, f'r Chrissakes?'

'You! The Mafia! The Sons of Al Capo . . . !'

He trailed to a diplomatic halt. All trace of amusement had vanished from the Colonel's eyes. Now they'd turned flintlike, deadly, and even Trapp had enough sense to recognize the virtue of silence on occasion. Particularly once he'd stretched the thread of tolerance by which his life hung almost to breaking point.

Apart from which – the Captain had already achieved precisely what he'd set out to do anyway!

From that moment on the intriguingly-styled Colonel Buck Whatsisname would begin to underestimate him: presume him an easily diverted simpleton – which Trapp *was* in my opinion, mind you: though I do seem to be the only man to have confirmed it through experience and still kept on living. But nevertheless to make such an elementary second mistake about the Captain when you've only just completed making your first: namely, threatening him with machine-guns in addition to – no matter what convenient justification Trapp's perverted reasoning had contrived for such a foul act of murder – wrecking one of Trapp's so damnably sacrosanct business deals by liquidating the other half of his contract . . . Well, that's the most reckless error you'll ever have made in your life.

For even though he'll continue to growl in beetle-browed negotiation, betray an unquestionably genuine avarice when you talk finance, blandly convey the impression that your deplorable lack of ethics has been overlooked in the mutual pursuit of profit . . .

Whether by one of the Captain's fondly imagined Machiavellian designs or, as is rather more likely, by sheer lunatic misadventure – no good can possibly come of it for *you*!

Now it may have been that the so-called Colonel Weston's tolerance was betraying signs of strain by then, but so far as lacking a sense of humour when negotiating a deal goes Trapp would easily score points off a Spanish Inquisitor. Take it from me, no such expression as 'Funny Money' has ever existed in the somewhat earthy lexicon of Edward Trapp.

Which was why, suddenly, that unconscious air of pantomime which Trapp always seemed to generate in times of hazard evaporated. He'd overcome his initial euphoria at the amount of funding on offer: it was business now. As a sort of tribute to Korky.

'This offer o' yours – what do I have to do to earn it, Mister?'

'Simply land me and some of my boys on a beach. Discreetly.'

'And roughly, where might this simple beach o' yours be located?'

'Roughly?' The Colonel shrugged. 'North Africa!'

Trapp pursed his lips doubtfully, displaying the pessimism which was his standard negotiating posture. 'You got any idea of what that coast's like nowadays? You got wall-to-wall gunboats from Syria clear round to Tangier, all driven by Ayrab fanatics, trigger-'appy at a dolphin splash.'

'We're talking two million US dollars, Trapp!'

'Oh, I appreciate that. An' that's what worries me – the limited budget!' The outrageous old miser actually managed to make such a sheikh's ransom sound like a social security handout. 'Course, it depends on what else you want me to do. F'r instance I might be able to trim back on overheads a bit; shave down the running costs . . .'

'That's mah wages he's talkin' aboot,' an outraged voice snarled from deck level. But Gorbals Wullie was still simmering over the *Beast from Twenty Thousand Fathoms* slight. 'Och but ah'm gettin' bluidy fed UP wi' him, so ah am!'

'Your little friend's not the only one!' the Colonel snapped harshly. It seemed his cool American posture was coming under strain, too. 'Now you cut out the hard-to-get act, you hear? I know all about you, Trapp. Two million bucks says "yes" in your language even if I wanted to charter you and your barge f'r a voyage to Hell an' back!'

'If that *was* where you wanted to go,' Trapp countered mildly, 'then me "barge", as you choose to call her, Mister, would be aptly named if nothin' else.'

Which simply proved that the Colonel didn't know that much about the Captain after all because, had he really done his homework, then he should have been a very apprehensive man. Trapp Mild was Trapp at his most unforgiving.

'Meaning?'

'Just that I call her *Charon II*. After me first ship what got lost in the war.'

'So?'

'So: accordin' to legend Charon was the mythical blue-jacket who used to ferry a certain cargo across the River Styx. To Hades!'

'What certain cargo?' Weston growled, somewhat at a loss again, but Trapp just grinned his most amiable grin. A close observer would have noted however that it didn't extend to his eyes.

'Souls, mister,' he said softly. And with only the merest hint of promise. '. . . the souls of The Damned!'

Just for a moment it seemed as though a shadow passed over the man in the white suit. Abruptly he gestured and the *Uzi* barrels lifted for the first time. It was a small but significant victory for the Captain.

'I specified a voyage to Hell *and* back, Trapp. You'd be well advised to remember that.'

Trapp deliberately chose to ignore the qualification. 'Then we'd better examine a few more specifics – like, where exactly Hell does lie accordin' to your charts, mister?'

Weston shrugged again. Rather too casually. 'Libya.'

'Oh, aye? Well, count me oot!' the intrepid Wullie immediately informed the ceiling.

'By Saint Elmo's fire, but it does get more an' more appropriate,' Trapp beamed. 'Finish up in one o' Mu'ammar al-Qaddafi's jails an' you might well wish you 'ad chose the other place.'

Gorbals Wullie lifted his head experimentally. Nobody shot him so he hauled himself gingerly to his feet. 'Dinnae lissen tae him, Captin. Thon Qaddafi's a nutter,

27

so he is. Since he took charge Libya's got mair polis than bluidy camels: most o' them religis fruit-cakes . . . The polis, that is – no' the camels.'

It was the one sensible comment Gorbals Wullie had ever made in his totally misbegotten life, but ignoring sound advice also happened to be Trapp's particular forte. The Captain's eyes narrowed calculatingly.

'Well, you claim you don't intend stayin' – an' I can't say as I blame you f'r that – so it can't be illegal immigration you have in mind. While Libya ain't much of a magnet to the tourist trade nowadays, especially not for US citizens. And spies is out on the principle that they don't usually get landed by the coachload . . . so these, ah, "boys" of yours who aren't Mafia, mister? What exac'ly *are* they then?'

The Colonel hesitated. 'Let's simply call them "a military formation", Captain.'

'You mean they're mercenaries?' Trapp translated bluntly, never a slave to euphemisms other than those he coined to describe his own activities. He couldn't resist a small jibe either; just to square away for the 'barge' insult. 'Which jus' makes you a mercenary colonel then? Not exac'ly like bein' a proper army officer.'

Strangely his adversary didn't react as strongly to that slight as one might have expected. But there again, Trapp was too busy being clever as usual, so any significance it may have held was also missed.

'I didn't come here to argue semantics, Trapp,' White Shoes retorted mildly. 'Anyway, what the hell difference does it make, what we're called?'

'It's an important contractual point, that's what,' Trapp insisted dogmatically. 'It's the diff'rence between chartering my *Charon* as a warship or just as a passenger liner, mister . . .'

'A *passenger* liner?' Gorbals Wullie struggled to overcome sheer disbelief. 'You talkin' aboot the same heap o' rust doon the dock as I am?'

Trapp directed a vitriolic glare towards his Chief Officer before continuing. 'All right. But I gotter know if they're all goin' to be kitted out with firepower like your two muppets there? Or d'you just propose to send Hermann in as a one-man *Panzergruppe* to knock out Qaddafi's local home guard when we arrive?'

For the first time in a while the Colonel smiled bleakly. 'We'll be suitably prepared I can assure you, Cap'n. By the time you land us at the target.'

'Ahhhhh,' Trapp breathed. 'I *sussed* you was expectin' to buy a bit more than a P & O cruise f'r your two million dollars. So where – an' what precisely – is this "target" you have in mind, mister?'

'A small harbour on the Gulf of Sirte – Ras al Djibela?'

'I know it. Up Shit's Creek.'

'I guess you mean Shi'ite's Creek, sir?'

'I know what I'm sayin',' Trapp countered levelly. 'Used to act as a sea link to the Trigh Capuzzo – the old bedouin caravan route across the Western Desert. But apart from a few Ayrab houses there ain't nothing there now 'cept flies, *agam* scrub an' dust devils.'

'Plus a bank.'

It was Trapp's turn to blink uncertainly. 'A what?'

'A bank, Cap'n. A small branch of The Bank of the Socialist People's Libyan Arab *Jamahiriyah*.'

Volatile as ever, Trapp immediately began to flush with fury. 'A small branch o' the . . . ? You SAID you wus payin' me in Uncle Sam money, mister – not Mickey Mouse dinars filched out o' the pockets o' half a dozen bedouin bloody CAMEL dealers!'

It was then that White Shoes delivered what must have been his long anticipated *coup de grâce*. Straight to Edward Trapp's Achilles' heel.

'It also happens to contain three . . . *billion* . . . United

States dollars, Captain. In genuine, legally circulated bills!'

There was a very long silence. Until: 'Ohhhhh, Jesus!' Trapp was heard to mutter faintly.

Weston's expression was almost restored to its original good humour with, perhaps, just an added *soupçon* of malice. But you could hardly blame the Colonel for savouring his little triumph, could you? Not after the way in which Trapp had looked his original gift-horse straight in the mouth.

'We intend to take out precisely two million to meet your expenses, sir. And then . . . '

'An' then?' Trapp echoed numbly. But he already felt an appalling presentiment.

The veil of dry amusement lifted. The Colonel had known all along that he held the power to hurt Trapp – to wound the avaricious mariner to the depths of his very soul, in fact – and he did so with exquisite relish.

'Then we *burn* the rest, Trapp . . . to ashes!'

Chapter Two

The quite preposterous letter caught up with me in Rotterdam eight days later.

Under any other circumstances I would probably have ignored the wretched thing as a joke, but it so happened that I'd just found myself on the beach for the very first time in my life – a neat seaman's euphemism for unemployment, my previous British owners having finally succumbed to the Western shipping recession and sold out to Third World interests. It meant that my command of the past four years, which also represented the last vessel to sail under their once-proud house flag, was by then half-way to Chusan flying a Panamanian Ensign, manned by a cut-price crew and in the charge of an 84-year-old Korean master on a salary roughly equivalent to a bowl of fried rice per day.

I gave them a fortnight before they blew her up, ran her aground or collided with yet another fifty thousand tons of inadequately-manned bargain buy in the middle of the night.

. . . As it turned out I should've stayed with her. It would still have been a bloody sight safer than opening that damned letter.

Captain S. Miller, the dog-eared brown envelope was addressed in large, almost childish script. *Master, M.V. Andes Star, c/o Europoort Harbour Office, Rotterdam . . .*

Postmarked Istanbul?

Curiously, to say nothing of somewhat gingerly, I opened it. A trans-European rail ticket fell out. One-way third-class off-peak to the port of Brindisi on the heel of

Italy; heavily discounted in some Turkish bucket shop and thus representing the cheapest possible means of travel without actually using your thumb. Whosoever had purchased it hadn't exactly lavished megabucks on the creature comforts of its intended user.

There was also a scrap of paper torn from a cheap notebook and apparently stuck together with what looked suspiciously like jam. Once I'd carefully prized it apart the writing displayed the same lugubrious hand.

It said:

deer mister miller : if you
want to make a lot o money
be outside the trattoria Amico
opposit the stazione centrale
at Fifteen undred hours any day
from Nex tuEsday fr a week
after ··· you reely will make
a lot o money ⟩ i can
promis You
signed A Friend·····

PS this is ded serious that you
will make a lot o money··⟩···
otherwise i wouldnt spEnd a
fortune to get you ere
Would i ?

It was so outrageous, so utterly ludicrous to imagine that any mature recipient would treat it as other than a practical joke that, jobless or no, I laughed a lot before I threw it and its equally insanitary enclosure into my waste bin.

. . . I arrived in Brindisi at midday on the following Tuesday.

Well *I* hadn't associated that stupid train ticket with Trapp, had I . . . ? I mean, I'd neither seen nor heard from the bloody man for several indescribably precious years. Not since he'd virtually hijacked me into his lunatic brush with Zarafiq the Ice Man, the coffin ship *Kamaran* and Mister Chang's Hollywood–Oriental hoods – it seemed utterly inconceivable that, during the intervening period, nobody had contrived the wit to sink Trapp clear to the bottom of some satisfyingly deep ocean; preferably along with that Gorbals Wullie Thing of his, the one that still persists in leering at me from the middle of most nights – as well, for that matter, as Trapp's one-eyed and totally illiterate Second Officer Spew who couldn't recognize another ship on a collision course even when it was less than a heaving line's distance off; not even if it was lit up like a Christmas tree and firing bloody parachute flares . . . ! And his equally degenerate bosun, Choker Bligh, of course; who'd always hated me and only ever spoke to me in sentences of one word, all of which started with 'F' . . . Oh, and not to forget the gallant Captain's nauseatingly oil-marinated Chief Engineer Maabud something or other who'd seemingly been Chief on the *Cairo Flyer* for fourteen years before he joined Trapp's demented complement – which would, I concede, have formed a splendid testimonial to his expertise in maritime technology except it turned out that the *Cairo Flyer* just happened to be a bloody RAIL-WAY engine . . . !

33

But then, Maabud whoever-he-was had got himself killed on that occasion anyway, hadn't he? Or had he . . . ? See what even *thinking* about Trapp does to me? Death and disaster followed so routinely in the Captain's tortuous wake that it gets difficult to pick out the highlights . . . Oh God, but why did I ever go back to my bin to take a closer look at that *rotten* letter?

Anyway, I did. Then I sat toying with the insanitary thing and frowning thoughtfully.

'Face facts, Miller!' I told myself reasonably. 'Europoort's full to the gunnels with unemployed ships' masters right now, so prospect-wise it seems you've run hard aground anyway. It follows you're just as likely to pick up a berth in Brindisi as anywhere. Added to which, fate has provided you with an opportunity, however unlikely, of making . . . er, *a lot o' money*, was it? – while quite apart from all that irrefutable logic, you always have, by nature, been an inquisitive bastard who's never learned the sense to leave well alone. So . . . ?'

So I got on the train. And thus was I to be found shortly thereafter sunning myself outside the Trattoria Amico on Brindisi's Piazza Garibaldi with a dewy cold Italian beer before me, the seabag containing my wordly effects on the littered pavement beside me and, despite constantly niggling reservations about the sanity of whoever wrote that letter, a rising sense of excitement at what the future might hold. The guileless, *Boy's Own Paper* kind, it was. The pleasurable butterflies-in-the-tummy kind, the like of which I hadn't experienced since I'd left home as a first trip cadet.

Such blissful naïvety didn't last very long. I'd only sat for a few minutes before a starkly familiar voice from astern replaced all my happy butterflies with stomach-turning prickly things.

''*Allo* Mister,' it greeted sardonically. 'So you turned up after all then?'

34

Followed by an even more grating chord sparking memories thought long past.

'Och, but ah'm fair chuffed tae see yous again, Mister Miller sir. So ah am.'

I didn't turn around. I just stared fixedly at my drink and, the moment my initial panic had abated, assured it ever so carefully, ever so clearly: 'You do not exist. *I* am not awake! I am sound asleep and perfectly safe in my bunk aboard ship, and I am merely experiencing yet another cruel delusion.'

'Whit's Mister Miller talkin' tae his glass o' beer fur?' the still mercifully disembodied whine of one called Gorbals Wullie demanded uncertainly.

'Jus' shurrup an' show a bit o' respect f'r yer new Mate!' the this-time quite unmistakable growl of Edward Trapp retorted cheerfully.

There came a long and uncertain silence. Until.

'But *ah'm* the Mate.'

'You *wus* the Mate! Now a proper officer's turned up you're back ter deck boy which, considerin' you still 'aven't figured out which end o' the pencil's the one what draws the course on the chart, is all you're fit for anyroad!'

'Och, shit – demoted again,' the voice of Wullie-remote gloomed. 'That's mah career prospects wi' Cunard doon the tubes f'r sure this time. Ah keep tellin' you, Captin – ah'm gettin' *bluidy* fed-up, so ah am!'

I gathered too late that Trapp had sent the letter, largely because this ectoplasmic dispute on a sunbaked Italian piazza appeared to assume my own participation in disasters yet to come. Certainly I was forced to accept that I *had* to be awake by then. No common-or-garden nightmare could've contrived a fate so hideous as sailing as Trapp's Chief Officer yet again. Not for a third time.

'Go away, Trapp,' I pleaded. 'I'd rather not turn around to look at you 'cause it'll just bring on another nervous breakdown like last time ... *Please*, Trapp?'

'Now what you needs, Mister,' he beamed as he settled himself square before me nevertheless, 'is a nice bracin' sea voyage.'

Fighting rising hysteria I glared at the keenly remembered figure. He hadn't changed a lot. A little older, a little more unshaven and weatherbeaten maybe, but still Trapp the super-confident; Trapp the indestructible; Trapp the Ageless. Trapp the eternal Peter Pan of the high seas, though undoubtedly more like Cap'n Hook when it came both to aspect and morality!

On second thoughts – more like Hook's pet bloody crocodile!

He hadn't varied his rig of the day much either. While he'd never exactly shown himself burdened by sartorial consciousness I swore Trapp was still wearing the identical battered reefer and filthy once-white sandshoes he'd sported as a Naval Lieutenant Commander plaguing the *Kriegsmarine* out of Malta – and the wretched man had looked like a survivor from a sunken collier's engine-room even then. Certainly steel-grey eyes observed me calculatingly from below the peak of the very same battered seaman's cap with the more or less severed top which waggled jauntily every time he moved, reminiscent of the lid of a carelessly opened can of axle grease.

Then Gorbals Wullie shambled within the periphery of my dazed vision and . . . Oh, dear Lord, but how *do* you describe something dressed like a recently disinterred corpse?

'Is this no' braw?' the awful creature leered. But his long association with Trapp had taught Wullie fatalism if nothing else. Obviously he'd already come to terms with yet another instant demotion. 'It's jist like old times, Mister Miller sir. Are ye . . . ah, plannin' tae finish yon beer then?'

'Shurrup an' sit quiet, yer greedy git: din't I buy yer one las' month then?' Trapp bellowed loud enough to make every patron of the Trattoria Amico swivel in fright – and *they'd* all been screaming their heads off at each other in conversational Italian for ages.

'Anyroad,' the Captain continued, totally unabashed, 'Mister Miller here an' me 'ave matters to discuss which need brains, so that counts you out!'

'No we haven't, Trapp!' I snarled, fighting a desperate rearguard action. 'I don't want to see you, to hear from you, to have anything whatsoever to DO either with you or with your lousy crowd of seagoing hoodlums and cosmopolitan bloody cut-throats ever AGAIN!'

'Told ye it wis jist like old times,' Wullie said, looking pleased. 'He still gets on with yer good as ever, Captin.'

'You took me money quick enough,' Trapp grumbled, suddenly petulant.

'You mean that cut-price rail ticket?' I fumbled in my pockets urgently. 'I'll refund it. Look, I'll give you back twice the amount. I'll even give you a clean piece of paper to replace the one you wrote the note on . . .'

'It's not a question o' money,' Trapp dismissed heavily. He looked strangely sad then; sort of defeated somehow. 'It's jus' that . . . Ah well, but then again you say you ain't concerned with my problems, Mister: my misfortunes. An' you bein' the one ex-shipmate I reely thought I could call a friend, too.'

I knew I was beaten then. That all hope had finally gone. It was a new Trapp sitting before me; an even more subtle, lying, totally convincing reprobate – and *I* hadn't even been able to cope with the old one.

'Ohhhh, go ON! Purely as a matter of academic interest, tell me why you're here, Trapp. Why *I'm* here,' I muttered wearily. 'But I warn you now – if you argue your case till bloody sunset you *still* won't be able to give me one good reason why I should feel obliged to help you . . . !'

*

'You *sure* you've got cancer?' I queried suspiciously.

'The Big "C", Mister,' Trapp nodded sombrely then drew a deep, shuddering breath. 'Riddled wi' it, I am. All through me hull like Toledo Worm in a wooden frigit!'

'And you've only got one month to live?'

'Lookin' on the bright side – yes!'

I chewed my lip while Trapp watched me keenly. He must've seen there was still some doubt because he sighed bravely, then added, 'That's why I needs yer to sail as me First Mate one last time. I gotter have someone I c'n trust to take command o' the old *Charon II* if . . .' His voice broke a little. 'Well, if I should be called to sign aboard God's heavenly barge afore me current contract's finished.'

I eyed him in fascinated silence, debating the consequences of Trapp's joining God's ethereal complement. I strongly suspect that should such an unlikely invitation ever be extended, then even a hardline saint would find himself hard pressed to resist questioning the Lord's basic wisdom. Admittedly God's conscience may leave Him little option once Trapp's been turned down flat as a potential hand on the Inferno's watch and station bill. Satan's a sly devil: he'll foresee that the Soul of Trapp Damned will've seized command and be steering Hell itself to a profit before his diabolical crew gets the grasping Captain half-way across those Stygian waters.

I've always reckoned that's the reasoning which lies behind the myth of The Flying Dutchman, actually – that spectral mariner who eternally sails the stormy seas off the Cape in search of safe harbour: an omen of ill-luck, doomed for ever to be sea-tossed and never to find rest . . . ? Now *he* was probably a disruptive old bastard just like Trapp. Neither Heaven nor Hades was prepared to gamble its future stability on offering him a berth!

'Don't yer see, Mister? 'Ow I gotter think o' my poor lads,' Trapp pressed bravely. 'How I gotter provide f'r them boys when they has to manage without me. A sort o' legacy of love, you might say. From a man who likes to think on 'em as a father.'

'That's the most beautiful thought you ever thunk, Captin,' Gorbals Wullie whispered with a little twinkling tear coursing down his filthy, unshaven cheek. 'Och man, but yon speech wis magic. Pure poetry, so it wis.'

'Aw, shurrUP!' Trapp growled, momentarily forgetting this was heavy melodrama he was into.

I simply had to force the prospect of my being nominated surrogate paterfamilias to Trapp's macho brood from my mind. Even the remotest possibility would've been enough to finally tip me over the edge of sanity.

Instead I concentrated hard on the positive aspects, curious as they appeared. He'd already told me about the unusual Colonel Weston and the fortune in US currency allegedly stored within the Ras al Djibela bank and – though it nearly broke Trapp even to speak about burning real money – what the Colonel proposed to do with the rest of the three billion dollars . . . I didn't believe that final part for one minute, but I wasn't exactly pro-Libyan bankers, I was still unemployed and, I have to confess, I liked the sound of the wages.

'*How* much did you say this contract is worth to you and your crew, Trapp . . . Honestly?'

His eyes became beacons of absolute piety. 'Wun million dollars, Mister. As God stands to be me judge, so 'elp me.'

Wullie's eyebrows collided roughly in the middle. 'Here, did yon Yank no' offer ye TWO mill – ?'

For some reason he fell off his chair and disappeared below the table just then, so I didn't quite catch the end of the sentence. I do remember thinking sympathetically that if the spasm which had suddenly caused Trapp's foot to lash out was symptomatic, then it must have been a

particularly virulent fatal illness the Captain had con-
tracted.

'And this odd-ball Colonel – he didn't happen to mention who was hiring him, did he?'

'The airlines, o' course,' Trapp said matter-of-factly,
giving the impression that I should've guessed that all
along.

'The what?'

'The *airlines*, Mister – they're the ones hiring Weston
an' his mercenary team.'

I gazed at him blankly. I accepted I was talking to
Trapp, but now we appeared to be advancing from his
routine bizarre to the utterly grotesque. He leaned forward confidentially.

'It's a secret concertina . . .'

'Consortium?'

'. . . o' internashnul airline operators. They're pickin'
up the tab for Weston's part o' the operation. Course my
share – er, ours I mean – gets taken out've the bank before
they . . . they . . .'

'Before they what?' I pressed enjoyably.

'You *knows* what! I already told you once,' Trapp
gritted.

I shook my head innocently. 'I've forgotten.'

'. . . before they BURNS the rest, damn you!'

A further shocked hush fell over the Trattoria Amico
while the locals all had another stare. Trapp's pained
whisper finally broke the silence.

'Oh, Gawd: three *billion* dollars. Uppa bloody funnel!'

'He's gettin' over it, mind,' Wullie volunteered encour-
agingly. 'First time yon Colonel telt him what wis tae
happen we couldnae get his pulse tae work f'r ten
minnits . . . He still wakes up cryin' in the night, though.'

'So,' I retorted meaningfully, and with feeling, 'do I!'

I sipped my beer for a minute or two, leaving
Trapp to suffer. Wullie's beady eyes watched my glass

covetously but I ignored the little wimp. For the first time I felt I was in control.

'I don't suppose it's ever occurred to you to wonder,' I said eventually, 'just why an alleged secret consortium of the world's top airlines should wish to hire some mercenary hit squad to break into a bank in Libya, steal enough US currency to pay off the Brazilian national debt – then simply incinerate it?'

He brightened then, and looked clever. But only Trapp's conceit was greater than Trapp's avarice.

'That's jus' where you're wrong, Mister. I drew it out o' him subtle like. Without his realizing it.'

'That,' I thought cynically, 'will be bloody right!'

Well, apart from Trapp's being about as subtle as the Hordes of the Vandals on the rampage I had a pretty shrewd idea that if Colonel Buck whoever-he-was hadn't wanted Trapp to know anything, then Trapp wouldn't have prized it out of the mercenary with a marlinspike.

Which in turn suggested that the Colonel had deliberately shown his hand. Or the hand that he wanted Trapp to see, anyway. And that suspicion worried me a lot.

'It ain't exactly a secret,' Trapp expounded triumphantly, 'that the Libyans are behind a lot o' the terrorist airliner hijacks. Nor that the airlines themselves are bein' hit hard by the consequent drop in business on account've the fact that, nowadays, passengers what planned ter go to Rome or Vienna are more'n likely ter finish up spendin' their 'olidays in the middle o' a runway being entertained by some nutcase Palestinian with a Kalashnikov.'

'So?'

'So the airlines have finally got thoroughly brassed off with Qaddafi, that's what. Only they can't get no real action against him from their own governments, so they plan to put the skids under the Colonel themselves – unofficially, o' course – by destroyin' all the funds he's secretly stashed away to finance the next round o' inter-nashnul terrorism.'

'Those funds being hidden in the Ras al Djibela bank vault?'

'God, you're quick, Mister,' Trapp retorted sarcastically.

I ignored him loftily. As Gorbals Wullie had said, it was just like old times, while the story did make sense. I didn't accept it totally, but it certainly sounded plausible. And I had to concede that the mercenaries' choice of attack transport was well conceived. Trapp, along with his awful ship and even more awful gang, was just the man to make a flash foray into Fortress Libya a possibility. Whatever I thought of the Captain he'd been conducting covert operations against the North African coast ever since Hitler's day.

I thought, 'What the hell? Being unemployed at my age – I might as well resign myself to the worst.'

'Well, are you in, Mister?' Trapp growled impatiently.

'One thing I must have your personal assurance on first,' I stressed firmly.

'What?'

'That fatal cancer of yours? You've got to *promise* me you'll be dead within the month.'

Chapter Three

Half an hour later, still dazed by the growing realization that I'd actually agreed to participate in one of Trapp's crazy adventures yet again, I found myself apprehensively following the Captain's pointing finger across a narrow stretch of polluted water towards his latest pride and joy, the undoubtedly not-so-good ship *Charon II*.

In keeping with Trapp's custom in every port where law and order maintained even a tenuous footing, it seemed that not only had he painted her name out but he'd also discreetly berthed her as far from the local *stazione di polizia* as possible: adjacent in Brindisi's case to a squalid shipbreakers' yard strewn with the decomposing remains of long-ago vivisected craft.

It was a depressing sight for any seaman to reflect upon, that desolate maritime abattoir. I brooded morosely that the Italian scrap business must, like myself, be suffering from recession. Apart from what had to be Trapp's second *Charon* only one other vessel, an ancient and rotting hulk of probable Greek or Cypriot origin in ages past, lay alongside the jetty of the yard itself, for-lornly awaiting the torch. Mind you, if trade was bad they'd probably decided against expending the effort. More than likely economics would eventually force them to tow the poor old lady back into the Med then sink her. It wouldn't take much to give her a decent burial – they'd only have to poke a hole in her side with a finger.

'Well? What d'yer think then?' shipowner Trapp

pressed deadpan, trying hard to keep the self-satisfaction from his voice.

My attention went back to the other ship.

'I'll grant you she's better than I expected,' I conceded grudgingly. But I wasn't going to let Trapp see my relief at finding his latest command – or rather more pertinently, my new First Mate's berth – not only managing to stay afloat without all bilge pumps working flat out, but with a hardly noticeable list at that. Someone was even painting her hull a pleasing blue. Once they'd finished and replaced her name on the bow she promised to be quite a respectable ship altogether.

'Din't I *tell* yer I'd gone up-market – that she wus a tiddley boat, Mister?' he beamed. 'There ain't a luxury liner afloat with a better pedigree than my old girl. Lloyd's One 'Undred A-One-Plus she'd survey out at, no bother.'

'Hmmmmm,' I pondered noncommittally. 'That lifeboat still looks as if it needs a damn good overhaul. And knowing you, her liferafts'll probably be well past their date for replacement.'

'What lifeboat?' Trapp asked blankly.

'Whit liferafts?' Gorbals Wullie echoed, frowning intensely.

I squinted along the line indicated by Trapp's grubby finger again. Out past the blue-hulled coaster this time until I focused once more on the incredibly ancient hulk moored drunkenly to the shipbreakers' jetty itself.

'No, please,' I whispered while my legs turned inexorably to aspic. '*Please* God . . . ? Not THAT one!'

She'd looked abysmally unseaworthy even from a distance. Viewed at close range Trapp's Mark II *Charon* appeared . . . well, I could only presume she must've been hard aground where she lay and was thus supported by the river bed itself, because surely no law of physics existed by which such a shapeless, broken-down caricature of a ship could conceivably retain enough buoyancy to float?

Naturally Trapp, complacent and big-headed as ever, had to misconstrue my trance-like stare.

'I know – you think you're admirin' the original *Queen o' the Seas*, don't yer?' he enthused, unable to contain his pride a moment longer. 'An' by golly but you're nearly right at that, Mister. Sound as a deep-sea divin' bell she is . . . Er, mind as you go aboard, by the way. There's a bit of rusted deckplate with a hole in it, just ter starboard o' the gangway.'

'I'd rather not,' I muttered. 'I didn't bring a lifejacket, and we'll probably have to abandon again just as soon as we set foot on her.'

She was older, if anything, than Trapp's first *Charon* – and *she'd* been sunk now for over four decades! Every single upright line of his latest acquisition – stem; masts; the break of her diminutive foc's'le; the whole ugly block of her rusted after accommodation – should have risen uncompromisingly at right-angles to the water . . . if it hadn't been for the fact that she fought against a fifteen-degree list to starboard, as well as having foundered so far by the head that her single distorted propeller actually broke surface beneath her dented counter.

Only her battered spindlestick funnel achieved a precise vertical. But that was only because it compensated for the rest of the ship's topsy-turvy attitude by leaning drunkenly both to port and astern all at the same bloody time!

I saw what they meant about the lifeboat and liferafts, too. Trapp had solved that particular maintenance problem by simply not buying any. A pair of corroded radial davits on the after deck gave doubtful support only to a line of noisome seamen's garments which had obviously, as a token to shipboard hygiene, been rinsed briefly over the side in waters sluggish with the weight of Brindisi's residential effluent.

'I warned 'em to smarten up a bit seein' as you wus comin',' Trapp volunteered patronizingly.

'He telt them you even had your ain razor, Mister Miller,' Wullie expanded enthusiastically. '*And* yer ain piece of soap.'

A massive figure shambled into view from the inner recesses of the accommodation, tripping myopically over the coaming as it advanced towards the brow. With sinking heart I recognized the anthropologically challenging frame of one Daniel Spew who, if the truth were known, gave the lie to the conclusion that Piltdown Man had been a hoax. He existed all right – it was just that the scientists had examined the wrong guy.

'Remember Second Officer Spew? Still with me, you'll note,' Trapp remarked meaningfully, 'even though P an' O 'ave been tryin' to get their hands on 'im f'r years now.'

'Only because 'e rammed an' sank wan o' their cruise ships comin' intae Singapore once,' Gorbals Wullie qualified jealously, showing that his pique at being demoted hadn't quite subsided. 'Mind yous, she wis only seven hundred feet long an' aboot hauf a mile high. The Second Mate widnae notice a wee thing like that through jist the wan eye!'

Mister Spew stopped dead and swung his pugilistic head in the rough direction of our voices. Suddenly, and rather flatteringly I have to admit, his singular optic lit up with delight.

''*Allo*, Mister Cooper. Fancy meetin' you out 'ere in Port Said.'

'Christ, an' he's supposed tae be the navigator,' Wullie muttered.

'He isn't a Cooper no more,' Trapp corrected, referring to our last association when I'd been forced to adopt a protective alias for reasons not too far from Trapp's door.

'You c'n call 'im Mister Miller from now on – 'is proper tally.'

'Congratulashuns Mister, er, Miller,' Spew said somewhat inexplicably, then lost sight of me and proffered his vast paw to Gorbals Wullie instead. 'I 'opes you'll both be very 'appy. I'd 'ave sent a card an' a present if I'd known.'

Wullie firmly guided Spew's hand back towards mine, upon which it promptly clamped like a hydraulic press. I winced and began to black out while Trapp, never a man to sidestep an intellectual challenge, asked curiously, 'Jus' what, exac'ly, are yer congratulatin' the Mate on, Mister?'

'Gettin' *married* of course, Cap'n!' Mister Spew retorted with complete logic. He frowned deeper and deeper in the ensuing silence broken only by my stifled sobs, then explained lugubriously, 'Well: if Mister Cooper's changed 'is name ter Mister *Miller*, then it c'n only 'ave been because 'e –'

'– got *married* to a Missis Miller!' Trapp deduced triumphantly. 'By golly but din't I tell yer Blind Spew 'ere's not daft, then? He ain't never right, but 'e ain't totally daft neither!'

I felt my reason starting to turn turtle. 'Ohhhh, let's get aboard the bloody thing and get it over with,' I snarled, clinging wistfully to the hope that the rest of them might drown before I did.

Well, hadn't experience already taught me that to survive among these lunatics I had not only to act positively, but also to look on the bright side, no matter what?

I stood gazing bleakly around the *Charon*'s well deck, undergoing a second phase of disbelief. Gradually I became aware of hostile eyes assessing me from the oddest places – through dirt-encrusted portholes; around

47

battered deckhouse corners; between the cracks in peeling, warped weather doors . . . ?

Glancing down at the rusted deck I chanced to sight
a grubby and overly muscular arm, tattooed somewhat
intriguingly with the letters POPE, slide snake-like from
under a winch before feeling experimentally inside my
seabag.

Philosophically I gloomed, 'Oh well, when in
Brindisi . . .' and stamped on it, hard and with a satisfying
malice. The muffled yell which ensued steadily increased
in pitch after Trapp leaned casually across the winch
barrel and began to drag a human ear into view. Eventually, once the ear itself had stretched to a strand of
transparent pink elastic, it was followed by a bald head
still fiercely clenching a corn-cob pipe in its lop-sided
mouth and, ultimately, a grotesquely over-developed
torso. There was something vaguely familiar about
Trapp's captive. In fact I formed the niggling impression
that I'd already seen it – the person to whom the ear
belonged – somewhere before.

'Meet me Chief Engineer,' Trapp volunteered, still
gripping the overstressed aural member delicately between finger and thumb. 'Excuse 'is tendency to kleptomania, but philosophy-wise 'e sees hisself as bein'
slightly to the left of Karl Marx – believes in equal shares
f'r all which, considerin' 'e hasn't got nuthin' of his own,
has a certain irrefutable logic to it.'

'A Marxist? Yet he's religious?'

I knew I shouldn't have bothered as soon as I ques-
tioned the inconsistency. Trapp looked puzzled.

'Religis . . . '*im*?'

'That tattoo?'

Trapp's mystification cleared. 'P O P E yer mean . . . ?
Aw, that wus only because when 'e went into the tattooist's in Piraeus 'e –'

'You letta me go, Capitano,' the creature croaked

menacingly through the pipe-free side of its mouth, 'or I cutta you to pastrami witha ma shiv!'

'– ran out've money before the tattooist finished his name.' Trapp beamed. 'Pop*eye*'s 'is tally: Popeye Bucalosie. Used ter be a *contrabandieri* on one o' them fifty-knot speedboats runnin' cigarettes inter Naples under the noses of the Eyetie customs – until 'e got too greedy anyway, an' tried to rip off 'is Camorra bosses by dealin' direct with the supermarkets. After that they put out a contract on 'im – the Camorra, that wus: not the supermarkets.'

'Contrac'?' Gorbals Wullie immediately pricked up his ears. 'Does that mean they'd ackshully *pay* f'r information on his whereaboots?'

'Amma warning you for the lasta time, Capitano Trapp – iffa you no letta go my ear I choppa you into the tiny pieces of the bolognese.'

'These Eyetalians do get excitable,' Trapp commented, quite ignoring his wriggling senior officer otherwise.

Wullie had sidled over looking conspiratorially shifty. 'Er, onybody got a few spare lire on 'em?'

'What d'you want that kind o' money for?' Trapp demanded suspiciously.

The oldest deckboy in the business shuffled his feet and looked diffident. 'Jist tae . . . well, tae make a wee telephone call.'

'YOU'RE planning to turn Popeye 'ere in to the Mob, ain't yer, you greedy Scotch grass?' Trapp accused. ''Aven't you never felt *no* sense of loyalty to yer shipmates – no principles at all?'

'Ah've never felt nae bluidy wages counted in mah hand from a certain ship's captin!' Wullie rounded in spirited defence. 'That's mair tae the point.'

'It's really disgusting: how low some people are prepared to stoop,' Trapp growled. Then added thoughtlessly: 'Anyway, there's no point. The local Camorra branch wus raided by the *carabinieri* las' week. They ain't answering the phone no more.'

'How dae YOU ken?'

'Oh, I 'aven't time to stand an' argue with CREW,' Trapp suddenly shouted, furious at being caught out. He returned his Chief Engineer's ear to its over-developed owner's charge while booting him towards the engine-room fiddley for good measure. 'You go an' bloody oil somethin', Spaghetti Brain – an' leave Mister Miller's gear alone from now on or *I'll* cutta da tripes from YOUR gizzard witha me fingernails – savee?'

'Pure Disney,' I said to no one in particular as I watched Trapp's cartoon of a Chief roll away in fascination

'Och aye, he's pure Disney, a' right,' Wullie muttered spitefully. 'Disnae *dae* nuthin' f'r a start!'

Suddenly a high-pitched animal howl echoed from starboard: a sort of yodelling cadence not entirely un-familiar to travellers through Tarzan country. I whirled in nervous anticipation just as Mister Spew remarked pleasurably, 'Aw, now *that's* nice. It's the Bosun come rushin' to welcome yer back, Mister Miller.'

I caught one stark image of Choker Bligh swinging towards me pirate-fashion, suspended by a rusty wire from a peeling derrick, his pugilistic features a mask of black-remembered hatred and, coincidentally, clutching his favourite marlinspike aimed straight for my skull . . . Wearily I unclipped the dogs of the steel door leading through the forr'ad face of the deckhouse and – after carefully opening it at right-angles to the hurtling Bosun's parabolic flight path – stepped behind the weighty shelter it afforded.

There came the booming *thud* of high-speed flesh meeting a totally inflexible hinged object, followed by a slithering sound as gravity took over from momentum. I returned to the Italian sun just in time to watch a spreadeagled and somewhat compressed Bosun Bligh slide vertically the last few inches to the deck.

It proved a most fortuitous public relations ploy. Quite unexpectedly someone began to cheer from the nether regions of the *Charon*, then someone else began to clap, and soon all sorts of unshaven and incredibly villainous sailors had appeared like rabbits out of a seedy magician's hat, jostling and shoving to shake my hand. Encouraged by such confirmation that Bosun Choker Bligh hadn't exactly established himself as one of the most kindly and much loved taskmasters in the world's merchant fleet, I kicked the moaning recumbent experimentally a couple of times; partly to make certain he wouldn't forget Chief Officer Miller *was* bloody well back in charge, but mostly to establish a bucko mate image with the rest of the crowd. One which could well save the real, marshmallow-centred me from getting myself heaved over the wall in the middle of some forthcoming night.

'Choker's been lookin' forward to your return f'r ages, Mister,' Trapp said drily. 'I think 'e wus worried in case yer working relationship might 'ave changed.'

'Well, it bloody *hasn't*!' I retorted viciously. And booted Choker again, this time partly for the benefit of anyone who'd missed my first show of strength but largely because I just felt like doing it. Then I gazed with loathing around the lopsided hulk that was now my only home; at the cretinous apparitions who were now my only family. At the unspeakably awful Gorbals Wullie and at one-eyed bumbling Mister Spew, and down at the ship's resident psychopath, Choker Bligh . . .

And finally at their buccaneering and utterly impossible leader, Captain Edward Trapp, beside whom by contrast all those previously described denizens of the *Charon* STILL stood as shining examples of human probity.

'Nothing's bloody well changed at *all* . . . !'

*

51

Two nights later we were lying half a mile off the Albanian coast.

Trapp was trying to figure out our next move: I was still trying to figure out how we'd even got that far.

From Brindisi we may have only covered a hundred plus miles across a mercifully calm Otranto Strait but even so, by the time we raised the not particularly welcoming loom of Cap Gjuhëzes light, I felt as though I'd already survived a major brush with the supernatural.

Well, that had to be the only logical explanation for the *Charon*'s continuing not only to stay afloat but to make good even that short distance through the water. I mean, surely no ordinary terrestrial force exists which could have achieved such a miraculous transportation of the rusted iron and rotted timber composite which represented Trapp's latest command.

For a start, her only means of propulsion consisted of a coal-fired, single cylinder, more or less reciprocating German *Spatz* main engine, which had been installed around the turn of the century and had probably reached the end of its practical life towards the end of the war – that's World War One, I mean. Now it indicated a degree of wear sufficient to allow a man's finger to waggle comfortably between its solitary piston and the cylinder wall.

Even the great adventure of starting the bloody thing represented a mini-miracle in itself, involving the strongest man on the ship, Mister Spew – who also happened to be the only one stupid enough to approach within spitting range of the evil Teuton – levering with a massive crowbar to overcome its dank and sullen inertia while Chief Engineer Popeye Bucalosie flexed his tattooed hamshank forearms and attacked the rust-squeaky steam-valve wheel when it was least expecting an assault.

Once under way the fiendish *Spatz* performed in a quite eccentric manner, hissing and chugging asthmatically at low revs for a few minutes while speed built up then, just as you got complacent enough to assume everything was all systems go, it would lose all compression and begin to race, clatter and vibrate at imagination-defying speed while our laboriously-achieved if somewhat minuscule bow wave would die inexorably away until the ship sat motionless in the water again, wearily awaiting another shove up the backside from its tortured propeller. The *Charon*'s progression between any two points was reduced, therefore, to an eccentric series of full ahead down to dead stop rebuilding to full ahead gyrations . . . and as full speed hovered around only seven knots going down a wave with the wind astern anyway, it was pretty safe to assume that the one thing Trapp never would be likely to get his greedy paws on – or not by legal means, at least – was the Blue Riband of the bloody Atlantic!

And all the time this pantomime voyage was proceeding Popeye Bucalosie, corn-cob pipe clenched defiantly in his crooked mouth, would warily circumnavigate the hissing, bubbling *Spatz* with a half-crouched, inward-facing wrestler's gait, squaring up to his loathsome metallic adversary until that tangible proof of Hun devil-ishness subsided into one of its less violent steam-spitting phases. Whereupon the excitable Chief, shrieking blood-curdling Mafia-style threats about what he woulda do to its big ends if itta don'ta *conformi*blood-*yeri*, would leap in and frenziedly squirt oil all over the momentarily dormant monster from a can presented in the fashion of a Camorran fighting knife.

Dear Lord, after less than one hour into the passage I'd already grown to HATE that ship.

Almost as much as those who sailed it.

With the *Spatz* stopped intentionally for a change *Charon* wallowed sluggishly off the dark Albanian coast, rising

53

to the onshore swell lively as a clump of oil-sodden waste. Out on her cramped port bridge wing and meticulously clear of any top hamper which might drag me down should she take a sudden dive to the bottom, I kept reassuring myself that we retained *some* vestige of buoyancy purely on the grounds that otherwise the surface of the Adriatic Sea would be above, rather than below, the level of my ears.

I felt uneasy. Unlike in other countries bordering the Mediterranean, few lights were evident to relieve the black mountainous shoreline, while it seemed that the oppressive atmosphere of that secret state to leeward seemed to hang in the night air like a shroud . . . in fact, that formed the basis of my unease. I couldn't help wondering why any mercenary force should consider such a location from which to mount an operation.

But then:

'D'yer see the Colonel's signal yet, Mister?' Trapp's voice niggled anxiously from the starboard wing for perhaps the fiftieth time.

'No.'

There was a short silence, then: 'What time is it now?'

For the fiftieth time.

Stoically I ignored him, having already responded on forty-nine previous occasions, then I heard my Captain clump through the telephone-kiosk-sized wheelhouse – within the mildewed confines of which a totally brassed-off Gorbals Wullie slouched grumbling behind the wheel – before materializing as a lid-bobbing silhouette beside me.

'I jus' *gotter* get a big 'and f'r that chartroom clock,' he grumbled ill-temperedly. 'Trouble is they costs money, them sort o' precision tools . . . What time *is* it, exac'ly?'

Just to keep him quiet I squinted at the luminous dial of my watch yet again. It showed twenty-eight minutes past three in the morning. 'Not quite seven bells. Still two minutes to go.'

'Sir!' he growled.

'Pardon?'

'Two minnits to go – *sir*!'

I sighed wearily. He hadn't mellowed with age. Courageous to the point of idiocy in physical hazard, Trapp was getting all nit-picking and pompous as he always did when under financial stress – like anticipating a client's failure to turn up at a contractual rendezvous.

'I'm here as a favour to a sick man, Trapp. Don't push your luck.'

''Oo's sick?'

I frowned. Surely not even Trapp could be that *blasé* about having only one month to live . . . ? Well: less than twenty-seven days now. With a bit of luck.

'*You* are, dammit!' I eyed him through the darkness suspiciously. 'Aren't you supposed to have canc – ?'

He dismissed his own impending demise with an imperious sniff. 'Never mind about that. Point is, I'm in command aboard me own ship. I expects me Chief Officer to call me "sir" as a matter o' courtesy!'

Even humbled by such undeniable personal fortitude I just had to draw the line at that. 'Firstly, this isn't a ship, Trapp, it's a failed naval architect's nightmare. And secondly, I haven't called you "sir" since I first began to detest you back in nineteen forty-two, and I don't bloody intend to start again now.'

The squat shape beside me bristled. 'Oh aye? Then do I also 'ave to remind you that I happen ter be a full three-ring Commander in 'Er Majesty's Royal Navy, Mister, while you're jus' a pipsqueak reserve two-an'-a-half striper? I could 'ave you onna charge under Queen's Reg'lashuns f'r starters!'

'Only because you didn't bother turning up for demobilization, and the Navy's manpower computer has kept promoting you automatically ever since.'

Unfortunately it was true. He never had been officially

discharged from the Service after the last conflict, which meant that, technically at least, Trapp probably did still hold the unique honour of remaining as the Royal Navy's oldest serving officer. I just prayed the Royal Navy itself didn't suddenly realize its oversight. Admirals would leap from the bridges of their flagships in protest; nuclear submarine captains would stubbornly refuse to return to the surface; sailors would mutiny by the frigate-load; morale, to say nothing of the nation's security, would be obliterated overnight.

There came another all too brief silence until: 'What time is it now?' Trapp demanded, will-o'-the-wisp erratic as ever.

I took a deep breath. 'Twenty-eight and a *half* minutes past three!' There was absolutely no point in continuing the argument; not with someone as predictably unpredictable as Edward Trapp.

Leaning circumspectly on the bridge rail – circumspectly in case it crumbled under my weight and precipitated me clear into the bloody Adriatic – I scanned the dark shoreline through my binoculars yet again, searching for the signal which would at least confirm that Trapp's Colonel Weston did exist outwith the Captain's somewhat over-fertile imagination.

'Here: which of youse is supposed tae be keepin' watch starboard side?' Gorbals Wullie suddenly asked from the wheelhouse.

'I am,' Trapp retorted; then, getting pompous, shouted, '*and* I don't need no bloody DECKBOY to tell me 'ow ter look after the safety of me own ship either!'

'Och, keep y'r hair on,' Wullie muttered, thoroughly miffed. There came a petulant silence interspersed with *sotto voce* grumblings from behind the wheel until, simultaneously, we both registered their gist.

'. . . no' even goin' tae *try* an' tell him there's a whole bluidy warship jus' cruisin' doon oor starb – !'

Wullie collapsed before our combined weight like a wind-blown sapling as his Captain and Chief Officer fought to pass through the wheelhouse at the same time. A moment later we were both staring speechlessly at the low sinister profile of what could only have been an Albanian naval patrol boat passing less than a cable's length to seaward. She was so close we could make out the silhouettes of men on her open bridge, even detect the occasional snatch of conversation above the throaty gurgle of throttled-back engines.

Not one of those heads turned in our direction. No voice raised a cry of alarm . . . it was as though we aboard our topsy-turvy hulk didn't even exist.

One minute later and she was gone; only her receding white sternlight a stark reminder of how close we'd come to sudden disaster.

Even Trapp was uncharacteristically shaken. He shuffled his feet, fighting for aplomb. 'Yeah, well, it's lucky they din't see us, eh? By golly, we'd've had ter run f'r it an' no mistake.'

Run for it . . . ? In the *Charon II*? When, powered by turbo-charged diesels producing forty knots plus, the Albanian Navy could have sunk us and been back in Himare or wherever drinking *zganje* on ice before Spew and Popeye Bucalosie even got our bloody engine turned . . . !

'Trapp, she was so close I could've spat on her foredeck,' I said ever so carefully. 'And she *was* a patrol boat! She was out here looking specifically *for* people like you. Uninvited capitalists who have a tendency towards committing illegal acts for money, and thus upsetting a carefully balanced Marxist–Leninist economy – I suggest to you that the only conceivable reason for their not seeing us was because they didn't bloody *want* to see us.'

'They might've thought we wus a . . . well, a . . .'

'. . . tide-washed rock? Semi-submerged WRECK?' I

took a deep breath. It was like trying to reason with a particularly dense bulldog. 'Hasn't it yet occurred to you to wonder *why* they didn't want to see us, Trapp? Doesn't it raise even one tiny doubt in that profit-tunnelled brain of yours as to whether your meeting – a curiously fortuitous meeting, it seems to me – with some self-proclaimed mercenary in Istanbul really *was* as singularly motivated as you so naïvely accept?'

'How d'you fancy a nice corned-beef an' pickle sandwich?' Trapp tendered uncomfortably, attempting to change the subject as he always did when trying to avoid an issue. 'Er, what time is it now?'

'So which wan of youse master mariners is supposed tae be on watch *port* side then?' whined a somewhat trampled helmsman Wullie from within his fœtid action station, this time not without a tinge of apprehension.

'The Mate is!' Trapp bellowed, secretly grateful for any diversion. 'But I've already told yer – you'll speak ter the ship's officers only when you're spoken to.'

'Och, STUFF IT then!' Wullie shrieked back in absolute resentment. 'Jus' FORGET ah wis goin' tae report ah've seen your bluidy rotten SIGNAL!'

Then he hurriedly took cover, cowering behind the wheel as the ship's officers once again surged towards him *en* gesticulating *masse*.

In almost total darkness, without marks and yet with a minimum of gruffly issued orders, Trapp felt his way into that rock-strewn and unfamiliar Albanian cove. I confess I watched with unstinted admiration as he coaxed the eccentric, wheezing *Charon* to an impossible landfall using that sixth sense of his which far transcended ordinary seamanship. For one all too brief period in that ill-conceived adventure I even found some small reassurance appreciating that, whatever else I feared, Trapp had lost none of his pre-eminence in the skills of navigational brinkmanship.

His ship handling would've been even more impressive if the Machiavellian *Spatz* hadn't clanked to a final grinding halt at the precise moment when the *Charon*'s rudder also fell off its corroded pintles, leaving the ship with neither power nor steerage, drifting aimlessly just beyond a heaving line's throw from the rude and unexpectedly deserted stone jetty which represented our ultimate destination.

'Dash it all!' Trapp commented – well, more or less anyway.

Surprisingly our usually somnolent Second Officer Spew was the first to react positively to this latest emergency. 'I know: I'll lower the ship's boat an' row the 'eadrope ashore, Captin,' he volunteered happily to Gorbals Wullie.

'Ah'm NO' the fuckin' Captin, ye great blind bat!' Wullie snarled at his superior officer, still fair boiling about Trapp's 'no speakin' till yer spoken to' remark of an earlier crisis. '. . . thon's the bluidy Captin over there – the bad-tempered wan jumpin' up an' doon wi' the purple face an' mah bluidy WAGES in 'is pocket!'

Undeterred, Mister Spew fumbled his myopic way out of the wheelhouse and over to us, then saluted. 'I know: I'll lower the ship's boat an' row the 'eadrope ashore, Captin,' he repeated. And to the proper authority this time.

'Ohhhh, bugger OFF!' the Proper Authority screamed, kicking at Spew in a vile tantrum.

'Permission granted, Mister Spew,' I grinned. Then lounged back and waited, beginning to thoroughly enjoy Trapp's discomfiture but also buoyed by the prospect of our drifting to irretrievable shipwreck on the far side of the cove, and thus being forced to call the whole ridiculous pantomime off.

'Aye, aye, sir!' Spew beamed, indestructibly amiable as ever, and shambled off down the ladder.

A minute later he shambled back up again.

'Silly ole me but I clean forgot, din't I? We don't 'ave a ship's boat!'

Trapp, by then approaching the terminal phase of apoplexy, promptly grabbed Spew's ankles and tipped his Second Officer clear over the bridge wing and into the water. Then hurled a heaving line after him and pointed to the jetty.

'What d'yer need a bloody BOAT for . . . ?'

Predictably it was to prove an unsettling event, that nocturnal rendezvous with Weston's mercenaries.

Flanked by black precipitous cliffs the crumbling jetty remained quite deserted, even by the time we'd finally dragged the *Charon* alongside by sheer brute force and recovered a panting, dripping Mister Spew. There seemed little indication that anyone, local or otherwise, had even visited there recently. Only that anticipated sequence of red flashes emanating from this source helped convince me there was any substance at all in Trapp's wild claim.

The captain leaned perilously over the bridge wing, frowning impatiently down the jetty to where it dissolved into threatening darkness – the thirty-years-in-a-Balkan-jail type of threatening darkness to my already overstrung mind, though admittedly if his Istanbul meeting *had* been set up by the Albanians themselves to inveigle Trapp into a . . . well, a *trap* in order, say, to square the account for some previous anti-State indiscretion which – Trapp being Trapp – must undoubtedly have existed, then our recent uneventful meeting with their naval patrol would certainly have presented less of a riddle.

Even less of a future too, come to that.

'What d'yer reckon then, Mister?'

I shivered. It was an eerie place. 'I reckon your would-be

passengers caught the first act of your berthing cabaret, that they've very sensibly changed their minds in favour of living a bit longer before paying you to drown them, and that *we* should get the hell out of here too – or soon as Bligh's crowd re-ship the rudder anyway, and Bucalosie gets that diabolical scrapheap you call an engine fixed.'

'I ain't goin' nowhere, Mister,' Trapp growled doggedly. 'I got one million US dollars at stake an' – !'

'TWO!' the vindictive cry of Gorbals Wullie shrilled from the blackness. Obviously the spiteful little cretin had remained lurking in the background, awaiting an opportunity to get his own back on Trapp. '*Two* million dollars thon auld miser wis promised, Mister Miller sir, an' thass a fact.'

Trapp's simmering frustration instantly fanned to white heat. Snatching up a shackle he hurled it recklessly in the general direction of Wullie-disembodied before taking off in enraged pursuit. There came a crash as it demolished the only wheelhouse window that still boasted glass, then Wullie's jeering cackle: 'Ye missed me, ye missed me!'

'Oh God, they're worse.' I leaned weakly over the bridge rail, closed my eyes and felt faint. 'They're getting bloody worse . . .'

When I finally reopened them I found myself quite alone on the *Charon*'s bridge and still gazing despondently down at the jetty.

But by then I also happened to be staring directly into the muzzle of a very large Colt service pistol. Presented by a seeming giant of a man who, I'd *swear*, hadn't been there a moment before.

Chapter Four

And thus did Trapp's second meeting with Weston – or
more appropriately perhaps, the Coalition of the Crazies
– come to pass. While for my part I was forced to concede
that Trapp had been uncharacteristically correct in this
case, and that the Colonel's mercenary group did indeed
exist.

Or a formation of military hard cases did, anyway.
Whether they really were simple old-fashioned soldiers of
fortune who, traditionally, had once fought other people's
battles and so helped topple governments but now, possibly driven by the same economic recession as myself,
apparently heisted banks on behalf of respectable airlines
merely to earn a crust, remained to be proved. I wasn't
being particularly cynical; I'd simply learned a long time
before never to trust Trapp's judgement, and most particularly not when it was coloured by the prospect of
making money.

. . . well, to tell the absolute truth, I wasn't *actually*
being anything but plain bloody terrified just at that
particular moment as I stared, suddenly feeling terribly
lonely, down a rock-steady forty-five calibre hole pointed
unswervingly at my forehead.

There followed a seemingly interminable period while
I hardly dared draw breath, never mind shout a useless
warning, during which time Trapp buggered around playing vitriolic hide and seek with Gorbals Wullie and the
rest of the *Charon*'s crew wandered back to bed, while
the balance of our passenger list materialized silently

and otherwise totally unnoticed from the darkness. Cover and fall back along the jetty; cover and fall back . . . Not a single verbal command was issued.

'I don't believe I've had the pleasure, sir?' an American voice called after what had seemed a very long time.

I dragged my gaze from the gun and eyed the second figure to appear below me on the jetty. He was dressed like all the others in camouflaged battle fatigues but there was nothing identifiable about them, no badges of rank: he could've been anything in anyone's army. Only a dark-blue baseball-style cap concealing iron-grey hair suggested vaguely US origins.

'Miller,' I croaked. 'First Mate.'

Baseball Cap smiled thinly but didn't order the pistol lifted. I decided there and then I didn't like him.

'Weston – Colonel! Where's Trapp?'

'If you mean Captain Trapp, he's busy pursuing a matter of on-board discipl –'

The matter, a most apt description on reflection, hammered past along the alleyway below puffing and looking flushed, then skidded to a stop, took one glance at the giant with the Colt, shrieked what seemed to me a totally incomprehensible, 'Och Jeeze, thon's that MELON squisher!' before promptly disappearing again like a bolted rabbit.

Whereupon Trapp arrived, completely ignored the gun which still happened to be pointed at me and, purple with fury, roared: 'You're bloody LATE, Mister! I won't 'ave my passengers late reportin' aboard . . .'

He hesitated then; glowering at the pistol while I thought gratefully, 'Thank God! So he's finally noticed I just happen to be at some risk here.'

'You let that bloody Hermann shoot my Chief Officer, Weston, an' it'll cost yer ten per cent extra – Penalty Clause Four, Para Seven B o' the *Charon*'s charter party

63

stipulates a cash penalty f'r interferin' with the day-ter-
day runnin' o' the ship . . .'

My more formal introduction to the Colonel took place
a few minutes later. It was to leave me as indifferent to
his sardonic charm as before, though had Trapp bothered
to forewarn me that, following their Istanbul meeting
his relationship with the man was already one of mutual
antipathy, then I might have been better prepared.

In fact I felt a certain agreeable surprise when he first
climbed the rickety bridge ladder to confront us. Weston
didn't conform at all to my previous concept of the rude
mercenary soldier. Immaculately dressed he exuded the
impression, despite his lack of insignia, of being more a
West Point or Sandhurst Military Academy man, from
the razor creases in his shirt all the way down to his
precisely laced combat boots.

'Meet me Chief Officer: Miller,' Trapp growled, still
simmering over Wullie's disloyalty.

'We've already met,' I snapped, every bit as put out as
Trapp, though in my case more by being considered a
mere penalty clause in a bloody contract.

'We have, sir,' the Colonel acknowledged. He was
smiling the kind of smile which belied any suggestion of
good fellowship.

A sudden disturbance forr'ad took me anxiously to the
bridge front. Weston's troopers were swarming inboard
of *Charon*'s bulwarks with complete disregard for our
gallant crewmen, the majority of whom were already
retiring at flank speed as was standard drill when faced
by the slightest hint of personal danger. Only Mister
Spew was brave enou . . . well, stupid enough to stand his
ground, waving his arms ineffectually while protesting,
'Permishun! Passengers is s'pposed ter get permishun
afore they comes aboard.'

'I'm goin' to have to 'ave a word with that one about

64

the real world,' I heard Trapp mutter. Otherwise he simply watched and even appeared to brighten. I eyed him anxiously. Trapp Happy was a Trapp To Be Suspicious Of, and he did seem uncommonly philosophical considering this arrogant invasion of his vessel.

But to stay with the theme of stupidity: our much-loved Choker Bligh, obviously sociable as ever despite his recent Mach Two confrontation with a steel door, chose that precise moment in which to burst from the foc's'le and extend his usual seaboard welcome.

'**** *OFF*, the 'ole ****ING *lot* of yer!' the Bosun bellowed with characteristic goodwill.

'I don't think 'e's –' Trapp began.

Two mercenaries matter-of-factly rifle-butted Choker amidships whereupon our pugilistic petty officer folded up, cannoned into the scuppers and started to be sick all over everyone. I quite enjoyed that part myself.

'– *ever* goin' to learn,' Trapp finished, then looked smug. I suddenly understood his unaccustomed tolerance – Trapp derived enormous satisfaction from watching someone else's collective discipline falling apart for a change.

'It looks like you should've given orders to your squaddies about how ter treat me crew, Colonel,' he sniggered pointedly.

'Oh, but I did, Trapp,' Weston smiled thinly. 'You'd better believe it!'

Whereupon Trapp immediately regressed into his earlier black humour and tried to think of an answer while I, sensing the growing friction between them, turned hurriedly for the ladder.

'I'll, ah . . . get forr'ad then. Take charge of the loading.'

'Negative, Miller!'

Weston's harsh correction stopped me dead.

Trapp's lid began waggle ominously. 'Did 'e say *negative*?'

'You copy me strength five, Captain – Miller stays well away from my men. And the same goes for the rest of your crew.'

I watched Edward Trapp turn three shades of purple and held my breath. 'Seamen stows their own cargo, Mister. It's my Chief Officer's responsibility to ensure this ship is in all respec's ready f'r sea . . .'

'Jesus, but this time you've *got* to be joking, Trapp,' I thought disbelievingly. Oh, he was right in principle: cargo must be properly distributed throughout any vessel according to the Mate's calculations in order to preserve both stability and freedom from excessive stress, but on this occasion I suspected Trapp was only being typically fractious. There really wasn't enough added weight aboard to matter one way or another, and certainly not in the case of his *Charon* Mark II.

Well, how the hell was *I* supposed to establish a safe loading for a maritime dinosaur which, computation-wise, couldn't possibly have continued to remain afloat after roughly mid-1923 even when empty? I mean, EINSTEIN couldn't't've come up with a mathematical formula to justify a phenomenon little short of an Act of God.

Pointedly ignoring Trapp, Weston eyed me grimly. 'You pass the message, Miller: no contact, no fraterni-zation of any kind will be tolerated, you hear? You just make damn sure your sailors keep their distance from our so-called accommodation spaces from here clear through to Ras al Djibela – and that goes double for all military stores!'

'Like hell it does! No bloody supercargo tells me or my Chief·Officer what to do, Weston!' Trapp finally exploded. 'Not on the bridge of me own SHIP!'

'I don't propose to argue with the hired help, Trapp.' It was as if Weston was dismissing two privates from parade. 'You and Miller may be driving this goddam

66

tour, but me and my boys are your safe conduct to picking up the tab. This ain't no social cruise for any of us . . . Now you'all remember that and we'll get along just dandy.'

'Oh, aye . . . Ohhhhhh AYE?' Trapp rushed to the head of the ladder and bellowed after the departing Weston. 'An' what if we bloody DON'T, eh?'

'What d'you mean – WE?' I interposed furiously. 'Just cut out the collective bloody *we*, Trapp!'

But by then the Colonel had gone. And perhaps it was just as well that I didn't catch his answer.

It was remarkable how Trapp always managed to bounce back.

His overbearing conceit helped, of course: the abiding conviction that he would always come out on top which meant that, to him, Weston and thirty-odd mercenary killers having virtually hijacked the ship merely represented a temporary irritation.

Either way, it had only required two minutes of disciplinary discussion after he'd finally caught up with a suddenly pleading, cringing Gorbals Wullie for him to reappear on the bridge in just an ordinary foul temper.

'What d'yer reckon that's for, Mister?' he mused a little later, eyeing a big container which now stood awaiting shipment on the jetty under the watchful gaze of two ostentatiously armed mercenaries.

'Speaking as a mere penalty clause, I really haven't the *faintest* idea,' I snapped. But I was secretly intrigued nevertheless. What possible military application could a stainless-steel box some two metres cubed suggest – particularly when it was connected to a small portable electric generator which puttered quietly beside it? 'Why don't you ask your Colonel pal straight out? Reticence has never exactly proved a characteristic of yours before.'

'I did,' Trapp retorted shamelessly. 'Weston jus' told me ter mind me own bloody business like before.'

'Well, he can't be all bad then,' I muttered, slightly mollified. Trapp wasn't pleased, I could see that. Then I began to worry even more instead: a devouring curiosity over matters which didn't directly concern him had already caused several of the Captain's many previous downfalls. This time I'd be going down with him.

Trapp frowned along the darkened foredeck to where our martial contingent, having loaded all their own equipment including seemingly inexhaustible boxes of ball, tracer and armour-piercing incendiary ammunition, were now proceeding to stow it below in number one hold. Again impassive sentries discouraged any undue interest on the part of the *Charon*'s crowd, largely by the practical expedient of pointing guns at them – a perfectly sensible gesture of mistrust to my mind which wasn't resented in the slightest by Trapp's pirates either. Being compelled to lounge in scruffy inactivity while watching someone else work was their favourite occupation anyway.

'Them self-employed brown jobs have brought a lot more kit than I expected,' Trapp complained grumpily. 'I could've charged excess baggage if I'd known.'

'For Christ's sake, you're getting two million dollars already – which is, it would appear, a whole million more than you're prepared to admit to for a start,' I pointed out, not unreasonably it seemed to me.

'What lyin' toad claimed that?' Trapp bristled as if he didn't know. But then pious outrage inevitably provided a reflex defence when faced by his own perfidy.

'That lying toad did.' I pointed to Gorbals Wullie who'd only just returned cautiously to the bridge holding a grubby hand tenderly over one eye.

'Leave me oot o' this,' the Lying Toad whined. 'There's some o' us cannae stand the truth wi'out getting violent.'

'You slander me again an' I'll poke me finger in more'n yer bloody EYE next time!' Trapp roared.

I tried to ignore them and focused uneasily on the hardware being brought aboard. There seemed rather a lot of it, even to my untrained eye. Trapp settled heavily beside me again and sighed.

'Funny,' he remarked pensively after a few minutes.

'Hysterical! Er, what is?'

'That gear they're loadin'. I mean, them's fifty calibre Browning M2 Heavy Machine-guns under the break of the foc's'le, f'r a start. An' M60 General Purpose dittoes. Then there's a heap of M203 forty mil Grenade Launchers over there. What's more, though most've Weston's troopers are slinging standard M16A1 Rifles, I noticed some of 'em are carrying the most recent Colt Commando versions . . .'

And, of course, the forty-five calibre M1911A1 side-arms holstered arrogantly on every camouflaged hip – now those I *could* identify without help, having formed a more than nodding aquaintance with one by courtesy of Hermann.

'I know guns form one of your less wholesome preoccupations, Trapp, but I don't really feel receptive to a homily from Illegal Small Arms of the World right now, thank you.'

'Illegal Small Arms of *America*,' he corrected absently.

'Huh?'

'That's the point I'm gettin' at. It seems they've brought one hundred per cent United States Army pattern equipment with 'em. An' current service issue at that.'

'Have they really?' I grunted, still uncompromisingly miffed. 'Well, you ought to know. You probably ran most of it in here yourself at some time.'

'Prob'ly,' he said, taking it as a compliment. 'But the point I'm *tryin'* to make is – d'you see one single non-US origin weapon down there, Mister? I admit Weston's heavies packed Israeli-made shooters las' time in Istanbul, but now? Not a single Spanish Parinoco, Soviet Kalashnikov or Belgian FN as you might've expected, even allowin' for his claiming his is a predominantly Stateside team.'

I saw what he was driving at then, and it did seem a bit odd. Didn't mercenary outfits usually have to take what they could pick up through the less respectable international dealers? Yet according to Trapp it appeared that Weston's crowd might well have drawn their weapons straight from the depot at Fort Bragge.

Which was, of course, an utterly ridiculous hypothesis.

And anyway, how did they then transfer them to Albania?

But then we observed a further clutch of sinister tubular objects being passed over the rail, whereupon the Captain gave an involuntary whistle.

'You an' me are priv'liged, Mister. I'd guess we're lookin' at the most up-to-the-minute kit in the US infantry armoury: Viper anti-tank rocket launchers complete with HEAT warheads. Now there ain't no way *they're* on the open market ye – !'

He halted abruptly and I guessed he could've bitten his tongue out. It suggested that Trapp, for the very first time, was actually beginning to question precisely what he had got himself into. Needless to say he was damned if he was going to admit it.

Not surprisingly I didn't feel privileged; just more threatened than ever. 'What d'you mean – no way? You telling me Weston couldn't possibly have negotiated those appalling tools of his trade from surplus Pentagon stocks? And if he couldn't, then where *did* he get them, Trapp – from bloody WOOLworth's?'

'Och no: frae Macy's surely?' Gorbals Wullie chipped in. 'Thon Vipers is mair the kind o' quality rocket launcher Macy's would sell, Mister Miller sir.'

And honest to God but I *swear* he was being perfectly serious . . .

'SHURRUP!' I screamed, snatching a leaf from Trapp's book of man-management while the Captain, for his part, tried weakly to cover up. 'Course not. More'n likely Weston stole 'em, Mister.'

'Oh? Then where FROM if they're so new, Trapp – the bloody Weapons Development Division of the General Dynamics Corporation of bloody AMERICA . . . ?'

I turned away feeling, well . . . basically hysterical? Apart from riddles already posed that night about why Albanian patrol boats were miraculously crewed by look-outs even more blind than our own Mister Spew, and maybe three hundred further doubts regarding who, why and just exactly what Colonel Buck Weston and his mercenary men really *were* up to, it now transpired that Trapp's antiquated hulk was about to shudder blithely forth carrying enough state-of-the-art weaponry, what-ever its source, to launch a pre-emptive attack on the bloody Kremlin, never mind knock off Qaddafi's private dollarbank!

Yet even those concerns represented only the tip of a worry iceberg already forming in my stomach.

By the time loading was complete I'd also come to reason that, because the act of approaching an inter-national tinderbox such as the Libyan coast even with permission could prove pretty damn risky, then surely to attempt such a venture illegally, in a six knot limping arsenal crewed by two non-fraternizing varieties of homi-cidal nutter, with command split fractiously between an all-American mini-Hitler and an accident-prone megalo-maniac – a category to which the *Charon* Mark II un-doubtedly now belonged – could only invite my reliving the nightmare that had been *Trapp's War* all over again.

Mind you, not by the time of our departure, nor subsequently during the increasingly frequent periods of manic depression which were to assail me as we inexorably — to say nothing of miraculously — closed with our destination, did I ever conceive of Trapp's actually managing to precipitate a whole brand spanking new international conflict.

Not that it mattered to Trapp, of course. But then he was all right. Having less than a month left to live, he could afford to take a shorter-term view than I.

In particular the enigma posed by that stainless-steel container and its attendant generator, quickly stowed out of sight in number two hold before we'd sailed, was to plague Trapp right from the outset. Even during that tense period immediately preceding dawn, while he conned the ship through the treacherous undertows which marked our return to the open Adriatic with an almost perfunctory expertise, I noted, and became haunted by, the likely consequences of his growing frustration.

I could practically see the wheels going around in his mind. I knew the way he figured it there was always an outside chance of imposing a surcharge according to the terms of his ridiculous contract. That prospect alone was enough to determine Edward Trapp to employ any device either subtle, unsubtle or — if really stuck for a ploy — plain bloody blatant in order to satisfy his grasping curiosity.

And having met the uncompromising Weston, I couldn't help but anticipate that any move in that direction could well prove fatal. Even as the scattered lights of Albania faded astern I was already beginning to wonder whether the greatest risk to the *Charon*'s complement didn't already exist inboard of our battered bulwarks, rather than from whatever unthinkable violence lay ahead.

It didn't make sense, not really: the ban Weston had imposed on fraternization. No more than did his troopers' implicit adherence to the spirit of the order. Certainly his command over them must have been remarkable for never once, from the start of that voyage, did I hear any mercenary soldier utter a word to one of the *Charon*'s seamen.

Though of course our crowd did try and draw them at first, despite my passing of the Colonel's edict and a by then somewhat bruised Choker Bligh's enthusiastic determination to enforce it with fists, boots and his rope's end: that being the first chance he'd had for ages to beat anybody up without getting promptly banjoed by something heavier than himself.

Oh, don't think I didn't appreciate the Colonel's desire to keep them apart to some extent – I mean, I myself invited as little contact with Trapp's misbegotten crowd as possible, and *I* was their boss! – but surely there had to be more to it than that. Weston would hardly have imposed such a determined lack of reaction to our seamen's sardonic banter on, for instance, purely moralistic grounds. His troopers *were* supposed to be mercenary soldiers, all said and done: hardly backward, one assumed, when it came to earthy sparring themselves and therefore unlikely to be further corrupted by verbal clashes with the denizens of our foc's'le, no matter how insanitary.

But as I said, his troopers simply returned expressionless stares until initially well-meant overtures deteriorated into resentful jibes and ultimately to open insults. To my intense relief the *Charons* eventually wearied both of being battered by Choker and of baiting an audience of apparent dummies, and throughout the rest of our passage to Libya I never heard one more word traded between the two factions.

It made for a disquieting relationship all the same,

73

though I confess that, as the voyage progressed and the mercenaries appeared to behave perfectly correctly in their self-imposed purdah on the port side of the well deck, I did begin to question whether my initial suspicions had been justified after all. Certainly after several uneventful days at sea – frequent breakdowns of both our diabolical *Spatz* and, as an inevitable consequence, of Trapp's equally unstable self-control excepted – I'd become rather less convinced that Colonel Weston and his somewhat colourless team did actually pose a direct threat to my future.

Whereas the warship which promptly appeared on the horizon within minutes of our entering the most vulnerable phase of our Ras al Djibela approach – now *that*, I could be absolutely certain, WAS about to!

Chapter Five

While the *Charon II*'s voyage may have scaled less than seven hundred miles when laid as a pencil line on a grubby dog-eared chart, in reality it still took seven days of on, off and belief-defying on-again steaming.

In fact thanks to Herr *Spatz* and our rudder, which regularly kept falling from its pintles to trail somewhat pointlessly astern secured only by a hastily rigged insurance wire, that passage was to provide the only instance of my career during which I found myself predicting our estimated time of arrival in terms of weeks rather than hours and minutes. And even then be forced to revise it continuously, to more or less the nearest day.

But eventually the erratic scrawl which marked our actual track moved closer to Libya until, one hot afternoon, I entered our DR position – *Dead* Reckoning: oh, very bloody appropriate! – as just north of a hypothetical line linking Misurata and Benghazi, before turning to glower at Trapp in one last appeal to common sense.

'That's it then! Another fifteen minutes' steaming – that I should be so unlucky – and we've entered the Gulf of Sirte . . . Now you do realize we shouldn't *be* in the Gulf of Sirte, don't you, Trapp? It's a sort of point of no return. I mean, that transit just ahead of us does happen to represent Qaddafi's so-called Line of Death. He's sworn to kill anyone who crosses that. Permanently!'

'It's all bluster,' Trapp returned confidently. ''E din't sink the US Sixth Fleet when they went in ter show the flag, did 'e?'

I didn't even dignify such tortured logic with an answer; just threw my dividers on to the chart and wandered to the front of *Charon*'s wheelhouse to stare moodily ahead. At least it was air-conditioned on account of the windows not having any glass, which, of course, started me reflecting that air-conditioned was precisely what the rest of the bloody ship – and most probably me along with it – would be too, if we happened to meet a Libyan warship from here on in!

A slothlike routine had settled over the foredeck because of the heat. Which was, when you came to think about it, much the same as the slothlike routine engendered by cold weather so far as Trapp's crowd were concerned. The few crewmen who'd summoned enough energy to drag themselves from their bunks now lazed in naked and repulsive abandon under whatever poor shade was provided by the break of the foc's'le instead, pointedly ignoring our mercenary contingent who, in their turn, sat carelessly under the blazing sun in tight forbidding groups, either endlessly cleaning weapons or simply gazing towards the shimmering North African horizon. They looked tough, nearly all of them younger than I would have expected, and every last one still smart as a lick of paint despite the cloying humidity. I didn't know where Weston had recruited them but, judging by the crew cuts, I couldn't dispel a niggling suspicion it wasn't too far divorced from the source of his all American state-of-the-art weaponry.

A sudden thought struck me as Trapp came to lean heavily beside me, wiping his shiny sun-baked face with a large spotted handkerchief.

'You ever heard any of them speak?' I nodded down at the troopers. 'Apart from our friendly Colonel, that is.'

The Captain shrugged, spattering sweat over everything like a big wet dog shaking itself. 'They ain't allowed to, are they? No fraternization, Weston said.'

'No, I mean to each other. Sort of among themselves.'

Well, I knew *I* hadn't. I'd skirted them on several occasions when I'd gone forward with Chief Bucalosie to engage in a hopeless struggle to free our rusted windlass which had probably last weighed an anchor around the time of the Spanish Civil War – not that success was ultimately to prove too crucial: I'd only discovered later that we didn't *have* a bloody anchor to weigh any more, either! Yet each time I'd passed within earshot of our passengers I'd never detected one single conversation taking place within their seemingly bovine ranks. Never a jest, not one surely inevitable soldierly curse; not even the brusque cautions and commands usually so much a part of military life. Either we'd shipped a cargo of khaki-coloured deaf mutes or Weston commanded a degree of discipline more appropriate to . . . well, to some sort of élite Service cadre rather than independent soldiers of fortune? Weird really, even by Trapp's eccentric standards.

'You always was one to let yer imagination run riot,' Trapp growled which, when translated, meant he hadn't heard them speak either but wasn't prepared to admit it.

'At least I do *have* some imagination,' I snapped. 'Not that I need any when I'm sailing with you. The reality's bad enough without giving it added colour!'

'Sir! Remember the *sir*,' he muttered lamely.

'And don't bloody start THAT again! Just stick to the poin –'

'I sees a SHIP!' Gorbals Wullie, who'd been keeping out of Trapp's range until his eye got better, sang out from the monkey island above us – a safe house not only affording a longer view to the horizon but also one most aptly named considering it was Wullie occupying it.

'Whereaway?' I yelled, lunging for my binoculars.

'Two points on the starb'd bow.'

'Prob'bly a mirage,' Trapp grumbled, childishly

77

petulant at Wullie's stealing a visual march over him yet again. 'That one claimed he seen cockroaches big as piglets dancin' in the foc's'le las' month.'

'Considering the state the foc's'le's in, I'd be more amazed if he hadn't,' I retorted, nervously focusing on the shimmering blob now adopting substance through the heat haze five miles ahead.

'What, with hobnail *boots* on?' Trapp jeered.

'If it's a warship and they're smart,' I muttered anxiously, 'they'll be changing into flippers and bloody snorkels!'

Trapp guffawed. '*Course* it ain't a warship. I know them Libyans. They wouldn't risk comin' this far out.'

The blob slammed into focus. 'Oh Jesus! It bloody IS a warship!'

Wullie came tumbling down the vertical ladder and collapsed at our feet. 'Jeeze, it's a WARSHIP!' he echoed hysterically.

There was a moment's silence while Trapp thought about that.

'All right, so maybe it is a warship,' he conceded eventually still positively brimming with self-confidence. 'You c'n take it from me she still won't bother us. We're flyin' the Libyan ensign ain't we? An' them Ayrabs is thick as two short planks: they'll figure us f'r locals an' ignore u –'

I saw an Aldis begin to stutter and anyway, I was getting bloody fed up with him. 'Then why's she signalling international code for "Stop"?'

'Ohhhhh *shit*!' Trapp shouted and promptly went back to his intriguer's drawing-board, refusing even to acknowledge Weston's unhurried arrival on the bridge. Coolly the Colonel surveyed the fast-approaching silhouette through his own field glasses – his US Army-issue field glasses.

'Libyan you reckon, Miller?'

'We've crossed Qaddafi's No-Go line into the Gulf,' I muttered. 'That almost certainly means affirmative.'

The Aldis flickered again. I couldn't make head or tail of the call, probably in plain language Arabic which at least suggested they were taking us at face value so far – as a corroded navigational hazard flying an Arab State's flag and utterly impotent in every respect. Which was exactly what we were!

'Thought you said they'd ignore us?' Wullie turned on Trapp with white-faced malice while still keeping judiciously out of range. 'Ah warned ye whit they Qaddafi polis is like but ye wouldnae lissen, would ye? All Islamic nutters hooked on rubber truncheons they are, whiles ah'm a devout Church o' Scotland Protestant.'

'Oh? An' since when wus *you* religis?' Trapp roared, goaded into furious response again.

'Since ah seen yon fucking WARSHIP, thass when!' Gorbals Wullie shrieked back.

I watched the white water under the approaching craft's bow rise significantly. 'She's increased speed. They're getting suspicious of our not answering.'

'Then flash them back. Any garbled reply will do.' Weston read my expression. 'It buys us time, Miller.'

Travelling at all of six temperamental knots I didn't ask what we could possibly hope to gain by delaying their next move. Nautical twilight was still nearly an hour away and offered no concealment against radar-directed gunnery anyway. To me such prevarication simply meant they'd be that much closer when they eventually did open fire.

But I couldn't think of a more practical move while suddenly minutes, even minutes spent in Trapp's company, seemed incredibly precious.

'Go ON then: pass the Aldis!' I snapped unthinkingly at Gorbals Wullie.

'Oh aye – an' whit Aldis might that be?' Wullie queried

79

with acid innocence. 'Mister Miller, sir: huv you forgot you're sailin' wi' a certain person who disnae spend money on wee essentials like lifeboats, anchors, bulbs fur the navigashun lights nor even buyin' a big haund f'r the ship's clock – tae say nuthin of refusin' tae cough up *anither* certain person's wage . . . ?'

'Get the panic party mustered on the foredeck, Mister!'

Trapp's capricious ability to rise like a phoenix from the ashes of his latest miscalculation had become evident once more. Affording the mischievous Wullie a glare threatening enough to freeze his turncoat henchman in mid-diatribe he turned to me and grinned cleverly, fully in command again.

'Jus' like we used to do in the old *Charon*, eh?'

I glanced forward over the dodger. The bulk of the mercenary force had seemingly been ordered below out of sight; only a few stragglers remained on deck crouched well below the level of our bulwarks while, for the crew's part, sloth had been miraculously banished. Now the *Charon*s were milling in terrified disarray around the exit to the foc's'le. Chippie and two sweating co-cretins were already half-way through building a raft; most of our renegade followers of Islam were prostrated due East and battering their foreheads off the deckplates as an abject last line of appeal while Thuggee Singh, much-wanted Bombay assassin and rather more practical sur-vivalist, was desperately trying to tie an inflatable beach lilo shaped like a rubber duck around his waist.

I couldn't help reflecting with a certain sardonic antici-pation that he just happened to be securing it in roughly the spot where, once he'd abandoned, the only thing that would float above sea level would be his backside. Chief Engineer Popeye Bucalosie, on the other hand, was doing sod all to help anybody, including himself, by running in aimless muscular circles bawling, 'We're a gonna die! We're alla gonna DIE . . .'

'It seems your panic party's already mustered,' I growled. 'And practising like mad.'

Now, in our old Q-ship days the idea behind a panic party was for half the crew to abandon ship in the lifeboat, thus presenting a disarming illusion of total surrender, while the remainder waited behind our concealed 4.7-inch gun for a by then theoretically unsuspecting enemy to close to within point blank range. It hadn't always worked even then, but I knew it wasn't worth drawing Trapp's attention to the other minor differences between our Second World War antics and this, his current Machiavellian Ploy Mark II – like that we neither sported the necessary lifeboat nor the aforementioned 4.7-inch bloody gun! Trapp must've noted the disgust on my face, though.

'Next we hoist the internashnul "W" followed by Zulu Victor, Mister,' he explained, adding smugly, 'There ain't never been an Ayrab yet I 'aven't 'ad the best of.'

I knew 'W' meant 'I require medical assistance', but Zulu Victor . . . ?

'"I b'lieve I have been in an infected area during the last thirty days",' Trapp supplemented with a broad grin. 'The power of suggestion, Mister. Soon as them Libyan matelots think our lot o' prime disease candidates down there are desperate ter board 'em for medical help, they'll be off like they wus bein' chased by Uncle Sam hisself.'

From the corner of my eye I noticed even the Colonel smiling tightly at the analogy.

But it wasn't until some time later that I was to learn precisely why.

From five cables, even bows-on and still approaching fast, I could identify her clearly: a forty knot Soviet-built Komar class missile boat flying Qaddafi's naval ensign, with the ungainly shrouded SS-N-2A launchers toed outboard on either side of her after deck. Old she may have been – it was an Egyptian Komar which had sunk the Israeli destroyer *Eilat* over twenty years before – this one still wouldn't need to waste a missile on us: she was more than capable of sinking the *Charon II* with her twin 25mm foredeck cannon alone.

Come to that, one full power run close down our starboard side an' the bloody wash from her *stern*wake would prove more than adequate to capsize us!

'Amma gonna die! We're ALLA gonna die!'

Trapp leaned reassuringly over the dodger and roared at his Chief, 'They got enough panic party on deck, Bucalosie. You stop actin' an' get back down yer engine-room in case I needs ter ring f'r full speed.'

'He isn't ACTING!' I bellowed. 'Apart from which we're already GOING full speed. Look! You can just see the water moving along our hull.'

Three cables off now, and heads clearly examining us from the Komar's open bridge: two more matchstick Arab sailors busy clearing the 25mm for action on her foredeck. A movement at the bridge rail made me look down sharply. The Colonel had swivelled his blue base-ball cap back to front, then casually gone down on one knee, observing the patrol boat through a split in the wing planking without being seen himself. I noticed uneasily that he'd drawn his Service Colt, but otherwise Weston betrayed none of the tension I was feeling, look-ing more as if he was resting easy between drill move-ments.

Gorbals Wullie had dropped out of sight too, but with rather less aplomb. He now lay curled in a tight ball behind the vegetable locker with his grubby arms shield-ing his skull, as distanced from the impending gunfire as our postage stamp bridge deck allowed.

One cable – two hundred yards off – and the Komar began to slow, turning towards our stern then sweeping wide to run along our starboard side. The signal flags requesting medical help hung limp from our drunken masthead while, on the foredeck, a frozen hush had descended as our panic party hoisted in the unpalatable truth that there wasn't anywhere to panic to. I sneaked a covert glance at Trapp as we waited for the Libyans to call our bluff. He just stood there, moving easily on the balls of his feet as the *Charon* lifted sluggishly to the first displacing pressures of the other vessel. There was a reckless and all-too-familiar set to his sweating, un-shaven jaw. I guessed then the old pirate was relishing every minute of our flirtation with death and couldn't quite make up my mind whether to hate him the more or admire him for it.

An iced claw gripped my belly as a staccato crackle slashed across the steadily closing gap until I realized with a surge of relief that it was merely an electronic loudhailer powering up. Then came the challenge, in guttural Arabic.

But then: we *were* purporting to be an Arab vessel.

Quite undismayed Trapp cupped his hands and roared back in a voice which conceded nothing in volume to the world of micro-chip communications. 'Me European master. Me no understand. You speakee English maybe?'

It was equally apparent that Trapp made no concession to the fact that he was talking to Arabs, not Chinese. But in Trapp's distorted view it didn't matter whether they were Wogs, Spicks, Dagoes, Eyeties, Pakis, Jocks or Taffies – they all understood the Queen's English if you yelled it loud enough!

And damn me if it didn't work. Immediately the Komar's hailer projected perfect English, probably the kind polished up at Britannia Naval College, Dartmouth while her commander was being simultaneously fine-tuned by RN specialists on how to kill Western ships more efficiently.

'You are in a restricted area belonging to The Socialist

People's Libyan Arab *Jamahiriyah*. You will consider yourself under arrest by a naval unit of the said Socialist People's Libyan Arab *Jamahiriyah*. Should you fail to give good account of your presence within this restricted area belonging to the Socialist People's Lib . . .'

'Is 'e f'r real?' Trapp hissed without changing expression. 'Or does Qaddafi switch 'im on by remote control from Tripoli, along with that bloody loudhailer?'

'. . . punishable by trial followed by death – as decreed by The Socialist People's Libyan Arab *Jamahiriyah* under the authority of Brother Colonel Muammar Al-Qaddafi, Leader of the Elfata Great Revolution . . .'

'Ah TELT ye they wis a' nutters,' Wullie's muffled voice wailed from the background. 'A' they People's Libyan Socialist Jammy-thingies. But och no, ye would-nae lissen would ye? So now you got us intae *anither* fine mess so ye huv, Captin, an' thass a fact!'

'Hang on a minute!' Trapp roared through his cupped hands, then ran over and booted Gorbals Wullie most pleasurably before galloping back. I watched with chilled fascination as the twin barrels of the 25mm cannon followed the Captain all the way until he returned to the rail. Particularly as I was standing right beside him.

The Komar was running parallel to and maybe fifty yards from us by then, drawing almost abeam.

'But I INSISTS you arrest us,' Trapp bellowed. 'We needs urgent medical assistance. I gotter sick crew aboard. This is a diseased ship, by Allah. Me Mate's got great black boils on 'is . . .'

'Oh, steady ON!' I snarled, but he was in full creative flow by then.

'. . . me Chief's all suppuratin' sores an' gangrene. I got six dead uns swellin' like porcupine fish down the lower tween deck. I only got four sailors what 'aven't turned mustard yellow all over – an' *that's* only 'cause they gone a sort o' mottled purple instead . . .'

I glanced down at Weston. He was still watching the Libyans with narrowed eyes but his expression was bleak now. He obviously placed little faith in Trapp's melodramatic tactic of presenting the *Charon* as a maritime leper to be avoided at all costs, even by the fanatical guardians of The Socialist People's Libyan Arab *Jamahiriyah*.

Trapp ran out of awful symptoms and waited confidently. 'You see, Mister,' he whispered in a voice about as *sotto voce* as a passing football riot, 'I knows Ayrab psychology like the back o' me 'and. They'll sling their 'ook any minute now . . .'

'You will heave-to immediately and prepare to receive a boarding party,' the missile boat's loudhailer crackled. 'They will guide you into Tarabulus where there is a military hospital. The Socialist People's Libyan Arab *Jamahiriyah* is not without compassion for the plight of those unfortunate enough to be contaminated by the scourge of American capitalist decadence.'

'Awwww *SHIT*!' a yet-again-thwarted Trapp exploded and started to flail his already pulverized cap on the bridge rail in black frustration.

'Ohhhhh *shit*!' I concurred with feeling, then began to work out whether I could maybe squeeze in behind Gorbals Wullie over on the far side of the bridge just as Mister Spew, utterly oblivious to the crisis reaching hysteria level around him, appeared at the top of the starboard ladder; eventually managed to focus a keenly interested eye on the forty knot prospect of death a mere spit away, then beamed delightedly. 'Party? Did they say they wus throwin' a *party*, Captain? An' yet there's our silly lads all upset an' thinkin' they isn't welcome . . .'

Weston faced Trapp bleakly. 'OK, so you've played your goddam games. Now we negotiate with the bastards my way.'

Unhurriedly he raised his Colt and squeezed three shots into the air.

Now I admit I couldn't really see much to be gained from shooting at a cloudless sky at first. Even allowing for the fact that it, too, had probably been annexed in the name of The Socialist People's Libyan Arab *Jama*-whatever-they-were. But, come to that, I had very little time to consider the Colonel's action in detail anyway.

It being instantly overtaken by the *whooshing* back-blast of three HEAT anti-tank rockets being triggered simultaneously from behind the cover of *Charon II*'s foredeck bulwarks!

At such merciless point-blank range each shoulder-launched Viper round bracketed the unsuspecting Komar with geometric precision: forr'ad; midships; and aft of midships.

The one which took out the Libyan's bridge deck sent four, plus what seemed only to be a half, scarecrow corpses whirling hideously on a swelling puffball of heat before flinging them contemptuously into the sea alongside the ruptured ship. The two matchstick matelots who'd been attending the foredeck 25mm simply cooked within their own flash-ignited skins as they stumbled blindly in whimpering circles before finally tumbling overboard, each causing a smoke-wisping hiss.

Her portside SS-N-2A surface-to-surface missile had already gone, blown clear of the wreck in the first instant. As I stared open-mouthed its twin reeled drunkenly within its cylindrical launcher then, trailing a shower of sparks, followed impotently to the bottom of the Gulf of Sirte. With a snort of compressed air a single orange-canopied survival raft, forcibly jettisoned by the explosions, inflated alongside like some writhing expandable sea mollusc to drift aimlessly on the otherwise mirrored surface.

There followed a momentary stunned silence broken only by the crackle of flames as the wooden-hulled patrol craft settled deeper into the water. Two dazed figures – presumably engineroom ratings and, as far as I could make out, the Komar's only survivors – had already begun to lever themselves through a distorted after deck hatch before Trapp finally found voice.

'What d'yer do THAT for?' he snarled at Weston, never prepared to concede failure. 'They'd've gone off happy to see the stern of us in another minute. I 'ad a few more frighteners up me sleeve . . .'

'It's done!' the Colonel snapped coldly. 'Just save your energy, Trapp, for getting us to Ras al Djibela.'

He rose and strode to the bridge front. The three mercenary rocketeers had remained kneeling behind the bulwarks, launchers still shouldered but gazing up expectantly now. Without a word Weston briefly crossed his forearms and impassively they stood down. Like everything else his troopers did it had been a mute and unemotional exercise: a silent routine of killing. I suddenly shivered despite the heat from the sun.

Trapp opened his mouth to say something argumentative, then diplomatically closed it again as he took uncharacteristic note of my frowned warning. I jerked my head towards the foredeck. Several more of Weston's clean young automatons had appeared from concealment and now stood, legs apart, weapons at a threatening port; some facing the bridge and the remainder our uncertain panic party which had now subsided more to an apprehensive shambles. No words were necessary to interpret our in-house militia's latest threat.

Sullenly Trapp turned his attention to the blazing Libyan missile boat, by then falling steadily astern as our thoroughly malignant *Spatz* – suddenly deciding to run like it had just been factory reconditioned – now took it into its head to propel us with Teutonic perversity ever closer towards a Libya infinitely more dangerous since we'd taken out a few of Brother Colonel Qaddafi's saltier revolutionaries.

'I only sees a couple of blokes left at her stern. How many d'you reckon made it, Mister?'

'The same. Presumably her engineroom watch-keepers.'

He sniffed, abnormally philosophical. 'Usually when a ship's lost it's 'er black gang go first. It seems their Allah c'n be as capricious as all the other gods us sailors put our faith in, don't it?'

I eyed him, strangely concerned. I'd never heard him refer to having faith in any god before and wondered if the cancer he claimed was in him had finally shaken even Edward Trapp's presumption of his own immortality.

Though he *still* looked remarkably healthy, mind you – for a man who was, by my reckoning, due to part his cable in just over a fortnight now?

Through my glasses I watched the surviving Arabs scramble into their jettisoned raft as the Captain leaned over the bridge front, contemptuously ignoring the trio of M16 muzzles which instantly swung to cover him.

'Bucalosie – you get back down yer bloody hole *jaldi*! I'll be wantin' ter manoeuvre soon.'

A great hissing and steaming arose as the Komar sagged by the bow then began to slide beneath the surface. Desperately the Arab sailors fended off until only they and the great orange raft were left, curtseying and revolving slowly amid a boil of flotsam and rainbow-hued diesel fuel.

'Right: that's it. Hard a port the wheel!' Trapp called matter of factly then, after a moment in which nothing happened, frowned around to observe Gorbals Wullie still preoccupied by his own determination to achieve immortality – having prostrated himself with as many people between him and the action as possible. Wearily

Trapp strode over and stamped on the little man's head.

'Gerron the bloody WHEEL then, ye spineless Scotch worm!'

'Ah'm *no*' scared,' Wullie shrieked. 'Ah wis jist huvin' a lie doon 'til youse made up your minds whit tae dae next, so ah wis!'

'Well we're goin' to pick up them survivors: that's what we're gonna do nex –'

'NEGATIVE, Trapp!'

'Ohhhhh, not *again*!' I thought apprehensively as Trapp slowly turned to face Weston. He was very calm this time, though. Ominously calm.

'*Negative*, Colonel?'

'We take no Libyans aboard,' the Colonel said flatly. 'I hired you for a secret mission, not a hands across the sea charity for goddam sailors.'

'Mission?' Trapp's eyes narrowed immediately. For the very first time he'd maybe rattled Weston's armour a fraction. 'I thought this wus just a robbery, not a "mission"?'

'Look, do I put the wheel hard a' port or no'?' Wullie demanded petulantly.

'Hard to port like I ordered!' Trapp said firmly.

'Keep it midships, sailor!' Weston countermanded.

'Ah'm gettin' BLUIDY fed up!' Wullie grumbled.

A sudden rage overwhelmed me. Brushing Trapp aside I rounded carelessly on Weston.

'And I'm getting bloody fed up too, Mister! With your silent gun-slinging majority and your sheer bloody arrogance, and the stink of deception you trail astern of you. So you hear this, and *you* hear it loud and clear this time, Colonel – I am a seaman, as is Captain Trapp. Thanks to your actions, two seafarers require assistance back there in that liferaft . . . We fully intend to rescue those survivors as our mariners' duty demands, no matter what colour, creed or goddamned NATIONALITY they are –

and the *hell* with your bloody bank heist or mission, or whatever else you damned well choose to call it!'

Even Trapp, who normally treated my occasional over-stressed outbursts with all the seriousness which a crocodile would afford an angry duck, looked taken aback. Weston, on the other hand, simply stared into my eyes for a long and thoughtful moment. Very intently. Without malevolence, though. Without any seeming emotion at all.

Until, abruptly, he shrugged before leaning indifferently on the bridge rail. 'Very well, Miller,' he said. 'You feel that strong, you do your sacred duty. You just turn tail and pull all the survivors you c'n find aboard.'

I blinked uncertainly, then turned to Gorbals Wullie. But I'd hardly repeated Trapp's helm order before I heard the Captain roar, 'Belay that, you BASTARD!'

I whirled with the shock of anticipation. Trapp was staring furiously down at the foredeck to where the biggest mercenary, the giant called Hermann, was single-handedly hoisting a heavy M60 General Purpose Machine-gun already trailing a 100-round belt loading, to rest on the bulwark capping.

Even as I swung to face astern and shout a pointless warning I heard the yammer of the gun and smelt the acrid drift of cordite. Through my glasses I watched the spatter of heavy-calibre ammunition cut a running fountain across the Gulf of Sirte, reaching towards and feeling for its so-frail target. One of the Libyan sailors saw it coming and turned to dive overboard: the bullets exploded his backbone and catapulted him twenty feet in a cartwheel of blood. The other simply waited for death. I registered his face in close-up: it was distorted with hate, the mouth revealing very white teeth and shouting something at us. Something terrible. I hoped to God I would never discover what it was.

And then Hermann's GPMG ate him up too, and pulverized the raft while I could only gaze, rooted to the spot, as they both disappeared from the field of view of my binoculars leaving merely a thin line of wavering horizon.

'No mariner's duty called for now, I guess?' Weston said without even shifting his stance at the rail. 'No survivors, Miller.'

I think it was in that moment that I first began to smile. Oh, not with any humour. No! More in a masochistic, thoroughly appreciative way as, ever so carefully, I caressed the focusing wheel of my glasses. Just to make absolutely certain. Before I shared my joke with the Colonel.

Finally I spoke, keeping my voice flatly conversational.

'Y'know, when he sees the bullet holes in that raft I'll bet he's going to feel *just* the same as you do, Weston . . . about survivors?'

The Colonel did glance up then, curiously. 'He?'

I pointed astern. Even while anticipating my own fast-approaching death, the exquisite irony of our predicament still appealed to me.

'The Captain. Of that next Libyan warship – a whole bloody frigate this time, Weston. Heading straight for us!'

Chapter Six

The bone in her teeth was dazzling white now, flinging high on either side of her racing bows while promising dreadful things. It made me think of the teeth of the murdered Arab.

I didn't know a lot about weapons, but by God I knew about ships.

'Origin: Soviet Riga class. Mine-laying frigate, Weston!'

He didn't answer – nobody had found tongue yet, not even Trapp – but I was gaining no satisfaction from watching the Colonel. He stood completely without expression, just gazing aft at the approaching warship: calculating the odds but betraying no fear of the consequences.

I was still grinning wolfishly. Probably a bit shakily too, by now: the irony of our predicament wearing thin as cold realization took root.

'Old maybe, like that Komar you killed back there, but a lot bigger. Sixteen hundred tons of angry frigate comin' at us like a bloody express train this time! Turret-mounted 3.9-inch guns backed up by triple torpedo tubes, depth charges an' a pair of 16-barrel anti-submarine rocket launchers . . . In your language she's a rootin' tootin' vicious bastard, Colonel. You won't bushwhack her with a few Viper anti-tank rounds – certainly not with a bloody GPMG!'

Trapp reacted then. 'Hard a STARb'd . . . Steady 'er on the coast!'

He swung furiously as the wheel blurred under Wullie's nervous hands. 'What the 'ell's SHE doin' here? There ain't never been a prime Libyan fleet unit out this far before. Qaddafi knows bloody well when 'e talks about his Line o' Death he means fur 'is *own* Navy, should they meet up with the Yankee Sixth.'

I was about to round on him in his turn and ask what we'd gain from holding a post mortem on current Libyan defence thinking at this somewhat critical juncture, but decided the balance of probability appeared more in favour of them holding the post mortem on us anyway – using high explosive as a substitute for scalpels!

'OK, you're the strategist, Trapp. What d'you propose we do now?' I snarled as a spiteful alternative to punching him. 'Build a getaway submarine?'

'I done it. We're runnin' for shallow water. It's only twenty miles off,' he muttered defensively.

I eyed the approaching Riga again. *She* was less than five miles away, and converging at thirty knots. We were fleeing somewhat erratically at six. It presented a straightforward time, speed and distance equation.

'Oh, we can cover that, can we – in roughly twelve minutes?'

'Calculashuns, calculashuns – you always WUS a nit-picker!' he shouted.

Distant as she was the Libyan had already begun to alter course slightly to starboard, the better to rake our exposed decks with gunfire. Through the glasses I could see she was already closed up for action: her A, B and Y turrets following us with gyroscopic precision as were her Soviet Muff Cob gunfire director and torpedo mounts.

Death would be quick when it came – which would make a change, being the only bloody thing about the *Charon II* that was! I suddenly noticed Weston had left the bridge and swung to observe him one last time; to see how he reacted to being helpless at the wrong end of a gunsight.

Again I was scheduled for a disappointment. They were all mustered on deck now, our mercenary contingent; the Colonel just leaning calmly on the bulwark capping and watching the overtaking Riga with an expression bordering on contempt. Whatever else Weston may have been, he was a brave man: every ramrod-straight inch the professional soldier. Or maybe he simply accepted there was no alternative; realized what the Libyans would do to us once they confirmed there had been no survivors from their sister Komar. Either way he intended to make a fight of it: I could count at least six troopers kneeling, Vipers shouldered and ready loaded with HEAT armour-piercing charges, while every other man crouching patiently – and silently, needless to say – along the Charon's bulwarks caressed either the butt of a GPMG or his automatic rifle.

It suddenly struck me that there wasn't a single crew member to be seen. It suggested that the pragmatic Weston had solved any potential risk of our panic-stricken panic party intervening in his mercenaries' field of fire with callous efficiency – by simply battening them all in the foc's'le, from within which various multilingual appeals, a colourful selection of threats in Choker Bligh's inimitable style, plus a few sundry screams accompanied by the battering of fists against the locked steel door now emanated.

It seemed a good idea. Those of us still in the open were due to follow the ship to the bottom of the Gulf of Sirte anyway, even if we did float around leaking blood awhile first. Trapp's crowd would just sink straight away, and leave a much more hygienic clutter of wreckage by so doing. The bonus for me was that it promised I could enjoy a distraction-free few minutes in which to ruminate over the better times of my life – which

94

basically covered any period which hadn't involved Trapp!

Even helmsman Gorbals Wullie in the wheelhouse, trying to steer to a compass from a huddled position on the deck – he wasn't speaking, being completely in a huff with Trapp for getting him killed at long last, an' wi'oot even *payin'* him f'r it!

. . . it became patently obvious that what little grace was left to us had begun to drag for Trapp, though.

Foolishly some industrious idiot once proclaimed that time meant money, and ever since he'd first heard the expression Trapp – who, needless to say, was quite prepared to impose upon other people's time with turtle-like efficiency when it suited *him* – had always argued time wasted was like money being thrown away . . . It now appeared he was bent on applying that ridiculous cliché to the present – my present, in particular – presumably being frittered by my simply hanging around and waiting for death.

''Ow long d'you reckon we got?' he speculated. 'About ten minnits?'

It rather depended on whether they settled for immolating us with their big guns, or closed so's they could exercise all their little ones as well. I just ignored him and concentrated on getting more and more frightened.

He wandered over and started fiddling with a splinter of wood hanging limply from the bridge rail.

'That container they brought aboard in Albania – you, er, ever wonder what they got in it?'

'No!' I snapped. Which wasn't true, but I wasn't in the mood for compromise.

'They ah . . . well, they're all sort've preoccupied right now – Weston's brown jobs? While the container's stowed nice and accessible down in number one, an' there ain't no sentry on it. Now *I* can't really be seen to leave the bridge while we're expectin' visitors, me being the Captain and everythin' . . .'

95

The frigate had closed to, maybe, four and a half miles. I suddenly twigged what he was driving at and began to back away, shaking my head. He followed me with the ingratiating persistence of a Port Said gillie-gillie man.

'. . . whereas you, jus' bein' the Mate an' not at all important, *could* slip away an' still 'ave a good ten minnits spare. So I wus – well – *wonderin'* if you couldn't . . . ?'

'NO!' I shouted. 'No WAY, Trapp! Quite specifically, quite categorically, and *most* bloody emphatically – *NO!*'

I was sweating profusely by the time I finally clambered under the corner of number one's tattered hatch tent and eased myself into the canvas-diffused gloom of the hold itself.

My distressed condition hadn't been entirely caused by the humidity either. For a start, practical terror had compelled me to crawl laboriously on hands and knees along the rusted length of the *Charon*'s port side foredeck while Weston and his laugh-a-minute team lined the starboard bulwarks less than a dead man's spit away, already fully preoccupied in pointing guns and things outboard with, it seemed to me, kamikaze determination – while secondly, every muscle in my body ached from the constant strain of anticipating the Wagnerian overture to several large Soviet-manufactured naval shells descending upon me from a great height.

Well, a Prokofiev overture maybe? I mean, a wind-up in the style of Comrade Prokofiev would surely be more appropriate under the circumstances, wouldn't it . . . ?

Once under cover I lowered myself hastily down the corroded vertical ladder to the tween deck where the container had, presumably, been stowed. Yeah, I could see it over there, lashed securely between stacks of ammunition boxes and other assorted militaria; gleaming sullenly in the half-light.

I frowned uncertainly. It seemed unexpectedly quiet in the hold; only the rumble and squeal of our miraculously still turning shaft allied with an occasional creak of protest from the tortured hull broke the tense silence.

Suddenly I realized what was missing. The generator, which had been coupled to the container when we sailed, wasn't running any more. Hurriedly I examined it. It was still connected by a heavy-duty umbilical but now the ignition switch was in the 'off' mode, and the fuel tap had been shut. Someone, presumably acting under orders, had deliberately shut down the power supply.

But why? It presented yet another unwanted riddle – what possible motive could Weston have had in cutting power to the container's user system several hours *before* we were due to arrive at Ras al Djibela?

Not that we ever would, now. But that was hardly the point.

How long did I have left – five, maybe six minutes?

Nervously I scanned the tent corner, half-expecting one of the Colonel's men to appear with weapon ready levelled, about to pre-empt the Libyans with a 500-rounds-per-second burst ... but I was also becoming perversely determined to satisfy my own curiosity now. Before everything became academic.

Urgently I inspected the container itself.

Made of what appeared to be stainless steel it stood rather higher than myself, looking more like a portable butcher's cold store than any form of weapon. That made it some two metres square and slightly longer in its fore and aft dimension. Snap retaining catches were situated around both sides – release them and I assumed the whole end-plate could be lowered to reveal the contents.

Whereupon, my own inquisitiveness fulfilled, I could cut back to the bridge just in nice time to get blown to bits by courtesy of Edward Trapp.

I decided that out of sheer spite I wasn't going to tell

97

him what *was* in it, anyway. I'd just smile secretively while Trapp jumped up and down in apoplectic frustration, so's I could go up in smoke looking all knowing and enigmatic.

BLOODY Trapp!

Taking a deep breath I unclipped the retaining catches and ever so carefully eased the pressed steel plate from what turned out to be a tight rubber seal. Even as I did so a wave of cold, unpleasantly fœtid air seemed to tumble from the container and spill over me, turning my own sweating skin clammy in an instant.

I hesitated then, just for a moment. Something deep inside me had begun screaming, 'Don't go any further, Miller. There's a horror in there: something awful. Something you're better not to know about!'

But then I countered savagely, 'Awwww, what the *hell*! You're dead anyway, Mister. Curiosity's already killed you: it killed you the moment you couldn't resist that bloody infantile letter in Rotterdam . . . !'

I wrenched the end-plate away . . . and blinked!

Instead of only one riddle, SIX now confronted me. Six metal sub-compartments, rather like a pair of over-sized three-drawer filing cabinets placed side by side. And each drawer front presenting both a dulled brass handle and yet a further unwelcome challenge.

. . . maybe four minutes left?

Savagely seizing the nearest handle – Lord, it felt cold: cold and all hazed with condensation – I pulled.

And came face to face with . . . a plastic BAG!

I think I cursed then: long and loud and quite uncaring for the consequence should the mercenaries on deck overhear me. Of course my near tearful rage was directed entirely at Trapp, as usual. He wasn't a mortal man, not even a particularly appalling man: he was nothing less than a monster, a shambling instrument of the devil with a cap like a half-opened tin of spaghetti, a warlock's familiar called Gorbals Wullie and an unlimited capacity for the perverse. I began to hallucinate then: that Trapp had been sent to condemn me to some eternal half-life in which I constantly wrestled with one of those diabolical Chinese box puzzles of the kind which, on opening the first, you come upon another box. Within which you discover yet *another* box. Within which you discov . . . !

The bag apparently filled the length of the drawer. Made of thick green plastic it at least boasted a zip-fastener: one of the very few examples – apart from weaponry, that was – of modern technology aboard Trapp's bloody *Charon*! Carelessly I gripped the metal tongue between finger and shaking thumb, and yanked.

. . . only to find I still couldn't see a rotten thing! It was too dark to discern detail down there in that sweltering hold while the bag, being stiff and unresilient, had parted only enough to reveal a shadowy slit.

How long *now*? Maybe three minutes at most? Suddenly a shaft of vagrant sunlight moved within the hold as the ship rose uneasily to a swell. Something glittered dully and I leaned forward, thrusting my face close to the plastic aperture, urgently seeking some recognizable feature by which I could finally identify the contents of that hateful cargo.

It glittered again. I wrenched the zip a little further apart and found myself staring at close range into . . .

'Awwwww JEsus!'

. . . an EYE?

A very mournful, very *dead* eye?

A very obviously HUMAN eye?

Well *you'd've* staggered back with a squeak of revulsion too, wouldn't you? If you'd just opened some filing cabinet at random, and promptly found yourself peering eyeball to eyeball with a corpse?

You wouldn't?

Not even if you considered it an odds-on bet that the cadaver you'd just met had five more part-defrosted associates stacked in the other drawers?

... or part-*frozen*, of course. I suppose it rather depended on your point of view.

Anyway it must have taken me all of thirty precious seconds to revert to a level of just ordinary hysteria. And another half-minute to steel myself to further investigate the contents of what, being wise after the event, had demonstrably turned out to be a green plastic body bag.

It appeared to have been shot through the head.

The corpse, I mean – not the plastic bag.

Male. White Caucasian male in fact, to employ the terminology so beloved by cinematographic enthusiasts of the American cop genre, like Trapp and Gorbals Wullie.

Trying not to gag I tentatively poked the pallid cheek, feeling, at the same time, ridiculously apologetic. It gave with the sullen plasticity of an oven-ready turkey, from which it hardly demanded a pathologist's expertise to conclude that Weston must have initiated the defrosting process some hours before. Though why on earth he should've wanted to freeze the guy in the first place I simply couldn't imagi . . . ?

Oh, by the way, its – the – cadaver's name was Jablonski. Initial W.

Moreover I deduced in a flash that Jablonski, W. had almost certainly been a military man for some time before his death. A sergeant, to be *absolutely* specific.

'Shades of Holmes', do I hear you gasp in utter amazement? Resurrected from the Reichenbach Falls in the cool analytical guise of Chief Officer Miller, the Hercule Poirot of the sea?

Not really.

I simply read his name tag, same as anyone would.

His army-issue name tag, that was. The one sewn above the right-hand breast pocket of the US Special Forces combat uniform the corpse was wearing.

I scrambled, heart still palpitating uncontrollably, back up the ladder to the bridge to find that the Libyan frigate had already overtaken us to the extent that she was now ploughing the long swells less than half a mile astern and broad on the *Charon*'s starboard quarter.

And that was the most cheering aspect of my hero's return. I also came face to black-scowling countenance with Trapp, whose heartfelt gratitude for my having risked my life a good ten minutes prematurely – and purely to satisfy HIS bloody curiosity at that! – was obviously matched only by his overwhelming relief at my safe delivery.

'I don't suppose it ever occurred to YOU,' he grumbled, 'that while you wus jollyin' below decks, Mister, *I* been carryin' all the strain up 'ere – so what took yer so long?'

I fought off my first impulse to storm back down to number one and invite a warmer welcome from Jablonski.

'Weston and his brown jobs,' I retorted sullenly. 'They're all set to defend the second siege of the Alamo down there.'

'He is headstrong,' Trapp agreed critically. 'Not subtle like me . . . Well, go *on* – what was in it then?'

'In what?'

'In the container?'

'Ohhhh, BUGGER the container!'

Needless to say my avowed intention of maintaining an aloof and tantalizing secrecy had dissolved the moment I confirmed how close the Libyan Navy actually was. Furthermore, advising Trapp he might conceivably have contractual grounds for levying some exorbitant surcharge in respect of undeclared passengers and/or unmanifested frozen cargo hardly came top of my agenda for discussion right then.

'Bugger the . . . ? But it's ship's *business*,' he protested, patently shocked that I should place selfish concern before the pursuit of profit.

'All right – bugger ship's BUSINESS then!'

Well, an attitude like that represented, for Trapp, utter sacrilege. It was also like waving a red rag to a particularly undiplomatic bull.

'Now you lissen, Mister. I'm the Captain an' you're jus' crew – I gotter bloody *right* to kno –'

It was then that Gorbals Wullie methodically commenced battering the wheelhouse door from the inside, indicating that Trapp had sneakily stolen a leaf from Weston's command philosophy to ensure his key personnel – Wullie, that was – also remained steadfastly at action station during our current crisis.

He'd turned the key.

'You damage it, you PAY f'r it!' the Captain roared, diverting his frustration towards his incarcerated helmsman instead.

'Oh, aye? An' what WITH – mah WAGIS . . . ?' the Key Personnel screamed back, provoked beyond reason, then began to employ his steel-capped boots on the bulging door panels as well.

'You've GOT to heave to,' I practically begged. 'They may hold their fire if we make it plain we're stopping, Trapp.'

'I told yer I knows Ayrabs like the back o' me hand,' he pursued doggedly. 'Specially them Libyan Ayrabs. They can't never come to a decision. You got plenty o' time yet: to tell me what wus in the contain – !'

A puff of smoke materialized from the Riga's 'A' turret. I heard the shell parting the air with the rip of tearing sailcloth then a plume of tainted water rose from the sea fifty feet ahead of the *Charon II*'s battered bow.

Trapp stood uncertainly for a second, revising his knowledge of Libyan Ayrabs.

Eventually: ''Alf a million roubles worth o' electronic fire control an' they *still* miss,' he muttered lamely.

'They bloody MEANT to miss!' I bawled. 'That was only a warning shot across our bows, Trapp. At this range a blind drunk could point a tenpenny bloody catapult and *still* wipe us out!'

I could see the inevitability of it was slowly gaining acceptance.

Not that it should have mattered that much to Trapp – the Libyans catching us. It was all right for him: he reckoned he had cancer anyway. So *he* wasn't likely to connive and make many more mistakes of judgement for very much longer either way.

'Oh, all RIGHT!' he shouted as if it was all my fault. 'You won't never accept you're aboard a grey'ound o' the seas, will you? I'm sayin' she could still outrun 'em easy, Mister, but if you insists on chuckin' your hand in, then I s'ppose we all got to.'

I rushed for the wing telegraph to ring down 'Stop Engine' before he changed his mercurial mind, but the verdigrised brass handle came off in my hand. Feverishly I began thumping to get into the locked wheelhouse and reach the engineroom voice pipe while Gorbals Wullie hammered equally frenziedly on the other side to get out.

Trapp watched us sourly for a moment, then indicated the gesticulating Wullie. 'Now 'im, he's thick: 'e's been tryin' to escape through that door f'r a good five minnits already. But you, Mister – you bein' a qualified ship's master an' a clever bugger to boot – I'd've thought *you* might've noticed there ain't no glass innit . . .'

A trifle sheepishly perhaps, but nevertheless with enormous dignity, I lifted my leg. And climbed through the gaping window.

*

Two minutes later we were hove-to and rolling sullenly while the frigate raced at full speed down our starboard flank. I knew they would be scrutinizing us minutely through glasses from her bridge so I tried to appear merely as a bewildered crew member of a typical unsavoury Arab coastal trader wondering what all the fuss was about.

I'd even begun to nourish a tiny seed of hope. Despite my earlier fears the Libyans obviously intended to hold fire at least until they'd asked a few questions. They'd been below the horizon and thus denied direct observation when we'd actually turned on their sister Komar while, judging by the speed at which they'd overhauled us, they couldn't have afforded more than a brief hunt for survivors when passing through the position of her sinking.

Possibly they harboured no suspicion yet of the cold-blooded manner of her black gang's dying. And Trapp Cornered always had been Trapp At His Most Devious, a past master at conveying injured innocence. There was still a slim chance he might pull off some form of outrageous bluff, even convince them to steam off in search of a more likely quarry.

Uncomfortably I watched as the Riga thundered past, every gun and mount still laying on us with robotronic precision – and not aiming fifty feet ahead of our bow this time.

She began to turn hard to port, decks leaning at a rakish angle, bows swinging fast to head back towards us. Abruptly the Captain broke the testy silence he'd lapsed into since we'd stopped, and looked pleased.

'She's slowin' to half-speed, which means they're not quite certain. I'll 'ave 'em dangling from the end o' me little finger in another minnit. You see, Mister: I knows them Ayrabs li –'

'Don't!' I snarled threateningly. 'Don't you *dare* tell

me you knows 'em like the back of your hand, Trapp. Ever again.'

'For a pipsqueak Reserve two-an'-a-half-striper you've suddenly got bloody uppity,' he complained petulantly.

'An' don't start THAT again, either.'

The Libyan steadied for a second pass. While we waited Trapp started picking more bits off the tattered rail and went back to looking morose. 'I really don't know what's happened to you,' he muttered petulantly. 'It's like you'd found somethin' nasty under your shoe.'

Which reminded me of the late Jablonski, W. which, in turn, raised a whole new generation of worries. It suddenly occurred to me that, even if we did escape retribution through some Trapp-engineered miracle on this occasion, and did eventually reach Ras al Djibela – then what? What further unpleasant surprises, what still undreamed-of horrors awaited us there?

I mean, for a start I couldn't even begin to imagine the connection six defrosting dead men dressed in military uniform could conceivably have with robbing a *bank* . . . ?

The frigate was returning at about fifteen knots now, still rolling synchronously from the momentum of her turn. I caught the flash of binoculars as they studied us uncertainly – probably wondering how the *Charon* even managed to float, never mind devastate a Komar missile boat. Her foredeck 'A' and 'B' turrets still laid on us, though.

Meanwhile Key Personnel Gorbals Wullie, finding himself redundant as helmsman since we weren't going anywhere, clambered through the wheelhouse window and crawled over to us on hands and knees before poking his head cautiously above the bridge rail. No one shot him with an anti-submarine missile so he stood up and looked cocky: tremendously pleased with himself.

'Ah should've been on the films, so ah should. Wis that

no' a braw act I pit on then, Mister Miller sir – kidding them on I wis panickin'?'

Rather than dilute my concentration by kicking him while there was so much going on, I determinedly ignored the lying wee monster. The Riga had stopped her own engines and had begun to lose way, gliding steadily abeam of us. Her grey superstructure towered above the *Charon II*'s eccentric masts while to my eyes each gun barrel had adopted the scale of a railway tunnel. Everything depended on Trapp now: whether we were going to live at least a little longer.

I held my breath as, cupping horny hands once more, Trapp adopted his most bewildered totally-innocent-of-any-misdemeanour, bluff and decent, hard-done-to yet, despite everything, transparently honest ship's master expression.

Now, whether Wullie was garrulously relieved at not finding himself in an advanced state of dismemberment yet, or simply too nervous to keep silent, I don't know, but of course he had to go and make some completely inane comment at precisely that critical moment.

Something broadly sub-Glaswegian and unintelligible, along the lines of: '. . . at you twa . . . heid tae heid wi' . . . matelots so 'e wull.'

I started to snarl, 'Shut UP for – !' then halted abruptly. 'Say that again?'

His thin weasel features took on a look of weary patience.

'Ah *said*: "Thon boot-faced Colonel'll be fair miffed at you two f'r stoppin' *his* lads havin' a proper go at yon Ayrab . . ."!'

'*Weston!*'

Trapp's frozen stare met mine.

'We've forgotten WESTON!' I shouted as the sleek warship came precisely abeam – and within point-blank Viper range.

. . . the multi-*whoosh* of six anti-tank rockets simultaneously leaving their launchers became submerged by a bedlam of drumfire as every heavy automatic weapon aboard the *Charon* opened up in concert.

The Riga's forward 'A' and 'B' turrets were taken out immediately, the mercenaries' HEAT charges melting through and exploding with devastating effect within the lightly armoured gunhouses. Her open decks became a firestorm of ricocheting, whining 7.62 calibre tracer and ball.

I watched hypnotized as a third and fourth Viper blew the topside of her navigating bridge into flaming, whirling cardboard while the blister-configurated twin 37mm mount crowning the frigate's superstructure simply detonated with a radiating flash as its ready-use ammunition exploded.

The final pair of rockets slammed into the base of her latticed mainmast, which tottered crazily before slewing to her port side, trailing the heavy Soviet Slim Net search radar scanner and most of her communications fit with it . . .

'Oh, 'ell,' Trapp muttered in an enormously shocked voice. ' 'E gone an' done it now.'

'Correction,' I swallowed. 'He's gone and done for US now!'

Because, unless some miracle occurred, I realized that any advantage gained through the initial surprise of the mercenary assault must shortly be negated by the Libyan's sheer size and speed. The pre-emptive savagery seemingly inherent in Weston's philosophy had hurt the frigate, but by no means mortally.

Already the sea was boiling under her flat overhanging counter as, below her waterline – and so virtually invulnerable to any weapon the *Charon* mounted – twin 20,000 shp steam turbines whined to emergency full ahead. Instantly the flushdecked grey hull began to kick hard to port and draw away like a taut-strung thorough-bred leaving the starting gate.

The acrid and already hatefully familiar stench from the hammering GPMGs was beginning to drift sullenly to the *Charon*'s bridge now. Bang, *whooosh*! Six more Vipers jetted from our foredeck within moments of each other, trailing white-smoke spirals as they chased the frantically evacuating Riga.

Lord but those troopers of Weston's must've been drilled to automaton standard. The conclusion again plagued my bemused mind even during those frantic few seconds – surely no ordinary mercenaries could possibly achieve such precise co-ordina – ?

The smoke trails overtook the violently swinging frig-ate to converge above her fantail like a swarm of enraged bees. A ripple of detonations defaced her after end, already presenting an ever dwindling target; three HEAT charges exploding uselessly within her angled funnel casing, two more melting at supersonic speed into her after housing where they must have caused further carnage, while the final rocket blew away the twin aerial array aft along with most of her second 37mm guncrew while she still clawed frantically for offing . . .

Gorbals Wullie started dancing up and down with unrestrained glee: 'By Goad but we've scunnered them, Captin! Och but huv we no' banjoed THEM good an' proper, eh?'

Neither Trapp nor I joined in. Only a rueful smile, almost apologetic, brushed his lips. 'I said Weston was 'eadstrong. I didn't claim he wus no Admiral Nelson, Mister.'

I just nodded dumbly. Weston's defiant gamble may have been impeccably executed but, in naval terms, it had been totally ill-conceived. The Colonel was a soldier, obviously didn't appreciate how modern warships are fought, but Trapp and I did: we were both grimly aware that control of the Libyan's remaining batteries would be effected from her electronic warfare space below decks as soon as her shaken crew finally got their act together.

And that vital target, like her engines, was proof against anything smaller than an Exocet.

Furthermore, we'd failed to neutralize her after 'Y' turret, already training uncertainly to counter the Riga's weaving and lay squarely on the *Charon*. It was a 3.9-inch bombardment weapon: alone it could dismember us from miles distant, while very soon her torpedo tubes could be brought to bear as well.

Not that she would need them. Not to puncture a rust bubble.

Trapp suddenly muttered, 'Ohhhhh shi − !' whereupon I saw Wullie stop dancing abruptly, noted the way his jaw adopted an even more vacant droop than usual, and whirled just in time to register the puff of grey smoke framing the particular 'Y' turret in question.

'INCOMING!' Trapp bawled. Entirely superfluously.

'*Geddown!*' I screamed at Gorbals Wullie. With even greater irrelevance.

'Ah'm on mah bluidy WAY . . . !' Wullie shrieked back from mid-dive.

There came a massive detonation from outboard before quite a lot of the Gulf of Sirte, warm and reeking of Soviet-manufactured explosive, thundered across the bridge in a long hissing cascade. I felt the tug of sea water drag me helplessly towards the end of the bridge until I brought up hard to find myself focusing hazily on our now distant adversary through a brand new shrapnel-torn gap.

I remember brooding dispassionately, 'The next one'll have my name on it − all our names on it . . . well, with *his* luck, all but bloody TRAPP's anyway!' then I heard the synchronized blast of Viper launch tubes yet again from our foredeck, and mused instead, 'How in God's name can those men know they are about to die, yet *still* fight with such cohesion?'

The bees, impotent now at that range, still smoked defiantly in ever-decreasing spirals towards the Libyan warship while Trapp began hauling himself to his feet.

'We *gotter* run f'r it now,' he grumbled with a touch of his old asperity. 'Like I wanted to at the start, remember?'

I watched our first rockets splash harmlessly astern of the frigate, and switched my absorbed gaze back to her 3.9. It would reply any moment now.

'Don't be *bloody* silly, Trapp,' I said.

. . . the climbing plume of water which suddenly appeared against the Libyan's hull was astonishingly white. Once again I thought absently of the teeth of the murdered Arab sailor.

There was something else familiar about that incongruous Excalibur of sea spray. Nothing to do with teeth, or even from my recent past. Just something which stirred a vague, half-forgotten sensation in my gut.

Then, almost in tandem, a second fountain seemed to rise from her waterline – alongside her bridge this time.

And *then* the low grey warship began to . . . well, to blow *UP* I suppose!

Spewing forth an ascending, monstrously interweaving ball of fire.

Chapter Seven

The Libyan must have been steaming at thirty knots when she broke into three separate pieces, the raked forepart immediately driving hard below the surface of the Gulf and carrying her already gutted 'A' turret with it.

Her midships hull section comprising 'B' gun, the bridge and most of her tophamper slewed demoniacally sideways then leaned further and further to starboard until we could just make out little white ants of sailors clinging stunned to their suddenly berserk world. A blink of a disbelieving eye later, exploding magazines fireballed up through her tiered decks to fling great shards of metal and minute scraps of instantly roasted men in a wide concussive flash which lit the sea itself and set tiny wavelets dancing and rearing back in fright for a half-mile all around.

Meanwhile the Riga's after part swerved erratically off course as if taking unilateral evasive action and, still propelled by the latent thrust of forty thousand Russian sea horses, kept on going for two or three cables with a great dam of boiling water mounting crazily ahead of it. Ultimately its foremost transverse bulkhead imploded with a thunderous roar, whereupon the sundered stern reared to reveal more white-ant men fighting to abandon that same 'Y' turret with which, a moment ago, they had proposed to kill us.

The part-ship's angle of descent quickly increased, exposing still slowly revolving screws which glinted briefly above the fire on the sea before being dragged below a bubbling black spew of fuel oil.

And she was gone.

On the *Charon*'s sea-washed bridge Trapp had been the first to break the stupefied silence.

'Them Vipers: they're *very* good value f'r money,' he'd mused in a small, even humble voice. Eventually.

'Jeeeeze,' Gorbals Wullie whispered, invariably pre-occupied more with consequence than conclusion. 'Thon Qaddafi's gonna be awfy mad wi' yous, Captin.'

I stirred uneasily. We'd survived, yes, but something was still very wrong: something a little less haphazard than your average miracle. Hi-tech weapons? Super-mercenaries? Prepacked cadavers? And now warships which conveniently self-destructed in the nick of time?

I just lay there pondering all of those enigmas – as well as the significance of the white columns I'd watched rise alongside the Riga as a prelude to her disintegration.

Trapp unlocked the wheelhouse and a moment later I heard him in pugnaciously familiar voice again, threatening to haul Chief Bucalosie bodily from engineroom to bridge via his own voice pipe if 'e didn't stop cryin' an' start the bloody ENGINE again!

Already the area of debris-strewn sea where the frigate had sunk was fast merging with the approaching North Africa night. Some crewmen may well have still been clinging to life among that churning flotsam: explosive could be a fickle agent of both God and Allah, but then I glanced over our foredeck to see Weston also scanning the desolate scene through field glasses. I further noted that, while the majority of his mercenary complement had already stood down with Viper tubes casually de-ported, Hermann and two others had laconically stayed by their GPMGs along the bulwark.

There was wreckage to cling to, the water was warm

and the Libyan coast less than twenty miles off. It suggested any survivors out there would stand a better chance of remaining so without *Charon*'s doubtful charity.

Trapp, it seemed, had arrived at much the same conclusion. He appeared beside me as the *Spatz* restarted with a great clanking and sputtering of soot from our spindle funnel, and gestured outboard.

'We'll take the humanitarian view,' he grunted bleakly. 'Leave the buggers to sink or swim. At least they'll 'ave the option without Weston an' that bloody 'Ermann around.'

'Wan o' these days ah'm goin' tae hae a square go at yon poofy Melon Squisher,' Wullie threatened darkly, though at the same time making sure his voice didn't actually carry as far as the foredeck. 'Ah mind once, when ah wis the ace hard man doon the Mocambo Ballroo –'

It didn't take anyone long to revert to lunatic normality. Not aboard Trapp's ships.

'You wus beaten up by a partic'larly vicious little girl?' the Captain led nicely.

'Two!' Wullie protested unthinkingly. 'Lissen, ah fought like a tiger, so ah did. Afore they played dirty an' pit the stiletto heels in.'

Trapp took him by his grubby protruding ear and marched him to the wheelhouse.

'You get stood steerin' on Tel Afrah shoals, Tiger, or I'll arrange f'r you to 'ave yer square go at Hermann right now. That monster could let yer borrow 'is *machine*-gun an' still leave you lookin' like a human Lego set before it gets built up.'

He wandered back. 'Square go! His idea of a square go is muggin' some blind old lady what's already been run over by a tramcar – an' then only if the bloody tramcar's still pinning 'er down . . . Right, Mister, we got a bit o' time now; what was in it then?'

113

I blinked. Sometimes his thought processes took a bit of catching up with. 'Say again?'

'The *container*. What was *in* it?'

I opened my mouth, then shut it again uncertainly. Suddenly a vision of the gunshot wound in Jablonski's pallid temple swam starkly to mind. Desperate to evacuate that claustrophobic hold or not, my fear of Weston's putting a matching hole through mine for challenging his orders had still been strong enough to ensure my leaving the container precisely as I'd found it.

But now, if I even hinted to Trapp that he'd been shipping undisclosed freezer cargo for free, then I guessed he would storm straight down to the Colonel and demand his bloody excess freight without any thought for the consequences – like how Weston would display considerable persistence in enquiring after the identity of Trapp's informant: probably by nominating Hermann as question master.

'I didn't manage to open it. It was . . . er, locked.'

'Shit!' Trapp erupted in renewed commercial frustration, kicking at an already blast- and age-eroded bridge panel which promptly fell off. 'Can't you do NOTHIN' proper either? You could've used a crowbar, Mister: a jemmy . . . !'

Or something equally subtle. Like a HEAT rocket charge.

. . . which reminded me – waterspouts! Climbing white columns of spray. Right alongside the frigate and just before she blew up . . . I knew why they'd stirred dim memories now. I'd watched much the same phenomena all too often a long time ago, and had felt the same clutch of apprehension then; the same sick anticipation. Plumes of water rising above lines of doggedly steaming and ever so much more gallant ships during a previous madman's conflict.

'Trapp,' I interrupted, even while hardly crediting what

I suspected myself. 'The Riga – look, I know it's crazy but . . . I think she was torpedoed!'

He must've been listening for a change as well as grumbling, because he stopped going on about breaking and entering. At least long enough to eye me derisively.

'You caught the sun or somethin?'

I shook my head firmly.

'I was watching the Libyan just before she blew. She took two hits on her starboard side.'

'Yeah – from the Vipers. The brown jobs had jus' launched a third salvo, remember?'

'Exploding *below* her waterline? Powerful enough to break her into three pieces? And anyway, she was out of range by that time, Trapp. I saw at least some of them splash well astern of her.'

His brows met in fierce recall. 'Nag, nag, NAG! I'll tell yer now, I'm gettin' *bloody* fed up wi' this.'

'Oh dear, I am sorry *you're* getting fed up,' I said scathingly.

But I could see him wavering; uncertainty matched only by his unwillingness to concede the mounting evidence that – to put it baldly – he'd really landed us in it this time.

'You've got to face it, Trapp,' I pressed. 'There are too many questions raised about the real motive for this trip: too many anomalies. Things can't be left to go on like this.'

'Oh, all RIGHT!' he shouted eventually. 'Jus' to please you I WILL do somethin'. An' now!'

'Thank God,' I breathed.

'Yeah – I'll jus' go an' have it out with Weston: demand bloody explanations!'

I stared at him in utter disconcertion. I mean, *I'd* had more a calm and balanced reappraisal of our situation in mind before we decided on what action to take, rather than Trapp's steaming off bent on purple-faced confrontation with thirty-plus armed killers.

But it was far too late by then. Trapp In Pique had long proved a Trapp Not To Be Reasoned With.

I watched him head furiously for the foredeck with, to say the least, some slight misgivings.

It was dark and the wreckage of the frigate had faded six miles astern by the time he returned to the bridge.

I knew the moment I saw his bear-like silhouette at the head of the ladder that Weston hadn't told him anything approximating to the truth.

Trapp looked far too good-humoured, far too pleased with himself to have elicited any plausible justification for why six dead men lay in macabrely pre-planned defrost down below.

Not that I could entirely blame him for that, considering I hadn't briefed him to ask the question. I'll even concede that my own privileged awareness of the Jablonski Factor did forearm me with more than my usual scepticism from the start – but there was still no possible excuse for the naïvety which he *did* display.

Or for his complete lack of concern to relieve *my* anxiety crisis.

For a start he just wandered straight past me and leaned over the wing on his own, gazing dreamily far beyond the dark horizon. Eventually I got thoroughly brassed off at being ignored and, swallowing my pride, moved to join him.

'Well,' I demanded acidly. 'What did he say?'

'Who?'

'Bloody WES – !' I had to fight hard for self-control before lowering my voice. 'Colonel Weston, Trapp. The tall person who kills people – what answers did he give you?'

He sounded as though probity was his watchword. 'Can't tell yer that, Mister. Sorry.'

'What d'you mean – you *can't*?'

'Nashnul security. I'm, ah, sworn to silence.'

I stared with incredulity at the two-dimensional black shape with the wagging lid that was the new Responsible Trapp. What in God's name *had* Weston promised to make him as docile – as bloody obnoxious in such a sycophantic way – as this?

'WHAT national security? You haven't *got* a nation. You've disowned Britain, other than when it suits you to claim you're still a Royal Navy officer . . .'

I could've sworn he smiled a little in the darkness then. In a sort of superior, infuriatingly secretive manner, but I was nearly biting the rail with frustration by that time and didn't follow it up.

'. . . and the last passport you ever felt the need to present in order to gain entry to anyone's country was probably written with a quill bloody PEN!'

'I've got seven actually,' he returned defensively. 'Down in me cabin. I got papers from Korky Tokoglu certifyin' I'm a white Tanzanian, a Brazil nut, a Polack, a Japane . . .'

'A JapanESE?'

'Rubber solution – Christ it does make yer eyes sting if yer dabs it on the wrong spot . . .'

'Stick to the bloody POINT! What nation's security have you suddenly developed this remarkable allegiance to, Trapp – and how much has it cost them?'

'Not a single dollar . . . extra!' he answered unthinkingly.

'Dollar? So we're talking about bloody America then?'

'We're talking about the Land o' Golden Opportunity: the United States of America, Mister, an' I won't 'ave my officers referrin' to Colonel Weston's roots as "bloody" anythin'.'

'Oh, it's *Colonel* Weston now, is it? Suddenly he's one of the good guys – a patriot, eh? While there was silly old me thinking I'd heard you claim he was just a simple old-fashioned mercenary person who robbed banks on behalf of international airlines.'

Trapp shuffled uncomfortably. 'Yeah, well, we still are goin' to hit the bank in Ras al Djibela an' . . .' He drew a deep, anguished breath; obviously rectitude still demanded a degree of suffering. 'An' torch the safe deposit.'

'But your sudden fervent allegiance to all things American: it isn't going to cost you *money*, is it? I mean, you're still convinced you're going to get paid two million dollars out of it before they light the bonfire?'

'One,' Trapp corrected with a certain prudish asperity.

'It wis TWA right enough, Mister Miller sir,' Wullie's voice insisted from the depths of the wheelhouse.

'You get steerin' an' stop lissenin', Bunny Bigears,' Trapp roared, briefly reverting to his original charm. 'I won't 'ave CREW eavesdroppin' on private conversations atween Officers neither.'

A sudden startling thought hit me; almost as stupefying as my still unconfirmed suspicion that a torpedo might have taken out the Libyan Riga. But it would answer at least some of the riddles which had plagued me – the superb cohesion of Weston's troopers; the unshakable discipline; the US pattern weaponry. It might even afford some link, however tenuous, with the dead Jablonski.

'Trapp, does Weston have any connection with US Special Forces?'

I could see his eyes grow wide even through the blackness.

''Ow did *you* know?'

Hurriedly I parried the question. 'You've been conned right down the line, haven't you? And by the US Government, of all people . . .'

The jigsaw pieces began to fall into place even as I

struggled to visualize the likely scenario. Even if US Intelligence really had pinpointed the location of Qaddafi's terror funds, the Americans must still have faced a political problem. They could hardly mount an overt strike against the Libyan mainland without once again inviting universal condemnation, as Reagan's 1986 raids had proved . . . but terrorism presented a constant thorn in the flesh of any President seeking eventual re-election. Some CIA-inspired clandestine operation might well have been authorized as an alternative, whereby an undercover mission – a group outwardly seen to be acting from purely mercenary motives, but secretly composed of US Special Forces personnel – sought to destroy the dollar cache of Ras al Djibela.

If they succeeded, then a White House leak was a powerful way of hinting at the truth. All Hail the President!

While if they failed – who'd care about a few stateless soldiers of fortune anyway?

Even Weston's 'admission', elicited so brilliantly from him by the cleverness of Trapp – about working for some vaguely defined consortium of international airlines – offered just the right degree of plausibility. Particularly to an idiot who'd just been offered two million dollars to encourage him to believe it.

. . . while, having once conceived the plan, all the Americans had to do was to figure how they could infiltrate that specialist team – as well, I fervently hoped, as *ex*filtrate them again once their mission had been achieved. But for that delicate task they could hardly risk employing any of the closely watched elements of the US Sixth Fleet, could they?

No. What they'd needed to come up with was some means of transport which would not only attract overwhelming indifference from the professional Libya watchers but, more importantly should things go wrong and the operation *was* compromised, would point no journalistic trail leading clear back to the Pentagon.

My hypothesis so far was at least tenable.

Presumably the President's men had then placed US Special Forces Colonel Buck Weston in command, given him *carte blanche* to commit international mayhem in the name of anyone but the United States, and promptly despatched him to scour the lowspots of the world in search of either a very gullible, a totally immoral or a myopically greedy man.

Or better still – someone who embodied all three weaknesses, with a few more cardinal vices thrown in as a bonus.

So if, subsequently, within the Istanbul emporium of Korkut Tokoglu the Fifteenth, Weston *had* perchanced upon such a paragon of degeneration: one who also happened to know Libyan waters like the back of his hand in addition to commanding the kind of nondescript hulk you wouldn't dare inspect too closely for fear of catching rust . . . ?

Yet it *still* didn't add up. And not simply because my feverish conjecturing hadn't yet explained how the frigid Jablonski and co-cadavers fitted into such a plan. Not even because I considered it barely credible that any US submarine commander's rules of engagement would have permitted him to go so far as to attack a major Libyan warship simply to prevent the loss of the mission – for it would have had to *be* an American boat in order to fit my scenario, if indeed a torpedo had caused the frigate's timely demise in the first place?

But no – my continuing scepticism stemmed primarily from my own intimate knowledge of Trapp's essentially rapacious character.

The bloody man was utterly obsessed, don't you see? By penalty clauses and surcharges and excess freight levies and any other argumentative means of extracting yet another few quid from a customer – Trapp would *never* have accepted so mildly the revelation that he'd been conned: that he'd actually been working for the US Government all the time . . . so why *had* Trapp suddenly become so defensive where the Colonel was concerned? He couldn't STAND the guy an hour ago!

And on top of everything else there was Trapp's 'Nashnul Security' patriotic crap. From a self-confessed blackguard with *seven* passports? Including one proving he was JapanESE . . . ?

'Trapp,' I said levelly. 'Come clean on what Weston has bribed you with, or I shall cast you forthwith into the Gulf of Sirte and subsequently run over you a great many times with your own bloody SHIP!'

There was a long and pensive silence during which his ludicrous silhouette seemed to swell both in stature and in pomposity.

'All right,' he smirked eventually, quite incapable of concealing the self-satisfaction in his voice. 'But you'd better start salutin' smartish when you sees me if I do tell yer, Mister. *And* callin' me "sir" like you should've been doing anyroad.'

'HUH!' Ordinary Seaman Bunny Bigears jeered in sardonic *sotto voce* from the wheelhouse. I, for my part, just glowered.

'If you're proposing to bring up that Commander RN argument again, Trapp . . .'

'Christ, no,' he protested with quite convincing innocence. 'That's incidental. Yer own conscience an' Queen's Reg'lashuns has to be yer judge on that one.'

I blinked uncertainly. Neither my conscience nor Queen's Regulations had exactly been uppermost in my thoughts right at that moment.

'Then why should I suddenly have to start saluting you all over again?'

He couldn't keep the secret any longer. It was predictable that, after even a few minutes, the constrictions of Nashnul Security were bound to prove too much for Trapp, what with his self-importance bursting to be recognized like that.

''Cause as a Service reservist yerself you now got another important reason to afford me a proper degree of respect, that's why.'

He swelled even more. 'Y'see, Weston – an' I means *Colonel* Weston, Mister: United States Army an' personal emissary f'r the President – has PROMOTED me, Mister. It's what he called a field promotion. All perfectly legal.'

I frowned, thoroughly confused by then. 'But we aren't IN a field, Trapp. We're on the sea.'

'A *battle*field promotion, smarty pants,' he snapped. 'And lissen, we're IN somethin' all right –, we're in a war out here, Mister: a real shootin' war . . .'

Well, I'd bloody gathered *that*! Anyway, Mitchum had used that line first – or had it been Errol Flynn?

'Pure Johnny Wayne, that wis.' Never a man to let personal resentment stand in the way of true cinematographic approbation, Gorbals Wullie's highly qualified critique pursued me through the darkness. '*Guadalcanal Diary* – we seen it in Djakarta, Nineteen Forty-eight . . . Och but ye acted that magnificent, Captin, so ye did.'

'All right, then just as a matter of passing interest what has Weston –'

'*Colonel* Weston, US Army,' Trapp persisted primly.

'. . . promoted you to?'

He drew himself up to full overbearing swagger. 'You knows how I'm already the senior Commander on 'Er Britannic Majesty's Royal Navy List, Mister?'

'Only by default,' I qualified grudgingly.

He cupped a hand elaborately behind one battered ear. 'Did I hear one o' my junior officers say somethin', *Lieutenant* Commander Miller?'

'Oh, get ON with it, Trapp!'

'Well now, in addition to that, I *also* happens to 'ave been appointed as . . .'

He sounded so nauseatingly pleased with himself, so complacently egotistic, that the first awful premonition hit me before he'd quite finished.

'No,' I pleaded inwardly, 'they wouldn't: not even the Americans – they COULDN'T?'

'. . . a full three ring, brass 'at Commander yet again, Mister. But this time in the United STATES Navy!'

Chapter Eight

Twice Libyan jets had made low, ear-splitting inspection passes above us since the sinking, then gone away in search of a more likely warship killer.

It had been an encouraging sign suggesting that, if any survivors from the Riga had been picked up, then either they'd been too shocked to be able to describe us, or had done so with such accuracy that the Libyan intelligence people had fallen off their chairs laughing before they'd locked them away as being out of their tiny revolutionary minds.

It was approaching midnight, with the *Charon II* running well inshore, by the time Weston himself finally appeared on the bridge.

Apart from a heroin-addicted sodomite pyromaniac – and, I would stress, those qualifications *still* made him one of Trapp's more socially acceptable pirates – called Backfire Joe, who'd only relieved a nerve-exhausted Gorbals Wullie at the wheel after being promised he would get to set fire to someone soon, I was keeping the watch alone: Commander Trapp RN – plus US Navy now and God knew what else by tomorrow – having briefly strutted off to bawl at people and generally behave like the intolerable paranoiac he was fast becoming.

It was typical of human illogicality perhaps, but Weston had assumed a grudging respectability in my eyes since he'd revealed himself as a US Army field officer. To my simplistic way of thinking, mercenaries fought and killed simply for money; regular soldiers served their countries. The Colonel had already proved his singleness of purpose and military competence beyond any doubt, as well as his ability to command those same qualities from his Special Force troopers.

I would never like the man: certainly I didn't propose to trust him to any greater extent than before, and not simply because of the callousness he'd displayed in gunning down the Komar survivors as a matter of operational expediency – we were up against fanatics who would offer little quarter should the situation ever be reversed. Colonel Brother Qaddafi himself had prescribed the rules by declaring his so-called Line of Death across the international waters of Sirte. It seemed reasonable they should apply equally to both sides.

So it wasn't because of that, though I'd been sickened by the murders. No, it was just that I could never, ever forgive Weston for encouraging Trapp to be an even more bumptious, thoroughly reprehensible pain in the neck than he already was.

. . . apart from which, the Colonel obviously hadn't spared even a *thought* to promoting ME.

Two soldiers accompanied Weston to the bridge, carrying a heavy military radio and remote aerial rig. He nodded when he saw me: a shade less curtly, did I perceive, than before?

'Wes . . . er, Colonel?' I acknowledged cautiously.

'Permission requested to establish my comcen, Mister Miller?'

'Please do, Colonel Weston.'

I wondered who he proposed to communicate with. How far away they were, for that matter: portable VHF was surely adequate to control any local operations whereas that radio looked powerful enough to raise the other side of the world, but it hardly seemed prudent to ask. It didn't strike me as being fruitful to test our new-found civility by refusing permission, either. I could hardly fail to observe that the troopers had brought along their M16s as diplomatic fire support.

While the antenna was being rigged Weston came and leaned beside me, gazing towards the faint shadow to starboard that was Libya. The conditions were ideal for the blatant approach Trapp had now committed us to: little moon to reveal our own possibly compromised silhouette, yet with several lights showing all around between which I was threading a discreetly distanced course. Most of them would be the Arab fishing boats which formed an unremarkable nightly feature of any North African inshore scene. With our own navigation lights hastily unearthed, refilled with paraffin from the foc's'le drinks cabinet, and now glimmering cheekily the *Charon* – proceeding at the most unwarlike speed imaginable anyway – would represent a hopefully insignificant addition to the many routine echoes cluttering the Libyan coastal defence radars.

Trapp's bellow came floating from aft. 'Choker, you jus' get stopped throttlin' that Lucille RIGHT now . . . ! Lissen, I don't bloody care if 'e IS wearin' the wrong colour lipstick: he's a bloody good greaser when 'e's normal!'

'I guess the Captain's in regular form tonight,' Weston commented expressionlessly. 'A little goddam louder and the Libs won't need radar: they'll hear him.'

I eyed him surreptitiously: either he was displaying a previously well-suppressed sense of humour or was, with a bit of luck, weighing the operational expediency of having Trapp garrotted by a very large commando. I risked a malicious jibe.

'You mean the "Commander", don't you? United States Navy?'

The Colonel smiled at that. Very drily. 'He told you then?'

I didn't try to conceal my resentment. 'He'll have it in

the *New York Times*, *Le Figaro* and bloody *Pravda* soon as he gets to a telephone.'

Weston looked at me a bit funny then, though I didn't really understand why. 'He also says you believe the Lib frigate might have been torpedoed, Miller. How sure are you about that?'

I frowned cautiously. How sure was the Colonel himself? That, for me, posed the more important question. If a Yankee submarine really had been shadowing us with orders to prevent interference, then surely Weston would have been briefed? In that case, however, considering his whole mission had been facing termination by the Riga, her torpedoing should hardly have come as a surprise. Yet here he was, apparently genuinely puzzled.

'I'm not certain of anything, other than that warships don't conveniently blow up without a damn good reason. And I don't think your Vipers hit her hard enough.'

'My Vipers deliver HEAT rounds with enough smack to take out forty tons of armoured T-72 Russki battle tank, Miller. Sure as hell those paper navy turrets brewed up good. Couldn't that have initiated an explosion in, say, her magazine?'

'Fire travelling down through her ammunition hoists?' I shrugged. Weston was again betraying his ignorance of ships. 'Unlikely. The Soviets must incorporate flash preventers in their systems same as any Western navy does. And anyway, she was hit below the waterline, Colonel.'

'Or hit something herself, maybe?'

'Like?'

'Like a sea mine. Qaddafi's worried by the proximity of the Sixth Fleet for all his sabre rattling. He also stretches International Law to the limit unless it suits him: the guy's quite capable of mining parts of what he believes are his own territorial waters anyhow. Hell, there was even a suspicion he'd strung the odd one around Egypt a few years back.'

I shook my head firmly. 'That frigate didn't hit any mine. Apart from the improbability of even the Libyans running into one of their own fields I saw two distinct and separate explosions.'

'Meaning you still hold to your torpedo theory?'

I shrugged, conscious of his close scrutiny. 'It's the only explanation which fits what I saw. I can't really prove it.'

There'd been something about the intensity of his questioning which finally convinced me that Weston knew even less than I did about the cause of the Riga's loss – which meant I had to face up to yet another riddle: a real Chinese puzzle this time. One that, I had a sneaking suspicion, was concerning Special Forces Colonel Buck Weston every bit as much as myself.

For if it really had been a submarine-launched weapon, yet it *hadn't* been fired by an American boat, then who ELSE might have attacked the Libyans?

Even more worryingly – WHY?

Weston stirred. 'OK, so when do you reckon we'll be there, Miller? It's time we got this show rolling.'

'Just before daybreak should see us in the Ras al Djibela approach – say zero five hundred if our luck and the engine hold out.'

'Trapp's famous Shit's Creek, huh?'

I must have been more tired than I realized. 'Shi'ite's Creek, Colonel.'

He grinned enigmatically. 'I guess Trapp knows where he's going, Mister.'

Still trying to work it out I watched him walk over to the wheelhouse where his troopers had left the radio, then thumb the transmit switch.

'Homer: this is Sunray. Over.'

'Sunray – we read you, sair. Over.'

128

The immediacy of Homer's ethereal reply suggested he must've been waiting anxiously. He sounded like an Arab, too.

'Zero five zero zero – confirm, then implement!'

The exchange was intentionally brief, too meaningless to hold significance for any chance ears monitoring the frequency.

'Roger OK, Sunray. Zero five 'undred. Out!'

So that was it. I'd committed us to an ETA with . . . what? A nervous Arabian bank robber code-named Homer? Who worked for the US Army, implemented unspecified things, was supported by tactical underwater weapons and awaited a consignment of chilled human remains?

Yes: it *did* sound about right so far.

Just about par for the course of any enterprise in which Trapp had a part.

We switched the *Charon*'s navigation lights off – well, we blew them out, really – just before Trapp finally ordered the wheel put hard over to alter for Ras al Djibela.

Gorbals Wullie, having been dragged back to the helm in his unwilling role of key personnel for entering harbour, began to bring the *Charon* gently to starboard.

Full of *bonhomie* as ever, Trapp complained, 'I said ter put her *hard* a st'bd, 'elmsman, not waggle 'er ass like a bloody ballet dancer's.'

Wullie suggested pithily, but nevertheless with re-markable tolerance I thought, that the bluidy rudder'd prob'bly fall off if he did *exactly* what Trapp demanded, whereupon Trapp shouted awful and thoroughly offen-sive remarks concerning the proper place f'r CREW, and about midgit Scotchmen bein' thick as mince, an' that *he* wus the bloody Captin an' he bloody KNEW what 'e was about!

Wullie spun the wheel hard over. Very hard over.

Twenty minutes later, having wearily recovered and reshipped our rudder yet again – another tension-fraught delay during the course of which I melodramatically tore up scores of calculations forecasting all my previous and equally irrelevant ETAs before scattering them pointedly over the wall – we commenced to clank, wheeze and vibrate erratically shorewards once more, still as suicidally bent on invading Libya as ever.

More suicidally, it now promised. What with submarines and Pentagon-sponsored skulduggery apparently beginning to crawl from *Charon II*'s rotting woodwork.

Having said that, Trapp conned us up Shi'ite's Creek – damn it, what *had* Weston found so bloody funny about that? – with his usual clairvoyant ability to read the wind and the scend of the waves better than any local pilot; to interrogate the surface of the water itself, even during the darkest night, on the sub-sea hazards it concealed; and to steer with terrifying confidence following only the most cursory reference to a dog-eared and criminally outdated chart, for some black humped desert feature which could hold no significance as a navigation mark to any other than the bedouin themselves.

Had the rudder detached itself again, or the *Spatz* coughed even to a momentary halt during some of the more hair-raising evolutions of that approach, then we wouldn't so much have visited Libya as taken up permanent residence there. But miraculously the *Charon* held together and, in the brief half-light heralding sunrise, we found ourselves threading a tortuous waterway between rush-lined banks from which carpets of waterfowl took flight in noisy resentment at our early-morning call.

'Port ten,' Trapp grunted. 'Steer f'r that clump o' *hillab* bush over there – THAT one, not *that* one, idjit! Steady . . . steady as she goes.'

As the daylight intensified I grew uneasily aware of

how exposed we had become to even the most superficial reconnaissance: a dishevelled smoke-belching anomaly sailing with splendid but thoroughly unpastoral aplomb across an otherwise featureless semi-desert. Should chance lead one of the Colonel Brother's MiGs to streak above the already shimmering dunes during this particularly vulnerable time, it wouldn't take longer than to shout the Libyan pilots' equivalent of *Tora, tora!* before Trapp's tireless crusade in search of profit finally terminated in a searing cascade of napalm.

Weston, too, had obviously considered the prospect of our being surprised in the closing stages of the voyage. His Viper fire teams squatted close by their weapons, while the carnivorous GPMGs sat ready-mounted on both bulwarks to enfilade the passing banks. I presumed there was little even Special Forces could do to combat a subsonic strafing from the copper sky but, by Allah, any local dromedary herdsman displaying undue interest before humping it for the nearest telephone box was really in for a depressing morning.

Which, in turn, brought the still hopefully unsuspecting residents of our imminent destination to mind; particularly such representatives of the Ras al Djibela Constabulary as might feel some small concern for public order at the lopsided approach of three score macho military desperadoes plus multifarious nautical hooliganry – sufficiently so, perhaps, to give the regional Ayatollah a bell and suggest he organized a few squadrons of Soviet-supplied T-somethin'-or-other *Panzerwagens* to lay on a traditional People's Socialist Libyan Arab *Jamahiriyah* welcome.

I conceived a chilling vision of Trapp Outraged standing immovably on the *Charon*'s bridge in the midst of a war of attrition between Weston's anti-tank Vipers and Brother Colonel Qaddafi's armoured corps, threatening contractual litigation for all damage caused to 'is Queen o' the Seas by any of the aforementioned parties – either jointly OR bloody severally!

'We're up Shit's Creek now, Mister,' Trapp announced cheerfully a few minutes later. 'All we got to do is go right round the bend an' we're in business.'

Then I DID begin to guffaw!

The Captain frowned irritably. 'What're YOU laughin' at?'

'I've just seen the joke.'

Trapp eyed Gorbals Wullie sourly. 'You seen 'im often enough before . . .'

The sun rose in those closing moments of the passage, a great red orb clawing above an already-shimmering silver haze to cast scorching feelers of light across arid stony steppes called the *hammada*. A horizon distant, the previously jet black faces of desert massifs suddenly reflected like the elements of a billion electric fires while, as the land heated up, so the dust devils sprang to dance, dervish-like, on the new-born winds of convection; softly wailing spinning tops, all chasing and racing and pacing each other hysterically across that vast dehydrated ocean.

I shivered involuntarily despite the already soaring temperature. I hadn't returned to this part of the world since the war, and I'd almost forgotten what a wild place it was, a totally alien environment for a seaman as well as being an area with ample cause to resent Western intrusion. Apart from oilmen, the last Europeans to make their marks here had been the men of the British Eighth Army and the Free French Brigade as they fought to stem the advancing tide of Rommel's *Afrika Korps*: a long time ago now, during a desert campaign in which Trapp and Gorbals Wullie and myself had played our own disreputable parts.

I hadn't liked those two any more then, either.

The marks were still in evidence all around. A sand

spit piled against the gutted hull of a Tiger I *Panzer-kampfwagen* over to starboard; the flash-suppressed barrel of a 75mm field piece, nearly half a century old now, yet still laying on some long gone target through that profusion of *agam* scrub. A battered jerrycan, a tangle of barbed wire, the burnt-out shell of a Jeep over there to starboard; a British army lorry wheel long stripped of its tyre by some bedouin forager . . . time moves infinitesimally for man's Second World War artefacts littering the Libyan desert: machinery corrodes at an unhurried pace, explosive deteriorates with lethal slowness – a myriad buried trip-wires still criss-cross the sand linking anti-personnel obscenity to fiendish device. A million anti-tank mines, most unstable enough by now to be triggered by the pressure of an unwary sandal, still lie below the constantly shifting surface. Countless Libyan bedouin have died – still die even today – from the scrapyard legacies of Bir Hakim and Sidi Rezeg, Mteifel, Knightsbridge and El Adem.

How ironic, I thought, that the husks of those men who had first brought and fought and died by their monstrous engines of war had been quickest to dissolve. Carrion birds could strip the flesh from a soldier's corpse before its dulling eyes had fully closed, its blood had properly congealed . . .

'Ahhhhh,' said Trapp, breaking with unconcealed satisfaction into my macabre reflection. 'Time to start fillin' in the bank withdrawal slip, Mister.'

Apprehensively I lifted my glasses. Focusing on the clutter of white and ochre buildings sliding into view.

Ras al Djibela looked tidier than I'd imagined: neat oval-roofed houses, most with curious lean-to's huddled by them like giant swallows' nests. A scatter of olive trees to landward provided an unexpected and verdant back-cloth to the shimmering settlement; even small produce gardens sucked whatever poor nourishment they could draw from plots scraped in the desiccated earth.

Some distance from the main habitations, and completely incongruous to any but the Libyan eye, what appeared to have been a giant supermarket – once a sort of super-*souk*, I supposed – rose in dilapidated plastic splendour from the desert itself, with its donkey park totally blocked by drifted sand and filthy, shuttered plate-glass windows bearing mute testimony to the Brother Colonel's New Socialist prosperity.

In the foreground awaited the harbour, another forlorn contrast to the town: just a crumbling sandstone wharf really, with a few apathetic fishing craft alongside and a trot of smaller, even more dejected *caiques* and feluccas nudging the clay at the water's edge. It appeared the al Djibelans were not a seafaring community.

A clink of metal made me glance over the bridge front. Weston had moved two Viper teams to the bow; now the sleek rocket tubes were laid with deadly menace to embrace the town. Anxiously I swung back to scrutinize the dust-laden stretch of wharf, trying to detect the flash of sun on waiting gun barrel, the glint of lenses trained back at us in our turn.

But there was nothing, no movement, no seeming evidence of danger. Not even, come to that, of the slightest passing interest in our coming. Gradually it began to dawn on me that, so far, I hadn't seen one solitary soul abroad throughout the length and breadth of that singularly placid landfall.

Which worried me a lot.

'Stop engine!' Trapp growled down the voice pipe then slouched at the wheelhouse window ledge, frowning beetle-browed through the glassless frames as *Charon II* coasted silently through the muddied water. I could tell he was uncertain too. Trapp liked things cut and dried: the prospect of a good old-fashioned lay 'er alongside an' get tore in to some tangible opposition he would have viewed with buccaneering enthusiasm; always the extrovert, this eerily silent acceptance of – no, total indifference to – our arrival disgruntled him as much as it unnerved me.

I suspected that mice felt similar twinges of doubt . . . just before they thought 'the hell with it', then went for the cheese anyway.

A movement forward drew my attention. Weston, blue baseball cap pulled well down on his brow, had climbed to the foc's'lehead and now stood right in the eyes of the ship, arms casually akimbo, carelessly exposed to any shoreside sniper.

'Oh, I do wish he'd keep 'is stupid 'ead down,' Trapp muttered anxiously. I looked sideways at the Captain: such uncharacteristic concern for other people, I gloomed resentfully, came strangely from one who'd recently considered the threatened demise of his own First Mate merely as an added lever to commercial exploitation.

Then I realized it was because Weston controlled the sole means of blowing Qaddafi's piggybank rather than any sudden onset of humanitarianism, and felt reassured as to Trapp's absolute rottenness again.

'Well, ah says we should shove off 'til taemorrow,' Gorbals Wullie, full of British grit as ever, encouraged hopefully. 'It looks like it's half-day closin' onyroad, an' there's naebody tae take oor heid rope or nuthin' . . .'

He broke off with a startled yelp as the sudden roar of vehicle engines shattered the oppressive quiet of Ras al Djibela. The tight rein I'd so far maintained on my phlegm finally snapped in the same instant.

'*Jesus!*' I choked. 'TANKS, Trapp! They've just been waiting to see the whites of our eyes.'

Slowly three ancient canvas-hooded lorries, preceded by a brace of ex-World War Two Jeeps which looked in worse condition than the one burnt out on the bank behind us, came chugging into view before drawing up on the wharf in great clouds of desert dust.

'Take her in, Cap'n,' Weston called laconically.

'Oh, get UP off've the deck, Mister!' Trapp hissed down at me, utterly mortified on my behalf.

'. . . really: there's times when you can be so *bloody* embarrassing!'

Other men gradually revealed themselves as we secured. Tall, dark, terribly fierce-looking men with beards, dressed in long goatskin coats and camel-hide sandals and black *tarboosh* on which the bright dangling tassels impressed me as being the only gay thing about them.

Criss-crossing each manly chest were sun-glinting bandoliers of ammunition, while supported casually on each hip were modern automatic weapons more suggestive of Eastern Bloc than Western origins to my untutored eye.

'Look, Mister,' Trapp grunted meaningfully.

I looked. A lone dromedary had materialized at the extreme end of the main track leading to the desert, ambling splay-footed across the road, expanding and contracting caterpillar-like through the curious optical effect of the shimmering heat.

'It's only a camel!' I said.

'Christ but you're hard to get on with,' he grumbled.

I looked again. From black-shadowed alleyways on each side of the dusty avenue stepped other terribly fierce men until I could detect a further seven or eight walking ammunition dumps in all. I fought the tendency to giggle again. It was all becoming so Hollywood-like: Cowboys and Arabs; a spaghetti Middle Eastern; a sort of *High Noon* and *Lawrence of Arabia* production all rolled into one.

So bloody *typical*, above all, of a Trapp-involved scenario.

'Is that no' magic?' Gorbals Wullie breathed in ecstatic and thoroughly predictable concurrence. 'Pure *magic* so it is, Mister Miller sir.'

It was also instructive. Now we understood why the regular citizens and lieges of Ras al Djibela had showed such restraint in their welcome. Either they were all keeping their heads down in case the sinister guys in the goat coats turned their oasis into a mini-Beirut or alternatively, acting on Weston's cryptic pre-arrival signal, Code-name Homer had implemented the entire Djibela electoral roll on a more permanent basis.

The more I thought about the second option, the quicker any impression of having become involved in some ludicrous black comedy evaporated. Particularly when a further discomfiting thought came to mind.

'The local bobbies, Trapp. What d'you reckon happened to them?'

For once the Captain didn't reply. Frowning, I followed his expressionless gaze from the wing of *Charon*'s bridge.

A little way along the wharf stood an ancient mud brick structure. Against its crumbling gable five Libyan policemen, still recognizable by their khaki uniforms and once white crossweb belts, had been crucified by sharpened thorn stakes. Each skewered man had had his throat cut from ear to ear but not, my gagging and sharply abandoned appreciation suggested, at the moment of overpowering. Cloud-swarms of desert flies now hovered and spiralled and homed in joyful exploration of the empty eye sockets through which each tortured corpse mutely contemplated its own already black-congealed plasma.

'That weren't necessary,' Trapp murmured with a terrible thoughtful look. 'I think I'll 'ave to kill that Homer before we leaves here.'

I'd only heard him promise a dreadful thing like that once or twice before, but I didn't have time to consider the full implications of Code-name Homer's already certain fate.

Weston appeared on the bridge at that moment, just as Mister Spew and Bligh had finished securing the *Charon* fore and aft with ropes as cheap and primitive as jungle creepers.

I must have stared at the Colonel for a full disbelieving minute before I finally found voice.

'Trapp,' I whispered urgently. 'Trapp, are you *quite* certain Weston's latest explanation was correct? That the US Government really *doesn't* plan to be connected with this operation officially?'

'*Course* I am!' Trapp growled, still preoccupied with his anger at Homer. 'I knows when a man's lying, Mister – I gotter natural sense f'r it.'

'Then why, Trapp, is *he* about to attack Libya,' I swallowed, pointing a shaking finger, '. . . wearing the full bloody UNIFORM of the United States *ARMY*?'

Chapter Nine

Trapp's features had adopted the choleric hue of a typhoon sky as we both struggled to comprehend what – this time – surely *had* to represent the quite incomprehensible?

Yet there it all was, for any Libyan to recognize at a glance. The Special Forces shoulder patches, the Service name tag stitched above the breast pocket – just like Jablonski's, I reflected bleakly: so's they know who they're bagging when you're dead . . . the neatly creased and undeniably US-cut combat denims; the US Service issue sidearm in its US Service issue holster: above all, the unmistakable green beret.

A regular, state-of-the-art doughboy in fact. Blatantly screaming 'American Aggression'!

'And what the hell,' Trapp growled ominously, 'are *you* tarted up like THAT for?'

Then the Pragmatic Trapp, being a great one for leaving his options at least slightly ajar, tacked on a grudging, 'Colonel?', just in case it *was* all a silly mistake, and that some perfectly reasonable explanation might shortly be forthcoming.

'. . . which, if it does, will make a unique bloody first on THIS rotten trip,' I thought savagely, mentally erasing all the answers I believed I'd found to some of the riddles posed so far by the *Charon II*'s voyage: mere teasers which, it now seemed, shrank to the level of mental limbering-up exercises compared to this most recent paradox.

The Colonel didn't say a lot; particularly considering Trapp was supposed to be a brother officer, even if of less than twenty-four hours' duration.

Just a simple: 'Shut it, Trapp!'

Tiny blood vessels began to pop in the Captain's eyeballs.

'You tellin' ME to shut up? *Me?*' Trapp's jaw thrust forward like a battering ram. 'I'm BUGGERED if I'll shu –'

A Master Sergeant and a Corporal – I knew they were a Master Sergeant and a Corporal because they were also inviting that very conclusion by wearing full US Army rig too – appeared at the head of each bridge ladder, M16s trained persuasively in support of Weston's point of view. It confirmed my earlier suspicion that, like the murder of the Komar survivors, Weston's brief mellowing had merely been a further operational expediency to encourage Trapp to continue the voyage with as little argument as possible.

'You'll be a helluva lot more buggered if you don't,' the Colonel promised in much more familiar vein.

I waited – not, I confess, without a certain thrill of ghoulish expectancy – for the master of the Queen o' the Seas literally to explode all over everybody. Somewhat anti-climactically he decided to be tolerant; offer Weston one last chance to apologize.

'You do realize you're not jus' talking to rubbish, Mister: that you are, in fac', addressin' a Commander of 'Er Britannic Majesty's Royal NAVY?'

'That's it, Trapp – now demand answers; use all the clout you've got,' I urged silently, consumed by then to learn the motive behind this, Weston's latest action. 'He's a soldier, hit him with the military argument: exploit the system.'

Weston shrugged dismissively. 'On this trip you're just the hired help, like I told you. Nothing more.'

'He's out of line, Trapp,' I blurted, prepared even to concede the Captain's sole and utterly scurrilous claim to respectability if it forced a showdown. 'You have the law of the sea on your side . . .' I nearly choked over that one. 'Don't let the bastard brow-beat you – sir!'

'Miller's right. As Captain o' this ship I still says what goes, Mister!' Trapp fired the very last shot in his locker. 'Damn yer eyes, I'm a Commander in your *own* bloody Navy an' all. You said so yerself!'

'Then you'll make the highest-ranking corpse pinned to that goddam wall,' Weston snapped dangerously: apparently the only field officer in the whole US Army who didn't give a damn for status. 'Do you really want me to give you to the Tuaregs, Trapp?'

'Oh, now he's *really* bluffing,' I hissed.

'. . . along with Miller there?' Weston added pointedly.

'For Chrissakes,' I yelled. 'Just listen to what the Colonel says and SHUT UP, Trapp!'

Three minutes later Trapp was off again, being high-risk awkward.

'Whaddyou MEAN – get some *shore*side gear on?' Trapp roared.

'Please, Trapp,' I implored wearily, 'don't start all that apoplectic stuff again.'

'You're coming with us,' Weston stated flatly. 'No way do we leave you aboard while we hit the Libs. This may be a pretty sad hulk but it's the only means of exfiltrating my boys: I intend to make damn sure it's still here when we need to re-embark.'

Again it struck me how remarkably perceptive the Colonel could be regarding the degree of trust he placed in Trapp. And anyway, even if Qaddafi's Fifth Camel Cavalry *did* arrive to defend the bank, surely, for Trapp, the consequent likelihood of getting himself killed was as nothing compared to this golden opportunity for him to enlist in – maybe even get to be a *general* in – the United States Army as well. And all on the same day?

'Go on, Trapp,' I encouraged on the principle that the quicker they went the quicker they'd be back, with or without Trapp in a green bag, and thus the quicker *Charon*, with Chief Officer Miller in temporary command, could clank and wheeze for saner parts. 'It'll be a run ashore. And besides, you can always help them count the money.'

'You're coming too, Miller.'

'Ohhhhh *shit*!' I snarled.

Trapp swung in frustrated desire to take it out on somebody: any-bloody-body. 'Well, what about THAT?' he bellowed, suddenly pointing to the wheelhouse chart table.

'We don't *need* a chart,' I yelled back, really fed up with the mess he'd got me into by then. 'The bank's only just UP the main bloody street!'

'I means THAT! That . . . that *worm*-like creature hidin' under it!'

'Och, *thanks* pal,' Gorbals Wullie's muffled voice squealed fearfully. 'But ah'll jus' stay aboard onyway if ye dinnae mind, Colonel sir. Ah'm no' awfy good at the marchin' an' the salutin' an' that – sir!'

Weston went down on one knee and sought out our cringing key personnel with, I thought huffily, a helluva sight more tolerance than he showed to us. 'We take you with us too, little guy.'

'Honest, sir,' Wullie pleaded, 'ah couldnae pass the medical. Ah've got flat feet an' a bad leg: ah'd jist be a liability . . .'

'Negative, sailor. The army needs men of your intelligence. And I mean right up front, son: leading the way for the very best pointsmen I got.'

I stared at Trapp, and Trapp looked blankly back at me.

So Weston wasn't simply power-crazed after all: he really was a complete raving lunatic.

'Och, is that a fact?' Wullie preened, trying with little success to look suitably modest. 'Well, ah do have tae admit, Colonel sir, ah used tae be a regular tiger doon the Gorbals: there wis aye a stream o' wild men hard on mah heels . . . You really see me out there as a leader, eh?'

'Every one of my guys will follow in your footsteps, I guarantee it.'

Wullie afforded a triumphant sideways glance at Trapp. 'Does that mean you're goin' tae make me an *officer* too, then?'

But Weston had tired of his little joke.

Meaning Wullie.

'No, I'm gonna make you a fucking MINE detector, sailor – if you don't haul ass out from under that goddam table *on the DOUBLE!*'

Ten minutes later all three of us were crammed uncomfortably in the back of the second beat-up Jeep as the convoy prepared to move from the wharf.

We'd given up protesting, menacingly overshadowed as we found ourselves by the massive figure of one who now turned out to be, according to his name tag anyway, Private First Class Stopf, Hermann, of both US Special Forces and – according to a still traumatized Gorbals Wullie – some not-inconsiderable international melon-squishing fame.

Trapp, always an absolute jelly of anxiety when it came to entrusting anything worth money – even worth as little money as his bloody *Charon* – to anyone else, had been given little option but to leave the amiable Mister Spew in, I fervently prayed, very short-term command.

Personally I wouldn't have left our Second Officer in charge of a tin of caterpillars, but I had to concede that Spew, who'd donned his best almost-washed and hardly-torn uniform shirt especially for the occasion did – apart from his missing eye and his mental black-outs and the disarticulated limbs and his rather curious tendency to bang into unnoticed things like bulkheads and closed doors and other ships and stuff – look every inch the sort of seafarer who'd spent most of his life training for this moment of glory rather than in escaping from various global prisons.

''Ave a nice time, Captin,' he waved with total sincerity from the *Charon*'s bridge. 'An' don't you hurry back if yer enjoyin' yerself.'

Then two troopers, those Weston had left aboard to ensure the loyalty of the rest of Trapp's crew, ushered Spew back down to the baking foredeck so's they could cover him, too, with the same machine-gun.

'An' don't you DARE try an' move me ship, Mister,' Trapp roared unappreciatively after him, and for the twentieth time. 'Not one heavin' line's throw, you hear?'

'Which is jist aboot all the distance yon banana heid *wid* be able tae move it,' Gorbals Wullie muttered spitefully, 'wi'oot a braille chart an' a white stick.'

Trying hard to look as though I wasn't really associated with them I wondered vaguely if, when and precisely how Sergeant Jablonski's somewhat unique squad were scheduled to fall in. Already the loading of ammunition on to the trucks was nearly complete; now most of Weston's commandos were supporting the Tuaregs in maintaining a loose defensive perimeter around the wharf area prior to moving out. Again I was struck by the silent teamwork: as on every previous occasion, not a command needed to be issued, or a word spoken. There simply *had* to be some very good reason – an almost certainly sinister if not downright macabre reason, I bleakly assumed by now – for Weston's imposing such rigid verbal discipline.

I gazed around uneasily. Would the Libyan Army

come? Or had Homer's pre-emptive occupation of Ras al Djibela been achieved with sufficient speed to prevent any alert being passed from the township to the local military command? The tortured policemen bore hideous witness to the ruthlessness of their pacification: the Tuaregs on the streets made it unlikely any other resident would risk carrying a warning – even if they thought it prudent. In Middle Eastern society one tends to hear all, see all, and say as little as possible. Certainly, half an hour after our arrival the only noticeable movement outwith the activity on the wharf was of a gaunt-flanked ochre dog snuffling through rubbish littering the sand-blown main street. It seemed barely conceivable that only a few hundred paces up that poor and deserted thoroughfare, an oil Sheik's ransom in US dollar bills lay concealed.

I frowned. That was, in fact, a point. Because if the bank *was* situated in downtown Djibela as Trapp reckoned, then why did we need transport at all? Why not just . . . ?

One of the fierce bearded men in the goat coats came by the Jeep casually cradling a Kalashnikov and, despite the buzzing proximity of five eyeless corpses, chewing with enormous relish on something sun-dried but otherwise – probably mercifully, in view of my already delicate stomach – unidentifiable: presumably some sort of desert fighter's K ration.

I just knew it had to be Homer.

As he passed he caught sight of us, and halted. I watched apprehensively as black, hostile eyes scrutinized us, then the Tuareg grinned insolently at Trapp, revealing stained and uneven teeth.

'You sheep's Captin, Mistair?'

'Fuck OFF, Sinbad!' Trapp snarled ill-temperedly, a greeting which typified his level of commitment to the furtherance of Anglo-Arabian goodwill.

145

. . . and to living to a ripe old age! I found myself abruptly at one with Gorbals Wullie as we both cowered closer within the, ironically, suddenly reassuring shadow of Pfc Mount Hermann.

Homer didn't seem to take offence though, having almost certainly, in pre-Qaddafi times, come to know and love other great British diplomatic institutions already. Like the Eighth Army, and merchant seamen from Newcastle.

He must've done because he just grinned even wider, then drew a grubby finger across his throat in an unmistakable cutting motion before ambling off to squat uncaringly at the fouled base of Djibela's temporary police station in order to finish his desiccated breakfast.

'Scared stiff of us, that one,' Trapp dismissed, again revealing precisely the depth of percipience which had got us, the British, flung out of the Middle East in the first place. 'I knows them Ayrabs like the back o' me ha –' He fixed a frowning eye on the *Charon*'s side. 'What's in them, then?'

I registered six olive-green shapes being passed across the bulwark before developing an intense preoccupation with a holding pattern of on-the-ball vultures which had begun to wheel directly above us.

'I really haven't the faintest idea.'

Trapp watched the sagging plastic burdens being loaded into the aftermost truck then growled dangerously, 'You wus down that hold, Mister, an' din't mention them. An' they certainly wusn't declared on no manifest. Yet they looks suspiciously like body bags to me – with bodies in'em!'

He didn't look shocked or surprised or anything: more, well, commercially alert.

'Don't', I laughed weakly, 'be *silly*, Trapp."

With relief I saw the Colonel approaching.

'Don't even say it, Trapp!' he warned sharply, alerted

no doubt by the crystallizing avarice in the Captain's eye. 'Time's pressing: we're moving out. And, whatever happens from here on in, I want no hassle . . . You read me loud and clear, you three? What*ever* happens!'

Private Third Class Wullie had obligingly shrunk so much by that time he was hardly noticeable. Trapp, on the other hand, just sat there simmering thoughtfully, thereby giving me more cause for apprehension than even the manner in which Hermann's sausage-like finger caressed – a little too bloody optimistically, it seemed to me – the trigger of his carbine.

And anyway – what, precisely, *had* Weston meant?

'. . . whatEVER' happened?

Leaving the Tuaregs to hold the re-embarkation area, and in the meantime, presumably, to slice bits off any unfortunate who happened to arrive wearing a Libyan uniform, the convoy started off with a protest of tortured gears and twanging springs. It all seemed so unsophisticated: so . . . well, so un-American. So characteristic, in short, of any venture involving Trapp. The mission's weaponry may have been state-of-the-art but, by God, its selected mode of transport was turning out to be more state of chaos.

Already the sun was a blazing furnace in the sky, while to add to the discomfort the Colonel's Jeep, positively bristling now with commandos and topped by a Rambo-cloned corporal manning a tripod mounted M60 in the back, whipped up a trail of limestone dust through which the rest of us choked and spluttered almost as convulsively as our vehicle engines.

By the time I'd ripped the tail from my shirt and tied it over nose and mouth – thus providing myself with, on reflection, a most appropriate rig of the day for a working bank robber – we'd swung into Djibela's main thoroughfare and were grinding threateningly past the scattered, notably silent dwellings. Even the ochre dog had disappeared, having either exfiltrated itself in favour of the lesser hazards of the desert or been already eaten by Homer's goat-coated dustbins.

'Aaaah,' Trapp suddenly breathed, cheering up remarkably. 'I told yer, Mister: there she rises fine on the port bow – the fount of all 'appiness to them who brings an army to 'elp collect it.'

I peered ahead through the grit-induced smog. It didn't look much of a bank to me: it didn't look much of *any*thing, come to that, and certainly not a building in which to hide three billion dollars – or maybe that was where Qaddafi had been clever until now. And American Intelligence even more clever. Few agents tracking down the source of terrorist funds would have suspected that sagging mud brick version of a Wild West saloon with crudely barred windows, a Visa sign lying in the sand beside its entrance, and peeling letters in both English and Arabic intimating we were indeed approaching the Ras al Djibela branch of the First People's Bank of the Socialist Libyan Arab *Jama*-whatever.

The trouble was, I *also* registered Weston half-turn to glance back from the front seat of his own careering lead vehicle just then, and something about the wary cut of the Colonel's jib afforded me immediate food for thought. It so happened we were travelling far too fast to allow the thought sufficient time to gestate – as any initial doubt concerning Weston invariably appeared to – into an outright clamour of warning bells before Trapp himself leaned forward anxiously, ignoring Hermann's pointed threat.

''Ere – you ring us to 'alf speed smartish, soldier!' he snapped to our driver. 'Take a bit o' bloody WAY off or . . .'

Twenty yards ahead Weston's Jeep roared full ahead for the Libyan desert without even slackening pace.

'. . . you'll take us straight . . .'

Ours followed suit. Boring straight PAST the bank.

'. . . *past* . . . the BANK!'

Trapp whispered.

So THAT was what Weston had meant by his cryptic 'what*ever*' happened?

Nothing particularly surprising, really. Other than it now appeared we'd steamed on a persistently disintegrating hell ship captained by an egotistical bloody fascist, all the bloody way from bloody Albania – whose naval patrol could have stopped us right at the start, but inexplicably didn't – and since then we'd been shouted at, and bloody shot at, and frightened half out of our wits. And had unwittingly carried a cargo of deep-frozen dead men while being shadowed by submarines that nobody wanted to own up to. *And* had been responsible, *en route*, for the violent sinking of two very expensive warships, as well as I couldn't even guess at how many Libyan seamen's deaths?

And all, it now transpired, so's we could completely ignore the one destination the whole rotten voyage was supposed to have bloody well been aimed at in the FIRST place?

. . . I remember staring numbly ahead while trying to figure out just where Weston really was heading for as we finally cleared the outskirts of Ras al Djibela before continuing to bucket crazily, deeper and deeper into that undulating, scrub-infested semi-desert I'd already considered so alien during the *Charon*'s final approach, and which ended only at the base of those awesome super-heated massifs over fifty miles away.

And with bugger all else between them and us as far as I knew – because I really *was*, you'll appreciate, beginning to give way to craven paranoia by then – except a few thoroughly unstable minefields populated by

149

vicious free-ranging camel-type things which, I'd heard, can spit in your eye at twenty paces before kicking the absolute shit out of you ... plus fifteen varieties of vulture, of course – a *terrific* place to study vultures very close up, I had to concede – as well as to find yourself eye-to-bulbous-eye intimate with scorpions like armoured bloody cars, and beetles and spiders and snakes and ... and all *other* desiccated forms of crawly, poisonous, utterly repulsive desert creatures ...

'Ah think the Captin's heart's stopped beatin' again, Mister Miller sir.'

Gorbals Wullie's voice halted me one shuddering sob from advanced manic depression. 'It's the shock, so it is – of passin' by two million dollars at sixty mile an 'oor!'

'Wun million.' Trapp's reflex protest was terribly weak, him being in a catatonic state like he was.

I eyed the Captain with concern. After all, the cancer he'd claimed was gnawing at his timbers – the progression of which had been most stoically concealed now I came to think about it – must surely be approaching a critical phase already. A further blow to Trapp's pocket of such magnitude could well be enough to catapult him clear into the terminal stage.

Apart from which, well, Trapp *was* the only one who could pilot us back out of the Shi'ite's Creek he'd only too clearly landed us in.

'I don't think, Trapp,' I swallowed, trying to be as gentle as I could, 'that Colonel Weston was telling you quite the whole truth about the money – about any of his reasons for this trip, for that matter.'

'Mister Miller means there's NAE loot, an' that there never bluidy wis,' Wullie supplemented with somewhat less tact. 'That ye've been ripped aff, Captin: yer contract's buggered. *Again!*'

'Oh, Gawd,' Trapp's ashen lips moved almost imperceptibly before his fixed stare dulled further and he didn't move again. I suspected that even Sergeant Jablonski, travelling in his green bag astern of us for whatever gruesome reason, must've looked two shades more animated than our Captain right then.

Eventually I got bored with trying to decide whether Trapp really was dying or simply holding a private seance for his profit and loss account, so I just clung to my seat for the next hour in gloomy silence, long after the Ras al Djibela road had faded to a track and eventually petered out into a nightmare terrain of rock and *agam* scrub linking either great hills of sand or sparkling white lakes of salt.

I still had no notion either of where we were heading, or why. But judging by the ever more set expressions on the dust-caked faces riding fore and aft of us, Colonel Buck Weston, US Army intended, sure as eggs were eggs, to start *some* kind of war.

And pretty soon.

Abruptly the convoy slowed to a crawl in order to reduce, I guessed, the dust storm raised by our passage and so avoid alerting . . . who?

A few minutes later we halted.

Immediately fire-teams dismounted to move swiftly and silently into their usual defensive perimeter. As the growl of the five vehicle engines cut, so the silence enclosed us in a stifling, airless shroud, quickly drying the sweat-dark dust on our faces to light grey casts which, in their turn, first cracked then flaked from the corners of sun-narrowed eyes like self-destructing death masks.

I don't think I've ever pined so much for the caress of a brisk sea wind and the familiar thresh of waves as I did in those first few moments of utter dejection.

Squinting uneasily around the floating horizon I could only make out desert followed by more desert above which stunted trees and impressionistic outcrops of baking rock appeared to hover in a silver shimmer of radiated heat. Hermann gestured indifferently with the muzzle of his M16, which I took as permission to abandon ship.

Stiffly, Wullie and I eased ourselves from the Jeep to stand uncertainly within the stark black periphery of our own shadows, the sun being so high in the sky. Trapp just stayed where he was, quietly barbecuing in a state of advanced financial paralysis, which was OK by me because he'd've just started another argument otherwise, and probably got all three of us left behind to debate breach of contract with the vultures when the trucks started off again.

Ahead of the convoy rose yet another slope of much the same mixture as before: stones, sand and flies with the inevitable scatter of dehydrated *agam* scrub. But there was a new urgency spurring the dismounted troops which made me suspect we'd finally arrived; that behind that unremarkable eminence awaited the ultimate destination of the *Charon*'s voyage.

The soft clink of equipment drew my attention. Weston had walked back from the lead Jeep to join me. He raised a quizzical eyebrow, obviously expecting some reaction. In deference to Trapp I didn't disappoint him.

'It doesn't seem much of a place', I greeted pointedly, 'to locate a bank, Colonel?'

Weston shrugged. There was no hint of apology, or even of embarrassment.

'So I exploited Trapp's cupidity: wove a little fiction. Some of us owe allegiance to causes greater than the pursuit of wealth, Miller.'

'Causes'? Ah, now that *did* worry me. I'd never liked the prospect of becoming involved in 'causes'. 'Causes' spawn maggots of hate: they tend to demand fanaticism from their followers and the random destruction of all others. Terrorists terrorize the defenceless for 'causes': religious and political bigots justify ever more thinly-

veiled incitements to violence by proclaiming 'causes'.
Day by murderous day the world over, the old, the young,
the children, the innocent are sacrificed on the spurious
altar of 'causes'.

But there seemed little point in saying so to Weston. I
just jerked my head towards our waxwork Captain. 'Tell
that to him. He's just a simple, old-fashioned exponent
of greed. He doesn't consider there is any other cause
worth pursuing.'

'Excep' me,' Gorbals Wullie chimed in gloomily. 'He's
aye pursuin' *me* roond the deck moanin' aboot somethin',
so he is.'

But Wullie always had tended to miss the thrust of any
conversation conducted on an intellectual plane higher
than that of a mentally retarded cockroach.

'Look, just go away and bloody melt!' I snapped so's
the wee monster wouldn't feel too estranged while Trapp
was *hors de combat*, then turned back to the Colonel.

'So what next? Or am I just inviting another operationally expedient lie from the President's personal
emissary?'

The grey-haired soldier smiled briefly at that and again,
just for a moment, I really did think I caught a flicker of
humour behind the hard eyes.

'Why don't you come and see for yourself?' he chal-
lenged. 'It's only a stroll, Miller: to the top of the very
last hill.'

I set my jaw pugnaciously. 'Yeah, why *don't* I?'

. . . I knew precisely why, actually. The mere *thought*
of attempting to scale that heat-shimmering slope, which
I swore grew steeper even as I looked, was enough to
make me want to curl up and die without going through
the wearisome formality of having a heart attack first.

The buildings were simply but efficiently camouflaged:
only just discernible against the dried and ancient

watercourse which formed the floor of the *wadi* below us.

They had a military look, yet I couldn't conceive of their military purpose, not deliberately concealed as they were out here in the desert. In the Middle East the Army represents Power; it maintains a high profile. It is there to be seen and respected and, to achieve that aim, tends not to hide its might under a bushel. Certainly not among a tangle of *hillab* trees in a valley of sand miles from any centre of possible discontent.

Sweat trickled behind my ears and into my eyes as I squirmed disagreeably, trying desperately to suppress the rasp of over-taxed lungs. After staggering to the top of that bloody ridge I feared I'd blown every natural thermostat in my aching body: to me the rocks now forming our vantage-point radiated little short of the heat from an open galley oven.

Weston, on the other hand, appeared quite indifferent to any discomfort, as did the two hard-looking NCOs accompanying him while they minutely scanned the scene before us through field glasses.

The physical security was high, no doubt about that. A double run of wire fence formed a broad defensive perimeter around the complex, an apparently innocuous strip of yellow sand which didn't require a soldier's caution to imagine concealed a minefield.

From within each corner of that formidable ring a desert-camouflaged heavy tank mounted guard, four in total with turrets trained to enfilade the surrounding slopes. Two further Soviet-origin tanks were parked with squat menace beside a guard post flanking what I took to be the main entrance to the complex.

Happily, their Arab crews didn't appear to be manning them so much as lounging idly in the shade of their lethal charges. I felt a little more encouraged: it was a bit like watching the crew of the *Charon* hard at work, and suggested much the same level of professional efficiency.

From the main gate a recently metalled road led away from us to cut through the opposite end of the *wadi*, presumably linking eventually with what Trapp had reckoned was the old Trigh Capuzzo bedouin caravan route across the Western Desert, almost certainly upgraded to a six-lane highway now, with potholes like dustbin lids and Little Arab Chef camelstops every few kilometres.

I noted a cluster of fuel tanks bordered a vehicle park holding a handful of light armoured cars and lorries on the far side of the camp. It seemed that several accommodation or office blocks surmounted by water towers and other less easily recognizable structures had been built fairly recently throughout the area, all painted in standard Libyan quartermaster's chameleon ochre.

But the focal point of the complex was unquestionably a large, windowless building within yet *another* high wire fence . . . ?

I sneaked a covert glance at Weston. When we'd passed the al Djibela bank, was it possible I'd been just a little too quick to jump to conclusions? Could he, after all, still be intent on neutralizing Qaddafi's terror funds? It at least suggested itself as a more likely location in which to stockpile several billion dollars. One thing was certain – that installation down there contained *something* of vital importance to the Libyans.

'Christ man, what *are* we looking at?' I muttered.

'A target, Mister: that's all you need to know.'

Well, I hadn't anticipated a straight answer, having long discovered 'Nashnul Security' didn't work that way. All I achieved was another sardonic smile when Weston surveyed my near-absolute state of physical disintegration. 'Just look on the positive side, Miller – it's all downhill from here on in.'

He rose, careful to keep below the skyline. Terrified of

being left alone up there I scrambled and skittered after him in a fury of sheer impotence.

'THAT,' I hissed as loudly as I dared, 'is roughly what the Captain of the *Titanic* said, Colonel. Just before she hit the bloody iceberg!'

Trapp's breathing had become almost perceptible; might even, on a more temperate day, have misted a mirror held before his lips by the time I got back, but the Captain still slumped in terminal dejection nevertheless, showing not the slightest gratitude for my second delivery from the jaws of suffering.

Which further indicated he was slowly returning to normal.

Not that it mattered right then. The Colonel just jerked his head at Hermann anyway, who lifted Trapp bodily from the Jeep and arranged him in the sand.

'Apart from the certainty of his causing us more goddam hassle than the Libs,' Weston said curtly, 'I need him safe to pilot the ship back out. He stays here under guard, out of the cross-fire.'

Which was yet another crushing setback to my hopes for a brighter Trapp-less future.

An what did he *mean* – CROSS-fire?

'Ah'll stay an' guard him, Colonel,' Wullie volunteered with instant selflessness. 'Seein' it's the Captin, ah'll stand the disappointment – gie up mah chance tae hae a square go at yon Libyans.'

'Negative. Get in the rear truck – soldier!'

'Och, *shit*!' Wullie grumbled and trailed off looking more like a disenchanted ferret than a commando. I derived only small satisfaction from knowing he, incapable of resisting his inbred tendency towards kleptomania, was bound to sneak an experimental hand into Jablonski's green bag to see if it contained anything worth stealing.

'And what about me?' I asked, bleakly anticipating the answer. 'Divide and conquer the hired help, is it?'

Weston grinned openly. 'The petulance of the enemy within, huh? Sure, you stay with me, Miller. In the Command Jeep . . .' Then, displaying his usual capacity for the unexpected, he added, 'But I guess you'd better draw a weapon. Temporarily. The Libs will come out shooting.'

I took a long hard look at Trapp, then shook my head. I was trying to give up tempting Providence.

'No. I'd better not.'

'Suit yourself.'

Pfc Hermann Stompf took over the M60 heavy machine-gun mount this time while the Rambo look-alike corporal crammed into the rear seat beside me, positively clanking with a lethal assortment of small arms and grenades. Weston stood up in the front seat, raised a clenched fist towards the burning sun, then dropped it sharply.

Immediately vehicle engines roared into life as the last Green Berets clambered over the tailgates. There had been no briefing that I knew of, no 'O'-Group necessary: Weston's very Special Force was clearly implementing a manoeuvre practised to perfection, more than likely against a detailed mock-up of that same Libyan installation located on some desert training ground back in the USA itself.

Only this time the Libyan Army within, inexpectant or otherwise, wasn't a detail.

While sure as hell those massive, ochre-yellow T-54 battle tanks I'd observed from the ridge weren't mock-ups.

We left Trapp, a hunched and utterly apathetic figure slumped under an equally apathetic tree and watched over by a clearly disappointed trooper who – understandably, on account of his having been ordered to forgo the fun of getting to kill people in order to babysit the Captain – looked fit to chop Trapp's ears off with a hacksaw blade if he so much as sighed out of turn.

Still resentful of Trapp's comparative security, I hoped the frustrated Green Beret would: just for something to do to pass the time. Those old Libyan T-54s may have been obsolete as Soviet front-line tanks but they still threw 100mm sabot rounds which would take a helluva sight more than *my* ear off if I got shot with one.

The assault force split into two sections immediately on moving out: the second Jeep and one lorry carrying Wullie and Jablonski's corps – corpse? – peeling off towards the starboard rim of the *wadi* while we set a curving port-hand course to take us towards the far end of the escarpment.

I frowned. Such a heading would eventually bring us to the Trigh Capuzzo feeder road I'd observed earlier, which in turn led directly to the complex gates, and it seemed quite obvious to me that a tactic like that couldn't be right – well I mean, I didn't have to be a *general* to know you don't attack a high security military installation by simply driving up the main road and knocking on its front door . . .

We arrived at the Trigh Capuzzo feeder road. And stopped.

'What now?' I asked with a mounting sense of foreboding.

Weston looked at his watch. 'In four minutes, twenty seconds our second group will cut the lines of communication to Lib area command. Then we . . .'

'. . . knock on the Libs' front door?'

'Neatly put for a sailor.'

'You'll *never* get to be a General,' I muttered.

We sat by the verge of that desolate heat-silvered road with the two lorry engines astern of us growling softly and me trying to occupy my mind by guessing which of the *Charon*'s crew would rifle my cabin first, after I'd failed to return aboard. The canvas cover of the nearest truck stirred fractionally and I could just detect the tubular maw of a Viper launcher readied and waiting.

I stole an uneasy glance at my own watch. One minute thirty to go.

The Colonel took off his green beret, snapped a neat fold in it with the edge of his palm, and laid it beside him. At least we had a bit of subtlety here. Expressionlessly our driver and Clanking Rambo beside me in the back followed suit while Pfc Stompf, Hermann, grudgingly relinquished his stance at the heavy M60 mount to squash down on the other side of me, presumably so's not to appear too aggressive.

Feeling like toothpaste being squeezed from a tube I gave Hermann as much room as I could. Personally I'd still've been scared-stiff-suspicious of the guy if he'd been sound asleep in bed!

Apparently that was the only concession to subterfuge that Weston intended, though what happened after we'd closed enough for the Libyan tankmen to identify positively the US-issue cut of my associates I didn't want to ponder: presumably nothing else left to us then other than Gung Ho, Hell for Leather and remember Guadal-bloody-canal.

Weston drew his Service Colt, holding it almost negligently under cover of the dash, then nodded curtly to our driver while I shrank further and further into my seat, trying anxiously to look as though the whole thing was nothing whatso*ever* to do with me.

The clutch engaged, the Jeep rolled forward, mounted the verge and, followed closely by two truckloads of US Special Forces, swung on to the metalled road leading to the *wadi*.

Maybe Trapp's next War hadn't started yet but, by God, mine was just about to!

Chapter Ten

I don't think anyone in the camp even noticed us cresting the rise and proceeding towards them at a quite unhurried pace: not until we'd approached to within a hundred metres or so of the red and white barrier spanning the main gate.

Two soldiers carrying buckets across the vehicle park to my left hesitated, idly bystanding as we cruised steadily past, then a third wearing an MP's armband, white belt and gaiters – which, for me, couldn't have served as a more untimely and discomfiting reminder of the crucified policemen back at al Djibela – also sauntered from the gate into the middle of the road, machine pistol inverted negligently behind his shoulder, to observe our coming with shaded eyes. Apparently still only curious rather than concerned.

Seventy metres . . . I sensed the rattle of a weapon being cocked surreptitiously under cover of the seat and started to feel sick with tension.

Previously masked by the gatehouse the first guard tank opened into view as we neared, followed by the second; both elliptical armoured turrets still trained fore and aft with, as yet at least, neutral menace.

Only one crewman could be seen aboard, perched on the edge of number two monster's cupola hatch with crossed forearms resting easily on the commander's co-axial PKT machine-gun mount. Four or five other khaki-overalled tankmen had casually begun to wander from the shade to lean against their matt-painted hulls, watching our approach with equally unsuspecting interest.

Sixty metres – those Arabs had to be BLIND, dammit! Or maybe Weston wasn't so crazy after all: maybe brazenness *did* defy belief. Maybe the Colonel *would* get to be a general after all . . . ?

Fifty metres! But the military policeman betraying sudden anxiety now. Shading his eyes more intently.

FORTY metres to go and the Jeep perceptibly beginning to accelerate in perfect tandem with my own heartbeats.

Oh, *Christ*! He HAD finally tumbled us!

Abruptly the soldier in the middle of the road whirled for the barrier, running for cover while struggling to unsling his weapon and shout a harsh warning all at the same time. With little sense of urgency Weston raised his Colt above the lowered windscreen and dispassionately shot the Libyan once . . . twice in the back as he scrambled for life.

Even as forty-five calibre rounds pulverized the running Arab's spine, slammed him face down on to the tarmac, I felt the Jeep surge to full throttle and the seat thrust forward as we began a race to cover the final and most vulnerable stretch of exposed tarmac before the Libyans got their act together.

Fortunately Weston's action triggered only initial confusion within the complex itself. Men appeared from everywhere, mostly, it seemed, not knowing quite where to go or what to do – whether to fight, retreat, or surrender to some still-unspecified threat.

I watched the two bystanders in the lorry park drop their burdens then inexplicably begin to run towards us: a tactic which, even to my non-military mind, appeared rather less than sound considering neither of them had thought to change his bucket for a gun first.

My reservation proved well founded when Corporal Rambo beside me snapped off a short burst with his M16 to tumble both squaddies helter-skelter into the sand.

Brief optimism was still-born, though, as the tank crews proved of sterner stuff. Caught literally napping maybe, but already they were swarming up and into the matt-ochre hulls of the monsters. Weston calmly shot two of them from their handholds in a flail of arms and legs, while bullets spanged and ricocheted around the cupola hatch of juggernaut number two as the Corporal ripped off a volley at the rapidly descending figure of the machine-gunner – but then the hatch clanged shut, I heard myself blurt an involuntary, 'Ohhhhh *Jesus*!', and we suddenly had six inches of partly manned and fully buttoned-up armour to contend with.

Meanwhile a tidal wave of white belts and gaiters began to pile from the guardhouse itself, one MP struggling desperately to hoist trousers as he hobbled bow-legged and chimpanzee fashion down the steps – obviously prematurely flushed from some small room, the nature of which I *myself* was rapidly developing an overpowering desire to visit . . . !

Someone must have hit the panic button before they turned out, all the same, because a siren started to wail across the complex just then, carrying eerily to the rocky slopes of the *wadi.*

TWENTY metres to the barrier!

Canvas covers being carelessly discarded from the trucks rumbling close astern: the first snarl of US automatic weapons strafing the complex. Hermann returning lovingly to the firing grips of his own Jeep-mounted M60, aiming, squeezing the trigger and swinging the hammering air-cooled barrel of the GPMG to hose the entrance ahead in one fluid, practised evolution.

A stark image of white belts exploding; the camouflaged stucco wall of the guardhouse splattering crimson between bullet holes; men screaming and going down – a dark Arab head abruptly detonating into a ghastly cauliflower stump of brain, bone and hair . . . I cowered, hands protecting my own skull as a clattering, smoking cascade of spent brass cartridge cases tumbled and bounced around me.

Whoomf!

The fiery tail of the first Viper to come into action licked from the truck hard astern . . . Please God, *please* let them take those tanks out as efficiently as they'd slaughtered the Libyan ships?

A dull explosion from much further away, TOO bloody far away, brought me scrabbling upright again in panic – the incompetent bastard had MISSED! Some quite innocuous building well away to starboard was puff-balling into flying masonry and yellow dust instead . . .

Then I registered a tangle of radio antennae collapsing inwards into the rubble while a dish aerial still spiralled crazily into the azure blue sky, spinning and wobbling like an out-of-control UFO, and realized that the destruction of the camp's communications centre had, of necessity, commanded tactical precedence. With the Libyan headquarters' links already severed, according to Weston, and the complex now deprived of all remaining radio contact with the outside world, no plea for reinforcements could be transmitted.

Neither – which, for me, was of infinitely greater importance than the success of Weston's mission – could any untimely warning be sent which might facilitate a pursuit force, or even air support, being deployed before we returned to the *Charon*.

Should we ever manage to extract ourselves from this desert hornet's nest so recklessly prodded in the first instance, of course. Currently we seemed to be heading for the heart of what had already become a gunfire bedlam interspersed with the tumult of snarling vehicle engines, strident alarms and the shrieks of wounded men.

CRASH . . . !

A section of splintered white timber caught my shoulder an agonizing blow.

We'd smashed clear through the flimsy barrier and were now driving pell-mell for the gap between the two guard T-54s . . .

Of course the advantage of surprise couldn't last for ever.

I remember dragging myself hypnotically above the level of the screen yet again, hearing the distant roar of diesels bursting into life while a great black cloud of exhaust jetted from beneath the nearest tank.

'Sod THIS for a game of soldiers!' I thought savagely.

Almost immediately its turret mechanism whined, beginning to traverse relentlessly towards us while at the same time the long barrel of that lethal 100-millimetre gun urgently depressed to close the range.

'S'all right for YOU . . . I don't even know why I'm bloody here,' I yelled impotently at the back of the Colonel's neck. 'But I'll tell you now, Mister – even if I bloody *did* know, then by God I'd STILL be getting bloody fed UP!'

I don't know whether he heard me or not but, quite calmly, quite deliberately, he replaced his green beret then, did the Colonel. Just like that, as we roared and bounced sickeningly straight over the bodies of the fallen guard detail – just put his bloody *hat* back on. Presumably so's they'd know he was a rootin' tootin' Yankee Commando when they shot his bloody head off!

Another *whoosh* of rocketry from astern. Already shattered nerves caused me to duck at least a micro-second too late as something burned the air above our Jeep with white-hot intensity.

I actually *saw* the Viper's missile strike the yellow tank just below its turret ring: registered the incandescent splurge of molten metal as the shaped HEAT charge instantly melted through toughened armour plate . . . then

164

nothing! Not a sign of concern from the rotten tank: even the turret continued to train remorselessly on target.

That target being ME!

'Oh, bloody MARVELLOUS,' I heard myself shouting – no: I'll be truthful, dammit, *sobbing* hysterically. 'All that bloody space technology and you can't eve – !'

A tiny wisp of orange smoke puffed from somewhere between the monster's tracks. The turret stopped uncertainly . . . then swung a little further . . .

Then stopped moving altogether.

Abruptly the cupola hatch clanged open and a rush of black oily smoke, tinged this time with furnace glow, jetted skywards. Then a man came out shrieking with his clothes on fire and Hermann deliberately smashed him like a chewed-up rag doll against the coaming with a burst from the M60 which might have been, but certainly hadn't been intended as, a kindness. There followed a sort of *whumpf* from deep inside the T-54's hull, whereupon most of its matt-ochre paint turned instant smoking black while the top half of the burning riddled tankman popped high in the air and the rest of him fell back into flame.

The starter motor of number two juggernaut was still whining desperately as two more anti-tank rockets bored into it: one smack through the driver's slit, the second into its after engine compartment.

By then I'd given up being surprised or resentful or even scared, having slipped into a thoroughly resigned state of shock, and hardly flinched from the explosion which followed. I still remember being morbidly fascinated, though, by the way in which ten tons of armoured turret were displaced convulsively on an expanding shock wave before rumbling monstrously askew with its long gun spewing a rather forlorn stream of black smoke skywards.

Ammunition began to detonate within the hull while

tracer from the PKT machine-gun belts flashed and crackled viciously as they snaked back into the fire below.

Our Jeep broadsided crazily, spraying a tidal wave of sand in narrowly avoiding the wrecks. The heat actually scorched the side of my face as we bombed past while I glimpsed the drivers of the following trucks dragging wheels savagely hard a starboard as they, too, were forced into reckless evasive action.

Then we'd bucketed clear of the tanks and were racing headlong, deeper and deeper into the Libyan complex and clearly heading – not without a certain lemming-like persistence, I gloomed – for the windowless building previously seen from the ridge.

Thinking back on that tortuous climb reminded me of other nauseating experiences I'd had to contend with recently. Like Gorbals Wullie, for instance: presumably still up there on that ridge as a stand-by mine detector with Weston's back-door assault team and thus poised on the threshold of what should prove the great opportunity of his bat-brained little life – to play John Wayne himself. Jist like oan the pitchers.

I did hope malevolently that Green Beret Wullie would experience just as much fun as *I* was bloody having!

It was becoming increasingly obvious that the camouflaged building situated within its separate compound represented Weston's primary objective. What the structure's function might be I couldn't even begin to imagine, but then, what was so unique about *my* being kept in the dark about things?

Anyway, the answer to that riddle would have to wait its turn in the queue. I hadn't yet caught up with trying to guess whose submarines went round torpedoing warships, apparently on Weston's behalf, when not even *Weston* seemed aware of their existence.

One myth I'd confidently discarded once and for all – that this mission ever had been mounted to neutralize some Qaddafi-inspired terror fund. Economic logic insisted that the Libyans wouldn't defend banks with tanks to this extent. The sheer cost of deploying the military hardware Weston's force was currently preoccupied with dismantling, armoured plate by bolt by rivet, must far have exceeded the value of any revolutionary gains achieved.

The Brother Colonel would've found it a hulluva sight cheaper simply buying up the world's major transport systems then giving them to the PLO or whoever to blow up in their own time, and without spoiling anyone's holiday.

So what other use coul . . . ? Oh, *damn!*

Pfc Stompf's beloved M60 began to shudder deafeningly yet again as an open half-track with a gaggle of steel-helmeted Libyans aboard shot into view from a side road ahead. I saw Hermann's initial burst spark and clang from the square bows of the creature as it swung towards us on a recklessly closing course, then Green Berets joined in from astern, the displaced air waves from tracer and ball *thwak, thwak, thwakking* above the Jeep – yet STILL the Libyan machine came at us!

I registered the wink of a machine-gun firing back, a bullet *spanged* off the lowered windscreen frame within an inch of Weston's hand: he didn't even flinch. But I did – in fact I tried to hurl myself to the floor but only managed an embarrassing list to port as my head made agonizing contact with my clanking associate's grenade belt.

. . . choking dust; a pandemonium tumult of automatic weapons; the din of high-revving engines all mixed up with the terrified rise and fall of that bloody siren. Libyans beginning to fall over and out of the troop carrier as it sheered crazily off course before careering clean through the wall of an accommodation block close along-side. A dull *whumf* and its gable blew out while the roof began to collapse into yet another instant furnace of fuel, men and exploding small-arms ammunition as we roared past.

. . . where WAS Wullie? More importantly: where was the rest of Weston's second and smaller commando unit, last seen heading for the *wadi* ridge? *Surely* they should've joined the action by now? Or were they being held in reserve; keeping the corps of Sergeant Jablonski on tactical – if no longer literal – ice, so to speak? Awaiting the precise moment to play its undoubtedly macabre role in the mission.

But when?

And, even more intriguingly – how?

Not to mention those other Libyan tanks, at least four to my knowledge, which I'd last observed guarding the corners of the mined installation perimeter and most certainly closed up and revving for revenge by now?

Abruptly our own Jeep broadsided to a halt: we were finally there – wherever and whatever 'there' MEANT, dammit!

Dimly I heard Weston snarl, 'OUT, Miller!' through the fog of swirling dust, and literally threw myself to the sand, grovelling enthusiastically as a creeping fountain of bullets immediately vectored towards us from the inner security compound . . .

A flash and report from the first truck astern as it, too, skidded to a halt: a fevered impression of a rifle grenade sailing skywards followed by another – two sharp deton-ations followed and the Arab gun stopped firing abruptly. American uniforms with green berets bright arrogant in the dazzling sunlight poured from the trucks and, bend-ing low, ran pell-mell for the wire . . . the sheer momen-tum of their assault was unflagging.

A flat, quite unexpected explosion to my left, somewhere from the rear of the complex, and a mushroom ball of smoke rolling and skying above the buildings. A momentary glimpse of more spiralling trails of incoming rocket exhaust: the supersonic tongues of Vipers being launched, this time from the ridge backing the camp – Weston's second team coming into action at last! – then a rippling shock wave of hits away over to starboard. I felt a bit better: hopefully the immediate threat from tanks had been removed.

Quite inconsequentially I found myself peering at my Hong Kong watch to discover how many hours had elapsed since my pulse had slipped into overdrive, then frowned and interrogated the timepiece again – it *was* still going, though its battery was obviously fading as surely as mine was.

It was trying to persuade me we'd only been inside the wire for just over two minutes.

I rolled on to my back, panting not to much from physical as nervous exhaustion. Smoke from the brewing Libyan armour had begun to mask the glare from the sun now, pyres rising almost undeflected from the torrid stillness of the valley. They must have been visible for many miles, but then we *were* many miles from the nearest military post.

I had little doubt that, already, every desert Arab within two days' camel ride would know something violent was happening in the great *wadi* north of Ras al Djibela, but I wasn't too sure they'd hurry to tell. The Libyan bedouin have little concern for the new revolution and, living as they still do with the explosive legacies of war, even less enthusiasm for armies, including their own.

Another staccato firefight began, this time with a concrete pillbox guarding the target building's sole entrance.

I wriggled to watch with renewed anxiety. For the first time the mission appeared to be stalling: Weston's force was still pinned down outside the compound fence, frustrated by crash-proof gates and a seemingly impenetrable back-up of barbed wire but already two Green Berets were doggedly crawling, bellies flat to the sand and dragging with them some form of tubular contrivance.

Until a growing desperation of machine-gun fire from the Libyan post reached towards the crawling men, ironically recalling those earlier fountains – albeit of sea foam then, not desert sand – which had so callously claimed the survivors from the Komar patrol boat . . .

. . . and then the sand jumped and became bloodied just as the Gulf of Sirte had, as young American soldiers lolled and jerked and came apart in death in precisely the same manner as young Arab sailors, while I felt nauseated beyond measure. And Weston's secret force had taken its first fatal casualties.

Someone did something, a bit bloody late and probably with a ubiquitous Viper, which blew the pillbox itself to lumps of concrete and steel rods and more ghastly parts of men, but I didn't have time to feel relieved.

Almost immediately a small armoured half-track of, I swear, World War Two *Afrika Korps* vintage careered somewhat erratically from the vehicle park; registered Weston's cowboys knocking the stuffing out of three-foot-thick concrete; changed its mind about playing Fifth Cavalry; skidded to a frantic halt before uttering a panic-stricken gnashing and crashing of gears as its driver tried to find emergency reverse.

. . . then, just before their reluctant *Schutzenpanzer-wagen* reverted to an incandescent ball of Krupps clinker after only just having made it to its next war, everyone leapt out and ran away arguing irritably with each other instead.

Which made them much more *my* kind of fighting soldiers!

*

Two more Americans had taken advantage of the brief diversion to race across the open killing ground, snatch the now bloodied clearance device from the sprawled troopers and, with random Libyan shots kicking sand as they sprinted the last few yards to kneel by the wire, thrust the tubular charge in below the vicious defensive tangle. Hurriedly I looked away, unable to endure the tension of their pell-mell race to regain cover.

. . . which was the moment when I saw Gorbals Wullie again!

Well, I didn't exactly *see* Wullie. Not your actual species himself in the unexpurgated, dirt-engrained flesh, so to speak.

To be more precise, as I'd hastily averted my gaze to the crest of the *wadi* ridge a few hundred feet above I also happened to catch sight of the third truck accompanying Weston's support group: the vehicle in which I had last observed Jablonski's sad company being conveyed to war, and aboard which a somewhat disenchanted Pfc Wullie had been ordered.

Etched clear against the skyline it appeared to be moving slowly towards us. Meaning it was *also* moving steadily towards the lip of the ridge . . . which was crazy, and why I thought for a moment it must've been an optical illusion because, if the heavy vehicle did pursue such a suicidal course much longer then the only way left to it would be down – and I mean STRAIGHT down!

Roughly equivalent to a five-ton bobsleigh embarking on a one in one rock- and scrub-strewn gradient. And with nothing at the bottom but wire fences, separated by a highly sophisticated MINEfie . . . !

Ohhhhh, *Jeeeeze*!

Incredulously I watched as the bonnet tilted forward, whereupon the heavy canvas-shrouded vehicle began to gather speed with a rush; bouncing and swaying crazily. Generating a whirlwind wake of dust and bounding, chasing boulders as it hurtled faster and faster, quite out of control already, down the steep incline towards me.

And towards the outer perimeter fence.

AND the minefield!

I remember the first thought which came into my head at that moment was that Trapp might never, ever speak to me again if I went back without his key personnel: Wullie being so cheap to run and all that.

But then, considering it unseemly to dwell overlong on the undeniable attractions of Gorbals Wullie's getting himself blown to high-speed mince, I prudently stuck my fingers in my ears, waited with bated breath for the careering truck to reach ground zero, and meanwhile updated the current list of riddles posed by this, Weston's latest and surely oddest eccentricity of all.

Because I didn't doubt for one moment that third lorry HAD been deliberately pushed over the edge in the pursuance of some coldly calculated plan. But what plan? I mean, why *bring* it all this way simply to write it off . . . ?

For a start, and always presupposing Weston's support troop hadn't confused determination with sheer bloody stupidity and so had sensibly dismounted before blast off, the wretched machine now only contained seven dead bodies anyway – well, six dead technically, plus one small Scottish person as good as – so what *possib* . . . ?

The truck rampaged through the outer defensive wire and began to detonate mines immediately: a great running sequence of fire and flame and gouting sand following its bucketing passage across the lethal strip.

As it lost momentum the devices began to trigger below, rather than astern of, it whereupon the juggernaut began to burn and disintegrate all at the same time. Then I saw a corpse flung hideously skywards as the cargo floor erupted, then another, and parts of others.

. . . I wondered sickly which bits had belonged to Gorbals Wullie and suddenly discovered I really *had* wanted to take the awful little man back to Trapp after all. Restoring Wullie as the Captain's disgruntled, whining shadow for the next twenty years would've achieved a much more subtle revenge on my part than any grief Trapp might feel over Wullie's death.

And he would undoubtedly mourn for Wullie. Well, for a few minutes anyway. Trapp wasn't completely insensitive, you know: not entirely devoid of tender feelings.

I remember he'd had a goldfish once. Kept in a plastic bucket in his sea cabin. It had died eventually – seasickness, I think – and the Captain had been terribly distraught for weeks, even months afterwards. It had looked a bit like Gorbals Wullie, on reflection, that fish: especially around the eyes; and I had a sneaking suspicion that despite all the contempt he pretended for his poisonous little familiar, secretly Trapp was almost as fond of Wullie as he'd been of his goldfish.

Even allowing for the fact that Wullie *hadn't* been quite as intelligent.

Incredibly I found myself stifling a sob; a tear coursed unheeded down my own dirt-encrusted cheek as I thought about Wullie lying out there beside the blast-distorted chassis of that blazing truck. I'd been plagued by him for a long time: he'd become a nauseous but almost intrinsic part of my life for too many years now to dismiss lightly. I forced myself to look for him, scanning the burned uniforms, the still plainly identifiable remains of American soldiers.

And all the time I wondered WHY, in God's name? Why *bring* dead men here? Why go to such secrecy to infiltrate Weston's Special Force if, when on the very brink of operational success, they'd intended quite deliberately to present Qaddafi with indisputable proof that

American troops *had* perpetrated this massive breach of Libyan sovereignty after all?

And to think that, before we'd docked at al Djibela, I'd just managed to persuade myself that the whole subterfuge had been intended to leave no trail leading back to the President or the Pentagon. Until Weston had turned up dressed like Super Yank . . . and now – this!

It seemed so utterly illogical. Not even Trapp could've planned a better catastrophe himself.

Thinking about catastrophes reminded me of Wullie again, and yet another tear squeezed from the corner of my eye . . .

'Here, is this no just like bein' on the pitchers, Mister Miller sir?' a voice echoed cheerfully at my elbow.

'Go away!' I retorted automatically. I was just beginning to get really maudlin: to truly appreciate how bad Trapp must have felt about the goldfi . . . !

I squirmed to eye the new arrival blankly. 'How the hell did YOU get here?'

'Same way as you – inna Jeep through the front gate,' the ghost of Gorbals Wullie leered. 'Christ, but ye fair sorted oot they tanks them Libyans wis usin' as door stops, Mister Miller, an' that's a fact.'

'Never MIND the bloody toadying,' I shouted resentfully. 'You're *supposed* to be dead. Blown to grotty little pieces.'

'Sorry,' he said, trying to look suitably chastened. 'They let me oot afore they shoved the truck ower.'

'I knew someone'd make a mistake before long,' I growled.

A sharp detonation from the wire of the inner compound, a shower of sand and little stones descended upon us and Weston's troopers began pouring through the gap made by the clearance charge. The assault was on again.

'C'mon!' I snarled, not relishing the prospect of being left alone with just Wullie to protect me.

A splintered noticeboard still hung askew on the wire as we passed, lettered in both Arabic and English. Brushing it aside I crawled nervously after the troops.

Gorbals Wullie suddenly stopped crawling though. 'Here,' he called uncertainly. 'See whit I've found, Mister Miller sir.'

'Come ON, dammit!'

'Ah'd rather no' – if ye dinnae mind, that is.'

I looked back. He was waggling the bit of board at me. It had a sort of stylized propeller painted on it in yellow. I vaguely recollected having seen similar logos before: displayed as warnings on the gangways of ships carrying radio-active waste, I think.

The rest of the board was heat-scorched, with little of its English language content still legible. Apart from the seemingly inevitable Socialist People's Libyan Arabwhatever, of course.

Oh . . . and just enough to suggest, for the very first time, the *real* truth behind why we were here.

Just a part-legend.

. . . UCLEAR RESEARCH ESTABLI . . . !

Chapter Eleven

Nuclear something-or-other, the notice definitely said! Referring, presumably, to that perfectly dull structure which still looked more like a battery chicken house to me than some academic beehive.

Yet, judging by the way satchel demolition charges were being hastened through the breached entrance, Weston's crowd was getting ready to kick the absolute SHIT out of it?

I became aware of a quite different sort of fear then: fear of the unknown . . . and the consequent dilemma such ill-informed aversion to getting my atomic particles all mixed up with Gorbals Wullie's insanitary nuclei posed regarding our next move.

Like where to hide next?

Certainly, now the Green Berets' goal had been achieved the emphasis had turned to defending the captured ground. Already the majority of Weston's assault force were digging in to throw a protective ring around the inner compound with GPMGs and Vipers outward-facing, ready for any attempt by the still demoralized Libyans to mount a counter-attack. So far surprise was still causing masterful inactivity within the Arab ranks: we'd only been going for four minutes even then according to my Hong Kong watch – which, incidentally, was waterproofed to a depth of fifty feet though I wasn't so sure about how it would be if I bled all over it – but nevertheless random shots did keep coming in.

Trouble was, what one man considered random could

prove fatal to the Chief Officer beside him. To deny myself the comparative protection of a reassuringly solid building, even for the short term, meant increasing my risk of developing a boringly conventional Kalashnikov-calibre hole in the head. On the other hand, electing to follow Weston and his rampaging demolition squad could mean I ran an odds-on chance of ending up glowing in the dark should they do anything to upset the radio-active balance of whatever infernal machine might lie within – and so far they'd proved bloody expert at upsetting everythin' ELSE Libyan!

I decided to stay in the clear air and chance getting just ordinary killed.

'Me too,' Wullie agreed. 'Ah dinnae fancy goin' intae a nukleer lavatory.'

'Laboratory,' I corrected absently.

'Huv you *been* in some o' they Ayrab places?' Wullie asked pointedly.

A shot fired from the surrounding buildings exploded sand between us. A second *spanged* off a steel stanchion within inches of my head before whining away into space.

'Talking of lavatories . . .' I mused, suddenly wistful again.

But Wullie had already gone.

'Bloody little *coward*!' I thought contemptuously.

Overtaking him.

Entering that sterile high-tech complex was most un-settling, quite unlike anything I'd ever experienced be-fore. More awful even than joining Trapp's *Charon*.

Wullie wasn't at all disturbed by the laboratory's sinis-ter ambience, of course. But then Gorbals Wullie had two great advantages over me: firstly he was a cinemagoer, which meant he knew all about scientific things, and secondly, the inescapable fact that Wullie possessed an

IQ roughly equivalent to that of a sirloin steak. To him danger had to evince itself in tangible form before it could be comprehended. A broken bottle in the hand of a fellow messmate; the glimpse of an approaching policeman's uniform; the mounting irritation of Edward Trapp ... but the futuristic array of stainless-steel piping and flasks and benches and computers which met us as we burst into the building implied no more threat to Wullie than had countless celluloid images projected on a wall.

Whereas to me it was a place which reeked of the malign. Somehow I sensed its purpose from the moment I entered – they either had researched, or were about to research, atomic weapons here. Oh, I admit to having no concrete grounds for such precipitate assumption; nothing more than a broken noticeboard really, yet I knew I was right – Israel was developing The Bomb independently: why not Qaddafi ... ? And what greater motivation for mounting a pre-emptive strike by US Special Forces? Christ, even the slightest possibility of the Libyans achieving nuclear capability must've had every Pentagon general chewing nerve pills like candy.

Apart from which Trapp had got himself involved: a factor which guaranteed the makings of a disaster of at *least* cataclysmic proportions for a start. Or more accurately, he'd got ME involved – him having opted out of this current nightmare on the grounds of fiscal and contractual breakdown, a peculiarly Trapp condition which *should've* been recognized as being certifiable as far back as World War Bloody TWO!

'... hysteria again!' I thought desperately. 'You've got to get a grip on this growing tendency of yours towards acute bloody HYSTERIA, Miller!'

Naturally such prospects of terrorist-inspired global holocaust concerned Gorbals Wullie not at all.

'Pure James Bond,' my noxious companion with the depopulated mind whispered, gazing about him

178

entranced. 'It's a' here, Mister Miller sir – SMERSH an' atomic warheids an' the secret scientists an' stuff. Here, dae you mind thon *Doctor No* film o' his? Och, it wis magick, so it wis – the way a'body got blowed up in a gigantick mushroom cloud at the end?'

A brilliantly timed allusion. Delivered with a lack of sensitivity almost worthy of Trapp the Master.

'Don't bloody SAY things like that!' I bawled. 'And for *God*'s sake, don't bloody TOUCH anythi . . . !'

A fusillade of shots came from further down the corridor as a man in a white coat with blood all over it ran sobbing from a side room and headed towards us, waving his hands imploringly.

He wasn't an Arab either. In fact he appeared to be more of German extraction judging by the way he kept screaming, '*Kamerad! Kamer* . . . !'

'Here, yous keep away fae ME, Mister!' Wullie squealed with remarkable intuition.

Pfc Stompf stepped unhurriedly from the same room and shot the fleeing professor or whatever he was with a calculated burst which nevertheless afforded all too little safety margin in my jaundiced opinion, the running target still being between us and Hermann at the time. The long corridor filled with cordite smoke; M16 rounds exploded the marble floor; I flung myself one way, Wullie the other; one suddenly posthumous physicist went down in a bloodied heap; the Libyan nuclear weapon programme took a giant step backwards . . . and a pair of broken spectacles skittered to a forlorn halt by my foot.

I remember thinking idiotically, unsympathetically, 'Now if you'd dedicated your life to finding a cure for something or other instead of being a clever bugger with bombs, you might still've been WEARING them, *Herr Doktor*!'

More shots ricocheted along the open hallway. The

mission's intention seemed clear: if it moved and wore white – shoot it!

I was wearing tropical whites – well, tropical greys maybe, after my tour of the Libyan Desert. But still . . .

I glimpsed an open door to port. 'Take cover in there!' I bawled urgently at Wullie who was already weighing up a large clock on the wall with the eye of a journeyman looter.

'Where?'

'THERE!'

We hurled ourselves through the doorframe to find Colonel Weston and two more Green Berets crouched behind an overturned bench. They whirled as we arrived: three weapons levelled as one.

'Don't SHOOT!' I screamed.

'GedDOWN, goddam it!' Weston bellowed back.

'What're THEY hidin' behind thon table fur?' Wullie snarled, dead put out. 'Isn't they the wans supposed tae be doin' the *fightin'* . . . ?'

A massive detonation from the far end of the laboratory answered his question, while a safe door zipped over our heads to disappear through the wall behind us. Wullie and myself fell over clutching tortured ears while a cloud of dust and charred technical papers floated gently down.

'Aw, Jesus CHRIST!' I blurted, partly deafened.

'Pardon?' Wullie said.

'You two better get the hell out of here. And fast,' Weston commanded bleakly as his troopers began to bundle the papers into a canvas bag. The sight was enough to have given Trapp another seizure; had the world been a more dishonest place, by rights they should've been US dollars.

I glowered at Weston defiantly. Well, I'd had quite enough by then. I was thoroughly brassed off with bullets and explosions and people in assorted khaki suits trying to bloody kill me. I didn't have the slightest intention of going back out into that shooting gallery of a corridor again.

'No *way*, Colonel. Me and him, we're staying put right here, safely out of the firing line – and there's absolutely nothing you can do that's gonna stop us!'

'Mister Miller means *if* that's a'richt by yous, Colonel sir,' Wullie supplemented, always tending towards prudence.

The Colonel shrugged indifferently. 'Please yourselves.'

'See?' I snapped at Wullie. 'You don't always have to be the servile little worm you are. Just stand your ground like me.'

Someone blew a long blast on a whistle. Immediately we heard boots doubling down the corridor, withdrawing fast. Weston nodded brusquely to his corporal who yanked the tape on a satchel charge from which white smoke instantly began to splutter. I guessed the fuse might have a built-in delay of around two minutes.

Drawing a deep breath I turned on my heel with, I rather like to think, considerable dignity under the circumstances. And it *certainly* wasn't my fault – the collision.

The selfish way Gorbals Wullie tried to shove in front of me. Just so's HE could be first through the door.

The Libyan fire was happily still sporadic, unco-ordinated by the time we evacuated that sinister place, a charnel house now with only the learned dead in possession. There hadn't been time to think, to absorb the full enormity of what had happened, but it was already clear that Weston's Special Force had perpetrated a coldly deliberate massacre in there. Little if any resistance had been offered by the scientific staff, yet two more labcoated technicians, both shot cleanly through the head

– and again, significantly, neither of them Arab – sprawled in the corridor near the late *Herr Doktor*. As I hastily withdrew past breached office doors I caught glimpses of further corpses huddled in bloodied pools, yet by then I felt strangely little concern for them.

I'd seen enough to satisfy myself that the development of warlike, not passive, atomic research had indeed formed the purpose of that remote desert complex. Drawings, sketches: a sectioned model showing rudimentary fins . . . I didn't have to be a nuclear physicist to interpret the gist of what I'd observed.

So if I had any capacity for feelings other than personal apprehension right then, it was for a bleak satisfaction rather than horror at what had occurred. Certainly I felt no inclination to question the event: to weigh the morality of those who'd ordered such cold-blooded executions against that of non-Libyan intellectuals . . . state-of-the-art mercenaries in effect: scientists of fortune – a neat irony in view of my initial misgivings regarding Weston himself – assiduously designing a weapon capable of holding the whole world to terrorist ransom.

More disconcerting was the realization that the Americans had been prepared to go so far. Or had Weston, by such murderous excess, simply overstepped the prescribed limits of his Rules of Engagement? Somehow I didn't think so: somehow I suspected those physicists had been assassinated to order. I didn't like the Colonel but I conceded his professionalism. I didn't consider him a psychopathic killer: just a chillingly pragmatic one.

Either way, even before the charges went off, Qaddafi's nuclear weapons programme had suffered a massive setback. Two-thirds of the world's governments would privately sigh with relief – well, they would before orchestrating their public outrage, anyway, at this further proof of American imperialist aggression.

. . . we began to withdraw as fast as we'd arrived. So far it had been a brilliantly executed lightning strike. Six minutes and thirty seconds from the 'off', my Hong Kong timepiece said, and already we were remounting the waiting trucks.

I do remember frowning in perplexity yet again though, even as I thankfully clambered back aboard that suddenly welcome Jeep. Careless of the risk from snipers a squad had already recovered the bodies of the two young Green Berets killed during the assault on the inner compound wire. I watched them passing their lifeless comrades over the tailgate of the second truck with surprising gentleness, while at the same time I wondered as ever at the inconsistency of it.

I mean, why take *them* home, however laudable a gesture, when the same force had gone to such bizarre lengths to ensure Sergeant Jablonski and HIS still plainly identifiable Special Forces team stayed behind as absolute gifts to the Libyan propaganda machine?

Wasn't it almost as if . . . ?

I shook my head firmly. Don't be so BLOODY silly, Miller! Speculation like that was too outrageous even allowing for this trip having turned out to be one of Trapp's most disastrous so far – such outlandish suspicions simply had to be my Chinese Puzzle paranoia evincing itself again . . . or my Pentagon Paradox, more like. Penetrate one enigma only to turn up a whole nest of others even more baffling.

And anyway, I had more than enough to worry about right then. Nitty gritty details. Like would I emanate a delicate blue aura when they switched the lights off? And precisely how long *was* the fuse on a demolition charge . . . ?

The Jeep's engine revved to life as Weston took one final calculating glance around before swinging into his seat. My clanking Corporal silently heaved himself and his grenades aboard to compress me into my familiar corner – which made me pray he wouldn't get shot because he'd probably blow up with a bigger bang than the bloody target was about to if he did – while Hermann, as chatty as ever, cocked his favourite killing tool with a metallic clatter.

And we were off at last, even though a long and undoubtedly fraught return passage still loomed ahead. Not only did we have to make it back to the *Charon* in one piece; Popeye Bucalosie also had to get that bloody sadistic *Spatz* started again before our getaway ship could leg . . . well, sea-snail it for the safety of international waters.

'Still, we're sort of homeward-bound, at least,' I thought, scraping the bottom of my morale barrel for the tiniest of mercies. 'Even if it *does* mean putting up with Trapp again!'

I even felt a little happier. Until I caught sight of Gorbals Wullie again, a burdensome spectre which had mercifully escaped my mind for the past few turbulent seconds, and got all depressed once more.

Of course he'd managed to get left behind as usual. But not *properly* left behind, you understand: just marginally left behind so's I couldn't simply ignore him and get a pleasant surprise later when I found he'd disappeared . . . ! Anyway, there he bloody was, sprinting awkwardly after the convoy while, at the same time, lugging that clock which I'd last seen on the wall of the laboratory building and yelling, 'Wait fur ME! Wait fur . . . !'

There was a screech of something unpleasant and incoming, then a sharp detonation as the first Libyan mortar bomb exploded less than ten yards ahead of him, whereupon Gorbals Wullie, all mixed up with virtually indistinguishable clods of dried earth by then, turned a complete revolution in the air, hit the sand with wee legs still going like machine pistons before, without even a break in rhythm, steadying to a gallop alongside the already moving Jeep.

I willed myself long and hard to do the decent thing – then stuck out a grudging hand and hauled him aboard anyway. The dreadful creature collapsed in a noisome heap on top of me while panting, 'Jeeze Mister Miller sir but ah *bluidy* near forgot the time, so ah did.'

I looked at the gigantic quartz clock still clasped to his thieving breast and wondered if he was being perfectly serious: which he was. There was a shrapnel hole clean through it – the clock I mean, not Wullie's breast where it would've been a bloody sight more practical – then sighed before I dropped it, the clock again unfortunately, overboard in strained silence. But there were occasions when it became impossible to think of anything really constructive to say to Gorbals Wullie.

. . . and then a second mortar came screeching in to detonate dead ahead. The lunatic driving the Jeep didn't even hesitate: just accelerated quite irresponsibly in my opinion, bursting clear through the hanging sand-fronds of the explosion, bouncing crazily into and out of the crater. Then another bomb landed twenty yards to starboard, this time with shrapnel fragments screeching like banshees to shred the smoke to whirling tatters and clatter ominously against the bodywork. I'd hardly had time to be properly sick with the terror of it before another came in. Followed by ANOTHER . . . !

Hermann began to fire above our dazed heads, beating up anything and everything Libyan in a wide killing arc around the bucketing vehicle with expended brass cartridges clattering and showering over Wullie and me: us two clinging white-faced together by then, each attempting single-mindedly to burrow under the other. Instantly the trucks astern returned fire as well and everything had become tumult and remote-controlled death and hammering weapons and roaring engines yet again.

BOOOOooooom . . . ! The shock wave chased us; disturbing the whirling sand devils, plucking at our hair.

'Jeeeeze, wull ye look at *that* then,' Wullie breathed, freezing abruptly with eyes barely raised above the back of the seat. I stopped punching him for a minute in order to watch as well.

The long windowless research building had begun to blow up in a series of running explosions which expanded its ochre camouflaged walls outwards before collapsing them into rolling, convulsing tongues of flame. I remember waiting tensely for the first indication of a radioactive configured cloud, but only reassuringly commonplace smoke rolled skywards.

Though I don't know – about the smoke being all that commonplace? I mean, as funeral pyres went that one must've had one of the highest IQs in the whole of the Middle East.

. . . and suddenly we were racing between the gutted hulls of the main gate guard tanks killed less than an unbelievable eight minutes previously, such had been the impetus of the hit and run operation.

A last fusillade of shots whipped above lowered heads as our Jeep broadsided in the inevitable spray of sand; a melodramatic form of progression but seemingly essential, I was beginning to conclude, to reckless devil-may-care exploits in deserts. The big corporal with the ammunition-dump belt leaned heavily against me under the G-force of the turn – then I heard tyres screeching on blessed tarmac once more as we bulleted down the straight with the second Jeep and both lorries hard astern, and the Libyan nuclear weapons programme already a fading nightmare.

A fading dream, too. For Brother Colonel Muammar Qaddafi. Though I gathered the Colonel wasn't the only one liable to disappointment, seeing how Gorbals Wullie also appeared inexplicably crestfallen right then.

Until I discovered what was niggling at him.

'Is that no' bluidy TYPICAL of mah luck?' he was muttering dead aggrieved while still craning to stare aft. 'NAE atomick cloud: no' even a wee smoke ring! Yet in the pitchers Double Oh Seven *aye* leaves a'thing blowed up inna gigantick mushroo . . . !'

'Stop being so BLOODY mindless and gimme a hand here,' I snarled awkwardly, struggling at the same time to shove the big corporal off because he seemed more than content to use me as a pillow. His grenades were pressing excruciatingly into my hip and I was just about ready to . . .

I stopped shoving abruptly, staring at my hand. It was covered in blood.

Uncertainly I examined my Clanking Corporal's face under the rather lopsided green beret, and noted a most unhealthy pallor. Along with a further trickle of blood coming from the ominously slack mouth.

' . . . an' whit aboot mah CLOCK that got heaved ower the wall then?' Wullie continued to ignore everything about him, obsessed only with the absolute injustice of his own colourless little world. 'Thon wis a perfec'ly good clock wi' only a wee hole in it, Mister Miller – ANN'it widda got blowed up onyway, so it wid . . . !'

Hermann hanging on to his machine-gun above me was still fully engrossed with the prospect of getting to kill a few more people before he knocked off for the day. I couldn't attract Weston's attention in the front seat either, because right at that moment he gestured with a map, whereupon the Jeep careered off the tarmac road without even slackening pace and began to roar south, back towards Ras al Djibela with our remaining three vehicles in close company.

More blood – pink-foaming, as from a lung wound – bubbled from the corner of the corporal's mouth, then suddenly he opened fast glazing eyes to gaze without

187

recognition into mine. I knew he had little time left and felt terribly inadequate because all I could think of doing right then was to place my ear close to his ashen lips when I saw them move slightly.

He whispered to me. Or to someone, I don't know who; but had his imagined listener been a military man then he would've been very proud of the corporal, the loyalty he proclaimed – the depth of patriotism so clearly evident in his very last words.

And then he died, still resting against my shoulder. But I wasn't aware of the discomfort caused by his grenades any longer.

In fact I didn't feel anything right then, other than a suddenly regenerated fear for myse . . . Oh, all RIGHT, dammit! For Trapp and Gorbals Wullie and Spew and the whole rotten lot of the *Charon*'s crowd as WELL, for that matter!

Because I was still trying to come to terms with unexpectedly having prized open the very last box in my puzzle aided by, of all things, the delirious indiscretion of a dying soldier. For not only had the corporal unwittingly exposed the *real* secret behind Weston's bizarre mission to Ras al Djibela; he'd also indicated why, despite having had access to the resources of the largest military power on earth, it had still been necessary for the Colonel to capitalize on Trapp's tunnel-visioned avarice.

And, of rather more immediate relevance: why the Colonel's orders must still require him to carry out one final task – an act dictated purely by operational expediency, of course; nothing personal – before concluding his mission.

Even I appreciated that Weston would be duty bound to do that, in order to ensure its success, don't you see?

. . . to execute us all, I mean. Every last man listed on *Charon II*'s watchbill.

Chapter Twelve

In the light of what simply *had* to happen, I was still slumped in utter disconsolation by the time we returned to the spot where Trapp had been left under guard.

Of course he wasn't there. And neither was his guard. But I couldn't even raise a smile of satisfaction over that discovery.

Weston raised himself ominously from his seat to scan the shimmering scrubland as the convoy halted, engines growling impatiently, while Pfc Stompf ever hopefully swung the muzzle of his M60 to cover the line of our withdrawal.

It seemed very quiet as we waited, and very exposed. Just the heat from the blazing sun beating on the vehicles, and the call of a desert bird and the distant occasional crackle from the *wadi* as ammunition continued to burn within the knocked-out Libyan armour. Still no sign of the feared mushroom cloud though, which, seeing I wasn't Wullie and so possessed a bit more than a reel of celluloid for a brain, did make me feel a little easier. Very possibly the Libyan weapons development programme hadn't yet reached a stage where the arming of fissionable material became necessary.

The good news, therefore, was that it didn't look as though I would expire from radiation poisoning after all.

The bad news . . . ? That I had only a few hours left to find out! Before the Colonel had me shot, stabbed, garrotted, hanged or otherwise terminated anyway.

I shifted uncomfortably as the sun barbecued the top of my head.

By then the corporal's corpse slumped against me had become a . . . well, a dead weight I suppose, so I coughed diffidently, trying to attract Weston's attention while not wishing to appear a complete nuisance. He may still have considered Trapp indispensable, required him to pilot the *Charon* back out to sea but, for all I knew, Gorbals Wullie and I could already be scheduled as 'operational immediate' on the Colonel's loose ends list and I wasn't too crazy about reminding him that we were still alive and relatively well.

Only Wullie responded though, the James Bond in him having finally accepted with stiff upper-lipped resilience that atomick clouds wis def'nitely oot f'r that day.

'Whit's wrong wi' you then, Mister Miller sir?'

'Nothing – yet!' I hissed. 'But keep your *voice* down: don't make Weston trigger-happy for God's sake. We've got to break it gently that his favourite corporal here's not breathing so good.'

Wullie stared. It didn't take Double Oh Six and a Half long to figure the bullet which killed the corporal must've passed within inches of both him and me first.

'You tryin' tae say the guy's DEID f'r . . . ?'

Of course I should have known: that the little tick would broadcast his alarm loud enough to cause *everybody*, never mind just Weston, to whirl with weapons levelled and trigger fingers already taking up first pressure under the tension of the moment.

'That's another way of putting it,' I conceded.

Soon as I'd recovered my power of speech.

Weston *didn't* shoot me of course, or you wouldn't be reading this now. It would have been nice, certainly jolly considerate of him if he'd thought to blow Wullie away as a token reprisal for destroying his concentration, but he didn't do that either.

He did manage to surprise me though, despite his disciplined lack of expression, while he watched them carry the corporal to join his other dead in the truck. His eyes gave him away, you see: the sadness they betrayed for one unguarded second which left me wondering whether delusion hadn't led the corporal to believe his own Colonel was the man he'd whispered his dying declaration to.

But then Weston abruptly returned to searching for Trapp, and his moment of human weakness had passed.

'. . . all right! So where's me bloody MONEY then?'

Everybody whirled nervously once more. Except me – I just sat there brooding darkly over proverbial bad pennies and not feeling the slightest surprise. Well, nothing had gone right for me so far, not since the rotten voyage had begun, so it was absolutely inevitable that HE'D bloody well turn up again before long. It was fortunate for Trapp that I was one of the few who *didn't* have their finger on a convenient trigger right then or I'd cheerfully have anticipated Weston's operation order by a few worthwhile hours.

Anyway, Trapp stood sticking out of a clump of *agam* scrub looking particularly irritable even for him. It was discouragingly obvious he was better – or worse really, depending on how you viewed it.

'Captin . . . ?' Gorbals Wullie called tentatively. 'Jeeze but it *is* you, so it is.'

'SHURRUP ye wizened little Scotch weevil!' Trapp bawled as fondly as if they'd never been parted.

'Och, but is thon man no' pure magick, Mister Miller sir?' Wullie whispered ecstatically. 'Whit a personALity the Captin's got, so he has.'

Weston frowned, trying to recover. 'Where the hell's my trooper?'

'Down behind the bush 'ere,' Trapp glowered matter-of-factly. 'I 'ad to tie 'im up with 'is own webbing in the end: 'im getting on me nerves like 'e wus.'

Well, I could have *told* the Colonel if he'd asked – that he shouldn't detail a boy to do a regiment's job. He'd have been much better advised sending one bloke off to wipe out the Libyans while holding the rest of his team back to guard Trapp. One paltry killer commando with a few guns and grenades an' stuff wasn't anywhere near enough manpower to prevent the Captain from causing havoc; not once he'd made up his mind there was profit at risk. I mean, not even *Rommel* had succeeded in preventing Edward Trapp from upsetting a perfectly good war, had he? And he'd had the whole bloody *AFRIKA Korps* to help him . . . !

'Anyroad, stick to the point, Weston,' Trapp persisted furiously. 'What about me contract? I'm goin' ter sue the pants off've –'

'For Chrissakes, just get in the goddam Jeep,' Weston snapped with, I must say, my wholehearted support.

But anyone other than Trapp would have appreciated that time had to be pressing: that we'd obviously upset *somebody* over on the far side of that *wadi* ridge from where smoke still billowed and ammunition exploded, and that a posse of hi-tech Arabian hardware could well be forming right then. Surely even his intransigent mind could hardly fail to understand the need to sail the *Charon II* clear of Ras al Djibela before a full-scale pursuit could be mounted.

But what Trapp understood, and what Trapp was then prepared to do about it, were two matters quite unconnected by logic. On this particular fraught occasion he simply folded his arms and looked grumpy.

'No. Why should I?' he refused, staying firmly where he was. In the middle of a bush. 'Lissen, *I* don't know what's happened, do I? I mean, *I* wusn't *INVITED*, wus I?'

'Yous got tae admit, Colonel: the Captin has got a point, so he has,' Gorbals Wullie nodded sagely.

I groaned, they were at it again: lunatics both of them. It was becoming plain as a pikestaff to me that nothing short of the exotic rustle of dollar bills as per contract stood the slightest chance of budging Trapp Thoroughly Bloody Disgruntled. Not once he'd settled on his Negotiation Ploy Number Fourteen A: the petulant, implacably stubborn response.

Unless Weston was prepared to consider some more subtle approach. Psychological. As with a fractious child.

'Last chance, Trapp – get in the goddam JEEP!'

'BUGGER off!'

'Hermann?'

I caught the flash of sun on steel above my head as the colandered barrel of Stompf's heavy machine-gun swung on Trapp, then heard the metallic clatter as the cocking handle slammed back.

'Kill the bastard,' the Colonel shrugged.

'. . . or then again, I suppose we *could* discuss a brand new contract on the way?' Trapp mused.

I moved over to make room on the seat.

'Sit here,' I suggested as the Captain clambered aboard.

'Very kind of yer, Mister,' he growled sardonically.

'Not really,' I said most politely. 'Its last occupant managed to get himself shot.'

Perhaps the most surprising feature of our return to Ras al Djibela was finding that the *Charon* hadn't actually sunk at her berth while we'd been away.

Oh, a few bits had dropped off in the intervening hours, but nothing vital; just the odd corroded rivet from her paper-thin hull and a few more worm-eaten spars from the wheelhouse, while now a vacant orifice below the break of the foc's'le indicated where her last surviving brass porthole had been earlier that morning – though more than likely that had simply been wrenched from its seating by one of Trapp's crew and sold to the Tuaregs at scrap value, seeing it had represented roughly half the total worth of the whole bloody ship.

But nevertheless, for our sole if somewhat lopsided means of escape to have survived both rust *and* Mister Spew's brief reign of command afforded some faint hope that miracles had not yet ceased.

Of course I'd tried to communicate with Trapp during our full throttle withdrawal from the *wadi* – not to be sociable or anything; good God, no: simply to mention how and why I predicted his outrageously tatty uniform cap was scheduled to get one last hole drilled through it to match the rest of us the moment Weston no longer had to rely on our maritime expertise to make good his squad's escape. But what with most of Libya choking me each time I opened my mouth despite my shirt-tail mask, and having to cling on grimly to resist the frantic gyrations of the Jeep buffeting from one dune crest to another . . . take all those difficulties then add 'em to the fact that, when I did finally manage to plead with Trapp to listen to me for a minute, I found he'd bloody well regressed once more into beetle-browed reappraisal of how to screw *some* small profit from what even he must've begun to concede was shaping into an unmitigated disaster – only HE still didn't know the *half* of it yet . . . !

'Oh God,' I thought feverishly. 'You're getting that panicky feeling again, Miller! You gotta control your HYSTERIA!'

The troops began piling out of the vehicles even before we skidded to a final dusty halt alongside the *Charon*. I jumped out. Wullie jumped out.

Trapp didn't.

Budge, I mean.

Oh, I really *was* getting so SICK of him.

I stared hastily around, first towards the direction of the sun-drenched massifs from whence we'd come, then even more apprehensively at the cloudless sky. It was all a question of priorities. While no dust clouds indicated pursuit by a land force as yet, at any moment a formation of the Brother Colonel's MiGs could still blast in above the poor dwellings of Ras al Djibela and mark us, in which case napalm backed up by Mach-one cannon fire would render whatever plans Weston cherished as totally irrelevant anyway. Either way it was vital that we began our tortuous trek towards the open sea without delay.

What happened then, once and *if* we ever made it that far, would have to take its turn in the worry queue.

We had maybe an hour of daylight left: probably the most vulnerable hour of all in respect of the Libyan threat.

'Please Trapp?' I pleaded, though I'd much rather have spent the time hitting him with the Jeep's starting handle. 'Get aboard and pilot us out of here. Don't get all awkward and childish like you usually do, huh?'

'Yeah, c'mon Captin: naething's basically changed,' Wullie had to chip in with his usual masterful tact. 'Ah mean, ye've only lost twa million dollars that didnae exist in the first place.'

'*Wun!*' Trapp flared morosely. 'F'r the las' time, both've yer — it was ONE million din't exis . . .'

Wullie struggled manfully to hold me back.

'OH GET ON THE BLOODY *SHIP*!' I bawled finally, driven beyond human tolerance.

'Did you all 'ave a nice day ashore then?' Second Officer Spew's cheerful greeting floated from the foredeck where he still sat amiably under the muzzles of two machine-guns.

'. . . AND YOU SHUT UP TOO, SPEW!'

Wildly I scanned downtown Djibela again, expecting to see Libyan tanks appearing any moment, but the goat-coated Tuaregs didn't seem concerned, still hanging about hugging their Kalashnikovs and looking as if they'd spent a thoroughly satisfying day working on rape, pillage and possibly a bit more torture.

The Djibela Constabulary still hung around as well. But I tried not to look too closely in that direction

Trapp folded his arms determinedly. I knew then nothing would get him out of that Jeep other than money, and my heart sank to its lowest point so far.

'If you've quite finished bullyin' my junior officers, Mister, I'd be obliged hif you would pass me compliments to Colonel Weston, an' ask if 'e would kindly step this way 'cause Commander Trapp, Royal *and* United States Navy both –'

'I, er – wanted to speak to you about that, Trapp,' I muttered, suddenly remembering the corporal again, but he was in full pompous flow by then and wasn't to be deflected.

'*wishes* to 'ave a word in 'is shell-like about certain contracshul arrangements what 'ave to be made before that ship there turns a single propeller blade homeward bound. Savee?'

'Mair like bluidy *dockyard* arrangements,' Gorbals Wullie interjected snidely.

'You do realize Qaddafi's crowd could arrive any minute in tanks and things, howling for our blood?' I tried to point out as a last-ditch appeal to sanity. 'And that money won't really help to rebuild you once they've cut so many bits off you look like a rugby ball, will it?'

Trapp shook his head deprecatingly. 'They'll be ages gettin' their act together. It takes that bunch a week just to organize what to 'ave f'r dinner – I *told* yer before, Mister: I knows them Ayrabs like the back o' me –'

'Don't!' I snarled, staring up at the sky in renewed terror. 'Whatever you do, don't bloody SAY it, Trapp!'

*

While I hated the *Charon* and her listing decrepitude with an intensity matched only by my loathing for her crew, I still confess to a deep sense of relief once I did finally return aboard, cautiously skirting the rusted hole in the gangway deck plating with near affection before climbing to her parody of a proper ship's bridge which again, for all its dirt and peeling brightwork, still felt more akin to my natural environment than any Jeep on that dreadful desert sea.

Once more able to lean over a bridge rail in the manner of generations of seamen past – though maybe with a little more care than most, seeing too much relaxation was liable to deposit me straight back on Ras al Djibela's quayside – I watched Colonel Weston approach Trapp with a certain pleasurable anticipation.

But nothing particularly stimulating happened. I mean, the Colonel didn't shoot Trapp, or have him beaten up or anything. In fact he and the Captain seemed almost on agreeable terms, though on reflection I suppose the dice were firmly loaded against Trapp. It had become perfectly obvious to me that Weston was prepared to promise the Captain anything he wanted, just so long as it speeded up our withdrawal. Trapp, on the other hand, being both gullible and feeble-minded when it came to money, would still be as anxious to believe any damn thing Weston promised just as earnestly as he had all that time ago in Istanbul.

And the really frustrating thing was that Trapp could quite easily have negotiated from a position of real strength: he being the one man under the circumstances truly capable of piloting *Charon* safely back to sea.

I couldn't have done it. In the absence of either chart or previous knowledge of the labyrinthine meanderings and sub-surface hazards of Shi'ite's Creek, to say nothing of that uncanny gift for achieving the nautically impossible which I unreservedly accorded Trapp, I could never have navigated the *Charon* so as to avoid the likelihood of stranding her like a particularly dejected duck in a shooting gallery: not without feeling my way by constant use of the sounding lead at least, and the consequent fatal delay such laborious pilotage must inevitably invite.

It must have been difficult for Weston to contain himself, all the same, to say nothing of containing Hermann, in order to keep up a tolerant pretence of negotiating fresh terms with Trapp in view of what he, the Colonel, intended to do.

And what *I* knew he, the Colonel, intended to do.

But what Trapp still didn't have a CLUE about . . . !

I glowered unhappily. One thing was for sure: the Colonel wouldn't have a problem disposing of the rest of the evidence, the ship herself. The *Charon II* had a sort of intrinsic redundancy about her which had been maturing for at least the past half-century . . . he wouldn't need to do much more than have Hermann stuff Popeye Bucalosie's olive-oiled skull into her bilge suction for ten minutes, or strike her a sharp blow, preferably with Gorbals Wullie, below the waterline to encourage her already long-overdue demise.

But that would come later; first we had to distance ourselves smartly from the Libyans' spleen. As I said: once Trapp had exercised his business acumen in a deal, the question of which other interested party killed us first simply became a lottery.

I made a conscious decision then to withhold my knowledge of Weston's real identity from Trapp, at least until we'd reached open water.

I couldn't have stood the tension. Him sitting down again and refusing to budge from Djibela until a week Saturday if that's what it took to change Weston's mind or at least negotiate a properly constituted massacre clause, while Qaddafi's army, navy and airforce drew leisurely straws to decide which of *them* was gonna get to banjo us first!

He was looking pretty pleased with himself, Trapp was, by the time he did condescend to join Key Personnel Gorbals Wullie and me on the bridge.

I'd already put the crew on stand-by for leaving harbour which meant, in the *Charon*'s case, that instead of lounging untidily all over the deck they concentrated on lounging untidily in vague proximity to her mooring lines.

All in all an impression of homely normality was being restored: GPMG and Viper teams had taken up their defensive positions along the bulwarks, with additional rocketeers closed up aft of the bridge deck to cover the line of likely pursuit. Choker Bligh had begun to shout at everybody again, and hit people with his rope's end, while Mister Spew had happily gone below with Bucalosie to renew hostilities with our malevolent *Spatz* just as soon as he'd been released from the muzzles of the guns which had, at least, ensured his brief captaincy was passive rather than destructive.

I'd even arranged a lifeboat for us, rather more in hope than anticipation: one of the little lateen-rigged Arab *caiques* which had lain grounded on the cracked mud beside the wharf. Now, dilapidated though it was, it still struck a note of incongruous cheer hanging between our previously empty davits; red, white and yellow against the uncompromising rusted gloom of the rest of its new mother.

Trapp reached for the engineroom telegraph, remembered its handle had fallen off hours ago then, unperturbed, walked briskly to the voice pipe to blow with rubber cheeks.

'Start 'er up, Chief,' he ordered with the breathtaking

complacency over lost causes that only he could generate.

'*That'll* be bluidy right,' Wullie muttered from behind the wheel.

Trapp shoved the cork back in its tube, cutting Bucalosie's rejoinder off in mid-invective, then turned to us.

'Right then,' he said, rubbing his hands briskly. 'You've both 'ad the day off. Now it's time to start earnin' yer wages again.'

I saw Wullie begin to turn a deep shade of apoplectic at the mention of wages and hurriedly stepped in.

'How much did he promise you this time, then?'

'Who?' Trapp frowned innocently.

'Weston!'

'You mean "Colonel" Weston, don't yer?'

'Cut the crap, Trapp!'

He hesitated. 'Quarter o' a million dollars.'

'That means *half* a million at LEAST!' Gorbals Wullie shouted.

'SHURRUP – *crew*!'

'Yer *always* sayin' that!'

'No bloody WONDER!'

'And you actually agreed?' I jeered. 'So what did he give you as a gesture of good faith, Trapp – a cheque?'

I'd meant it as a joke. Until I saw his expression.

'A promissory note, yeah,' he muttered, producing a tatty scrap of paper torn from a military notebook. 'But drawn on the Bank o' the United States o' America, see? 'E wrote it on the top hisself.'

'Jesus Christ!' I shook my head.

'Lissen, you think I'm *reely* stupid, don't yer?' Trapp glowered, beginning to lose his good humour. 'You think I'm completely bloody green when it comes ter doin' business, don't yer, Mister?'

'Yes!'

'Oh,' he muttered, a bit taken aback. 'Well, Mister

200

Clever Egg: f'r your information I also insisted on security – assets in lieu, so ter speak.'

'Like what?'

'Their weapons,' he said cleverly. 'When they've finished with 'em, o' course.'

'They'll be worn out by then,' I said involuntarily, nearly succumbing to the temptation to explain why. Fortunately, with him possessing all the perception of a cash register, he picked me up wrongly.

'It doesn't matter. Even used, them Vipers is worth twenty grand apiece on the gun-runnin' market. HEAT rounds – say another thou per rocket? We still got a stack o' satchel charges an' grenades an' assorted other explosives down number one hold, while there's them GPMGs an' enough ammo to have half the nutters in Beirut queueing down the beach at midnight, waving cash on the spot . . .'

There came a terrifying hiss and a bang from down below: the whole ship trembled as if stricken, Wullie flung himself to the deck while I debated the best line of abandonment for the wharf, firmly convinced that half of Trapp's assets in lieu – the explosives in number one – had just liquidated themselves.

Then a jet of soot and steam shot from our dog-leg funnel to coat the water around with a scum of mini-mal-grade coal dust as the *Spatz* rumbled to uncertain life.

'Lissen ter that,' Trapp bellowed proudly above the clatter of vibrating steel plates and things generally shaking themselves to pieces. 'Runs like a sewin' machine she does.'

'In the auld Royal Navy they used tae make ye change yer underwear afore goin' intae battle,' Wullie muttered, easing the seat of his pants uncomfortably behind the wheel. 'In this ship ye need tae change it soon as the bluidy ENGINE's startit!'

'You 'aven't *got* any underwear,' Trapp derided. 'You 'aven't 'ad none since Nineteen Sixty-eight.'

'Thass the bluidy TROUBLE!' Wullie shrieked back.

I left them to enjoy their reunion and stared moodily across the wharf to where the Tuaregs were congregating around the vehicles in anticipation of their pay-off. Weston, flanked by half a dozen of his toughest Green Berets with weapons at the ready, was handing over a wad of notes to that most evil-looking Arab of all, the one I'd already suspected as being Homer.

Trapp tired of baiting Wullie and came up behind me to watch through narrowed eyes. I assume the thought of all that money going to waste was eating into him, yet strangely he appeared genuinely interested.

'D'yer reckon that's Homer then, Mister?'

I nodded bitterly, somewhat put out by the fact that the Colonel was obviously prepared to leave the bloody Arabs on good terms, while it was a stone cold certainty we ourselves were due for disposal. But then we presented a security risk – no, let's face it: a guaranteed giveaway! It would've been facile, once Trapp's crowd were safely clear of Libyan reprisals and running amok in the bars of the world again, to pretend that any detail of what had taken place in Ras al Djibela would remain a secret for longer than it took to swallow a bucket of rot-gut ouzo.

Homer's Tuaregs, on the other hand, lived in Qaddafi's desert, had tortured and killed Qaddafi's own security forces. They would keep their mouths shut to ensure their own survival. Apart from which, such a hard-case team of resident insurrectionists offered a very attractive long-term investment to any foreign government seeking to maintain a covert finger in the Libyan pie.

Hands were shaken, *salaams* bestowed, and the Colonel's team withdrew expressionlessly aboard the *Charon* while the obviously well-satisfied Tuaregs congregated with much grinning of white teeth around the loot. Homer clambered into the first Jeep followed by as many of his Middle Eastern hoods as could cling to it, then stood there waving the fistful of notes triumphantly.

I eyed Trapp apprehensively: such unseemly display of other people's wealth might well, under the circumstances, have tipped him right over the edge of self-control.

But no: Trapp just continued to watch amiably, and grudge them not one dollar – and thus, by showing such gentlemanly restraint and good sportsmanship, to frighten *me* to bloody death!

Weston appeared behind us on the bridge. I gathered even he was feeling a little wary. 'You'll get yours eventually,' he promised.

But *I* knew that already!

'That's all right, Colonel,' Trapp shrugged meekly.

Another splurge of soot shot from the funnel as the *Spatz* gave faltering warning of horrors to come. Immediately a torrent of Latin-flavoured oaths arose from the engineroom fiddley accompanied by the furious pounding of a heavy hammer against metal. Trapp looked bored.

'There might be a short delay while me Chief's fine-tunin' the engine . . . er, do yer mind if I asks you a favour while we waits, Colonel?'

'Ask away, Cap'n,' Weston smiled sardonically.

I just looked anxiously at my watch, then again at the sky. Maybe our departing a week Saturday had been a bit optimistic, on reflection. And I did wish Trapp'd cut out the small talk.

'Yeah, well, I got to admit ter bein' a bit o' an expert on weapons – havin' had some small dealings with 'em on certain occasions when demand has exceeded legitimate supply, yer might say – but I ain't never had the priv' lege of examining yer Viper launchers up close before.

So seein' how they're a part of our new deal, I, ah, wondered . . . ?'

'Sure, Cap'n,' Weston shrugged. It was time for diplomacy still. He leaned over the back of the bridge and relieved a corporal of one, handing the sleek khaki tube to Trapp who took it reverentially.

'Feel the balance,' he breathed, easing it to his shoulder. 'An' there ain't no weight to speak of . . .'

'Careful!' Weston warned, suddenly anxious. 'The goddam thing's loaded, Trapp.'

'CAREFUL!' I yelled, just in case he hadn't heard the first time. 'The goddam thing's LOADED, TRAPP!'

'Beg pardon?' Trapp said, swinging to face me.

I could actually *see* the brass-capped HEAT missile winking at me from inside its tube. Approximately four feet from my nose.

Wullie dropped to his standard grovel with a terrified shriek. I stood frozen. Trapp began to look dangerously confused what with everyone aboard running round and shouting warnings and trying to hide under winches and things . . .

'Point it OUTBOARD, Trapp!' Weston snapped tensely. 'And keep your finger off the trigger for *God*'s sake, man.'

'Trigger?' Trapp appealed, turning hurriedly to face the wharf. 'D'yer mean *this* . . . !'

The Viper detonated with a WHOOOOOOSH which licked a great tongue of exhausting fire clear across the after end of the bridge which immediately set the desiccated planking crackling and burning with merry little blue flames. Still hypnotized I caught a blur of supersonic flame leaving its bell-mouthed muzzle, pushing enough high explosive to kill the heaviest front line tank stone DEAD . . . !

'. . . trigger?' Trapp finished lamely.

The rocket hit Code-name Homer's Jeep right under

the front passenger's seat. Which in turn supported Homer and was still surrounded by triumphantly gesticulating Tuaregs.

The detonation became a swelling incandescence with parts of a large number of Arabs and nearly all the Jeep flying in opposition directions, then subsided to a writhing column of grey sand from out of which a solitary wheel rolled drunkenly before bouncing over the edge of the wharf and into the water.

There followed a stunned silence aboard the *Charon*. Until.

'Oh, gosh,' Trapp said, utterly mortified. 'Oh, dash it: what *'ave* I gone an' done?'

... I sneaked a covert glance at him a few minutes later, as we finally shuddered and clanked away from Ras al Djibela. We were alone on the wing once more; admirable if perhaps barely disciplined self-control having compelled Weston to leave the bridge for fear of what he might do to Trapp and the hell with exfiltrating the goddam mission!

The Captain was gazing astern towards the place where the five crucified constables still hung, ironically blanketed now by the smoke from Code-name Homer's own destruction.

It struck me then that, for someone who's sheer bumbling incompetence had recently caused such a tragic accident, the expression on Trapp's lips was, well . . . a little too angelic?

It was dark by the time we'd cleared the really tricky narrows of Shi'ite's Creek and again sensed the smell of the sea in our eager nostrils.

There was a freshening wind carrying warning of a gale soon to come, but I didn't care: even bearing in mind the corroded instability of the *Charon II* I welcomed it after the stagnant misery of the Libyan desert. And anyway, we still had some considerable time to run the gauntlet before we were truly out to sea and clear of Qaddafi's naval presence in Sirte – heavy weather would make their task of locating us that much more difficult.

But eventually our greatest threat still had to come from Weston himself. When would he make *his* move? Where, for that matter, did he intend us to head for once Trapp found deep water? So far no mention had been made of the voyage back, so was a fraught return to Albania in the offing, maybe? Or even to . . . ?

'Starb'd ten the wheel,' Trapp called gruffly to Wullie for no reason at all that I could see, though I accepted that somewhere close ahead the channel must veer, or some unsuspected shelf of rock must lie just below the wind-ruffled surface, such was my confidence in Trapp the Navigator.

He watched her head critically as Wullie eased the wheel, then grunted, 'Midships. Steady . . . Steady on nor' nor' east.'

Professionally intrigued, I scanned the surface to port through my glasses. Yes, there was just the slightest disturbance of the water there; evidence of a sub-sea hazard quite invisible until far too late to ordinary seamen such as I.

But there were other even more acute dangers lurking ahead which Trapp as yet couldn't possibly suspect. He had to be told of what I'd learned from the dying trooper some time.

I hesitated. Even I was reluctant to break that bit of news.

Trapp, of course, misread me as usual to grin derisively. 'You're forced to admit I 'aven't lost me sea sense, aren't yer, Mister? Not like you seems ter think I lost me commercial flare?'

Oh, it *did* irritate me, the bumptious way he said it. His crass ego.

'Never once have I suggested you've lost your commercial acumen, Trapp,' I defended stiffly. 'So far as I'm concerned you never bloody *had* any to lose in the first place.'

'Ho yus?' he said superiorly. 'An' what about the Colonel's bank draft, then? A quarter o' a million dollars profit, less fuel costs . . .'

'An' WAGES!' Gorbals Wullie shouted. 'Dinnae yous forget mah wages this time.'

'. . . don't seem too bad f'r a chap what hasn't got no business sense, eh?'

'Worthless,' I dismissed.

'What d'yer mean: worthless? It's signed by 'im as the personal emmissary o' the President of the United States of America, dammit.'

'It's bloody WORTHLESS, Trapp,' I snarled. 'Will you just shut up and listen to ME for a minute?'

'Go ON then, Mister Clever Dick!' he jeered. 'You jus' give me one good reason why Weston *can't* sign a proper legitimate note on be'alf of the US Army? Go ON then!'

I took a deep breath. 'Because . . .'

'Go ON! I challenge yer!'

'Because your Colonel Weston – all of them – *all* of his Special Forces crowd down there, Trapp . . . They're all bloody *Russians*. THAT'S why!'

Chapter Thirteen

'He definitely spoke to me in Russian,' I asserted as soon as we'd got Trapp breathing more or less regularly for the third time on that voyage.

'It wus a joke,' Trapp appealed, clutching at straws. ''E wus havin' you on.'

'He was *dying*, Trapp. Shot in the lung.'

'It didn't mean he had ter lose 'is sense o' humour, did it?'

'He also used the term *Rodina*. I'm no linguist but I do know that has a very special connotation to a Soviet. It means "Motherland". More than that: it's an expression of patriotism, of fealty to the State. For God's sake *believe* me for once, Trapp: those are very dedicated Ivans down there, and while their Colonel may be a top *Spetsnaz*, he sure as hell isn't acting for any US President!'

'Whit's a spitzniz?' Wullie squealed apprehensively.

'Soviet Special Forces . . . their equivalent to our SAS and the Green Berets. Except they're mostly KGB and even nastier.'

'It don't make sense,' Trapp muttered. 'The Russians support Qaddafi. What would they want to shaft 'im for?'

'Because if you'd bothered for one moment to show some interest in what *we* were doing while you were playing petulant out there in the bloody desert,' I explained acidly, 'you'd've learned that Brother Colonel Qaddafi just happens to be developing his own nuclear capability, Trapp.'

Trapp looked blank, not having thought a lot about

Wullie and I nearly getting ourselves killed *in absentia* nor, until then, about atomic weapons either, seeing there weren't that many being traded around the illegal arms markets.

'So?'

'So THAT sort of national enterprise is sheer anathema to the Superpowers, that's what! Any smalltime dictator brandishing that kind of threat frightens 'em to death. And to make matters worse, Qaddafi's a revolutionary to start with: a fanatic. It would be like giving a religious maniac a machine-gun in a witches' coven . . . the Soviets couldn't hope to control Libya with the Bomb any more than the Americans can now. They'd lose their influence throughout the Middle East; probably even be at risk themselves eventually.'

'Oh, Gawd,' Trapp croaked listlessly, still indifferent to the global repercussions. 'Weston's promissory note. The United States Treasury won't *never* agree ter cash it. Not signed by a Russian. All them crisp green dollars . . . right down the tubes again!'

'Stop harping on about your bloody MONEY – it's *us* goin' down the tubes you should be worried about. He's got to eliminate us all, you do realize that? Before he leaves the *Charon*.'

But to be fair to Trapp, I'd had longer than he to consider it: to appreciate how substituting *Spetsnaz* for Green Beret so neatly answered many of those riddles plaguing me from Day One.

Why they'd joined us in Albania – a Communist state. And why that first naval patrol had sailed past with eyes averted despite their undoubted desire to have a rubber-truncheon chat with Trapp themselves, over certain other long-standing differences.

Why Weston's men had maintained their otherwise inexplicable silence throughout, broken finally by my corporal but even then only *in extremis*. No doubt many of them spoke English, but probably not all nor with the right accents. They were Soviet stormtroops, not linguists. It was an obvious precaution to observe, particularly within earshot of Trapp's super-nosy crew.

Mind you, half of *them* couldn't speak proper English either, come to that. I mean, well – take Gorbals Wullie, for instance!

... and then there'd been Sergeant Jablonski and his fellow travellers in suspended animation: undoubtedly genuine American Special Forces corpses. Where might the Russians have got them from, and in God's name why?

I thought I'd worked it out at long last – the pathology of intrigue, I suppose you might call it. First obtain a supply of ethnically appropriate cadavers . . . well, most commando forces have some involvement in subversive operations: it wouldn't prove impossible for the other side – the Russians in this case – to pick up agents who shouldn't have been wherever they were in the first place; execute them, then put them on ice awhile. Certainly no one was going to complain. The *New York Times* could hardly be encouraged to headline 'Pentagon spies missing' any more than *Pravda* would advertise, 'Wanted: the return of certain KGB saboteurs'.

So Jablonski and company probably had been working under cover in some foreign field until recently – maybe compromised initially in Eastern Europe or Vietnam; Cambodia, one of the Communist-controlled South American countries . . . ? It didn't matter to the Russians because the rest of the world didn't know about them anyway. Not until they turned up publicly dead in Libya, and thence acted as incontrovertible proof of US involvement in the Ras al Djibela massacre – particularly once interrogated by the pathologist's knife.

Because that was where leaving authentic American corpses while removing their own dead from the battleground added a brilliant twist to the KGB's already considerable expertise in misinformation. Post mortem examination would undoubtedly provide evidence of the United States origins of those blast-torn remains eventually retrieved from the *wadi* minefield . . . it was unlikely that the actual *time* of the combatants' death would be called to question – but even if it were, then sure as hell the Libyans wouldn't publicize that curious anomaly, even though they did suspect it differed by a few weeks.

It was an ingenious plan. They achieved their objective, the Americans were acutely embarrassed yet again, while relations between The Socialist People's Libyan Arab *Jamahiriyah* and the Kremlin stayed untarnished. On the surface anyway.

But the whole operation, its quick and its dead, still had to be infiltrated in the first place. So, being denied the use of the actual US Sixth Fleet itself, the Soviets then had to find someone unconnected with themselves yet who was capable of skulduggery as its very highest level. He would have to be an independent shipowner, voraciously greedy, 100 per cent egotistical and utterly gullible. He would further need to be a man who harboured absolutely no allegiance to any cause other than self.

Someone totally amoral, in fact. A right pain in the neck: your complete anti-social pariah.

. . . which brought me neatly back to Trapp, and the moment when he'd bumbled, a super-confident fly entering a particularly artful spider's web, into Korkut Tokoglu's rancid emporium on the Alley of the Tassel-makers in the Great Covered Bazaar of downtown Istanbul.

Ironically it was the one bit of ingenuity the Soviets had wasted. Weston, or whatever the Colonel's real name was, could easily have levelled with Trapp right from the start. The Captain would have been equally happy to deliver *Spetsnaz*, Green Berets, common-or-garden mercenaries or creatures from Uranus so long as the price had been right . . . even now, despite the minor setback of going to heist a bank which wasn't there, he would still be quite content to take them out again having satisfied his ego with a new contract – if only Weston had been a little more straightforward. Had come out with the unvarnished truth and made his bloody promissory note out to roubles.

But Weston hadn't. Ill-advisedly he'd continued to treat Trapp like the contemptible idiot he was, only Trapp knew that now so, despite all the odds stacked against us, I didn't go much on *Spetsnaz* Colonel Westonski or whoever's prospects of survival either.

Or no more than I would've done for Hector the Torturing Tuareg's anyway. Trapp would've killed him for what he did to those policemen if he hadn't been so tragically blown away to Allah by sheer accident.

'Och niver mind, Captin,' Gorbals Wullie was consoling. 'It's no' as if going bankrupt again wis onything special. Ye've aye said yerself that soon as wan door closes, anither slams shut in yer face.'

Trapp shook his head stubbornly, still searching desperately for a straw to clutch at. 'No,' he muttered. 'I don't accept it, Mister. I ain't no dummy: I'd've sensed from the start Weston wus a Russian if 'e had been. Lissen, I knows them Ivans like the back o' me 'and!'

That's when the panic hit me. I knew we were doomed, the moment he said that.

'For Christ's sake he's *Spetsnaz*, Trapp!' I exploded uncontrollably. 'He's bloody well TRAINED in delusion, perfidy, intrigue . . . ! In other words he's exactly like you only *he's* bloody COMPETENT at it!'

'*Maskirovka*, we Ivans call it, Captain,' Weston's voice reached us calmly. 'Strategic deception. The ultimate trickery.'

'. . . an' *you* bloody well keep OUT of THIS!' Trapp bawled without thinking.

There followed a silence. A very long silence.

Until.

'Excuse my asking, Colonel, but, er . . . how long *have* you been standing at the head of that ladder?' I asked unhappily.

I didn't actually add, 'eavesdropping'. It didn't seem politic right then.

There were three of them. Weston, the indispensable Hermann of course, and another trooper. All had guns.

'Long enough, Miller, to appreciate our *maskirovka* has outlived its usefulness.'

The *Charon* rolled sluggishly as the first of the rising storm seas nudged her bluff bow. The weapons, however, remained levelled as if gyro-stabilized.

'Oh!' I said, acutely aware that his bloody *maskirover* or whatever wasn't the only thing about to outlive its usefulness. Especially now. Now he'd confirmed that his mission secret had been compromised.

'It would seem an opportune moment for me to introduce myself properly, gentlemen?'

'Yeah, you just do that, Mister,' Trapp growled. I shot him a sideways glance. As ever he'd recovered his gruff aplomb with remarkable flexibility. But then Trapp, being utterly impervious to his own countless failings, had got so used to deals going pear-shaped on him it wasn't so much fortitude as routine psychological crisis management in his case.

The man we'd previously known as Weston bowed slightly, an oddly formal touch. I noted his accent had become less overtly American too, though his smile remained cold as ever in the falling darkness.

'Thank you, Captain . . . Then I have the honour to be

Colonel Aleksandr Chernyshev of the Fourteenth *Komitet Gosudarstvennoi Bezopastnosti* Special Forces Diversionary Group, South-Western Strategic Directorate.'

'Here,' Gorbals Wullie deduced, he being a regular little Aristotle when it came to head-work. 'Ah'm beginnin' tae think he's a *Russian*!'

'Oh, that's bloody brilliant f'r a start,' Trapp jeered caustically. 'Where 'AVE you been f'r the last ten minnits?'

'Lissening to you, that's where – arguin' that he *wisnae* a bluidy Russian!'

I glowered at them both. I would have much preferred Wullie not to have referred to them as 'bloody Russians' under the circumstances, while Trapp always had allowed himself to be rather too easily diverted from the essence of any problem – like how to avoid getting us all terminated within the next few minutes. Personally I'd lost my appetite for understanding by then, having decided I didn't want to know anything about Weston: certainly not that his real name was Chernyshev, and all the stuff about Strategic Directorates. That was highly contentious intelligence: the more we knew, the more imperative became our executions.

'Oh, port the wheel. Just stop being a smarty pants an' bring 'er to nor' by west,' the Captain grumbled, ominously mild, then he turned to Weston ... Chernyshe ... ? Oh dammit, Weston was still as good a name as any seeing I probably wouldn't have much time to get used to his real one anyway.

'Right, Colonel,' Trapp said with a philosophical acceptance which should've struck an immediate chill through the inner corridors of the KGB. 'So you ripped me off proper, which is fair enough – you done the same to Qaddafi: love an' war an' that, eh? So what next? Back to Albania with guns at our heads all the way, or hard a starb'd at Gib, straight up to the Baltic an' home to

Leningrad before you hammers in the cartridge cases?'

'Whit does he mean, Mister Miller sir – cartridge cases?' Wullie squealed from the wheelhouse.

'Look, *I* don't bloody know, DO I?' I shouted back irritably. Well, hell, *he* was the one who went to the movies.

'An old KGB tradition,' Trapp amplified, watching Weston sardonically. 'When it comes time to pay you off they hammer an empty cartridge case into the base of your skull. A nice, cost-effective Chekist method of terminating ship's articles.'

The Colonel looked genuinely amused. 'It also happens to be unsophisticated, time-consuming and forty years out of date, Captain. Only our predecessors of the Stalinist General Beria's NKVD employed such brutish methods – but even then largely as a concession to the ammunition shortages of World War Two.'

'Well, thank God it's peacetime,' Trapp grunted, rather too mildly I felt. 'At least we can count on gettin' the whole bullet now.'

Weston shrugged. 'More than that, surely? Our arrangement was that I leave you all assault equipment other than personal weapons. I see little to be gained by either of us in not continuing to honour that agreement.'

Even Trapp's eyebrows raised perceptibly. 'You don't?'

'Don't trust him,' I hissed, suddenly concerned that Trapp's judgement was about to prove as feckless as it usually did. We still held one slim hand – Weston had already proved he wasn't a seaman, yet the *Charon* was still in Libyan waters. Without us he couldn't even hope to clear the danger zone of the Gulf, never mind set course for wherever he ultimately intended to disembark.

So despite the ever-increasing risk of our being overtaken, now *had* to be the time to stop the ship and negotiate some cast-iron guarantees, though quite what form they might take was still outwith my comprehension.

But Trapp, as usual, dismissed my warning with lofty contempt.

'It seems we're still in business then, Colonel. Where to?'

Expressionlessly Weston handed him a slip of paper. 'My orders are to keep a rendezvous, Captain. At that position.'

I watched Trapp's eyebrows lift for a second time. He waggled the paper thoughtfully. 'Yer mean you just wants me to take you *here* . . . Nothin' else?'

'Affirmative. We will be met at that point. From then on you're on your own, Trapp.'

Well naturally, after a cryptic conversation like that my inquisitiveness knew no bounds. Neither did my cynicism. The more accepting Trapp looked, the more apprehensive I became.

'Well, go *on* – let's see where it is then!' I muttered, curiosity finally overcoming my determination never to speak to him again.

'In a minnit,' he said pompously. 'This is top executive stuff just now. I'll brief me officers later.'

God, he could be so bloody *irritating*.

I tried one last effort to reason with him: much as I would've done with a human being.

'You simply can't trust him,' I whispered urgently. 'Not again; not for a third time, Trapp – and don't you DARE say you knows 'im like the back o' your . . .'

This time he pretended not to hear me at all: basically the same as his usual habit of listening, considering my argument at length, then bloody well ignoring it anyway.

'PORT twenty! Steady 'er on nor' by nor' east if you please, 'elmsman.'

'Are you speakin' tae *me*?' Gorbals Wullie queried blankly. But in all fairness, Wullie hadn't ever actually

216

heard an order being given politely aboard the *Charon* before.

'*Course* I am, silly,' the Captain laughed tolerantly. 'Nor' by nor' east me request wus. Just a little correcshun to save us from goin' hard aground – IF you would be so kind, that is?'

'Oh dear GOD,' I thought. 'Now he's even started being nice to *Wullie*.'

I really started to panic then. Trapp's suddenly becoming Mister Nice Guy underlined, more than anything else, the truly desperate predicament we were in. The ploy suggested the Captain hadn't been foxed by the Colonel's charm: things were much worse than that – the bloody man had started to think for himself again! Having obviously decided he *didn't* trust West . . . Cherny . . . bloody WESTON, it seemed he was enthusiastically reverting to what he, Trapp, no doubt considered was ingenious plotting.

Which explained why *I* was panicking. Trapp's intrigues never quite turned out the way he intended, invariably because his idea of subtle artifice displayed all the *finesse* of a thousand bomber raid – bitter experience had long proved that Trapp Playing Clever Buggers would be infinitely more dangerous to the *Charon* and all who shuddered forth in her than any trivial coalition between rust, complete instability and a mere few dozen professional KGB assassins ever could.

. . . though I swear to you that, not even then, did I dream for one moment he'd managed to escalate the situation to a crisis of *quite* such global proportions.

I mean, there we were, literally minutes away from ground zero as events were about to prove – yet the possibility of Trapp's managing to go and start a whole real shooting Third World War between the Superpowers *still* hadn't entered my head.

*

There was a wild yellow storm light in the southern sky by the time Westo ... Chernysh ... *Weston* left the bridge.

Hermann didn't. Nor the other Russian soldier. They both stood impassive as ever with M16s at the ready and eyes taking in every single move Trapp and I made. For some inexplicable reason Weston didn't appear to trust us any more than we did him – only he had all the cards now: we'd good as cleared the Ras al Djibela shoals and were finally lumbering into the Mediterranean itself with the seas beginning to break in excited flurries of spray over the *Charon*'s battered bow, and every part of the ship creaking and squealing in geriatric protest.

'Go ON then,' I snarled at Trapp. 'Where's that position?'

He looked innocent. 'What position?'

'That position Weston gave you.'

'Oh *that* position,' he said infuriatingly.

I peered at the scrap of paper, already grubby from Trapp's pocket. It prescribed a latitude and longitude only some twelve miles distant.

'Christ,' I muttered, 'we'll be there in a couple of hours if the engine keeps going. Then what?'

Trapp shrugged airily. 'I'll think o' somethin'.'

'Oh, that's all right then,' I said heavily. 'As long as *you're* thinking of something I don't need to worry about getting shot a hundred and twenty-one minutes from now then, do I?'

There was a huffy silence until we only had a hundred and nineteen minutes left to live. Then Trapp mused, 'What d'yer reckon's waiting at the rendezvous to take them off, then – a Russian sub?'

'So far as I'm concerned they can catch a bloody bus: it's BEFORE they disembark I'm worried about ...' A sudden thought struck me. 'Did you say "submarine"?'

'It's most likely. They'd 'ave a job slipping through the

Yankee Sixth radar pickets in a surface ship. Unless it's another one like this, o' course.'

'There couldn't possibly *be* another one like this. Not actually floating.'

'Yer dead right, Mister,' he conceded after some serious thought. 'They broke the mould when they built me old *Charon*. Perfection only comes once in a lifetime . . . an' anyway, they'd 'ave to find a very special kind o' Russki matelot to be 'er captin.'

'Yes, they certainly would,' I agreed with total sincerity. I sneaked a surreptitious glance around: Hermann was still there but well out of earshot even if he did understand. 'But if you wouldn't mind sticking to the point seeing decision time is becoming just a little pressing, Trapp: I'm still convinced that Libyan frigate was torpedoed by a submarine on our way in – yet Weston really seemed genuinely doubtful.'

'So?'

I hesitated, gazing past him out towards the north-west horizon. Just for a moment I thought I'd seen something: only a faint shadow breaking the already nearly indefinable skyline. But there was nothing . . . I shrugged. Lost.

'So . . . I dunno. It's just odd, that's all. I would have thought he'd've been briefed if a Soviet sub had intended to ride shotgun on us all the way, both in and out?'

Trapp looked knowing. Basically that meant he didn't understand it either. 'Don't worry. I knows them Russkie's like the . . .'

'DON'T, Trapp,' I snarled dangerously. 'Don't you *dare*!'

'I wus only goin' ter say them KGBs won't let their right 'and know what their left hand's doin',' he protested, hurt to the core.

'Well, don't! Every time you *say* that something's bound to happ . . .'

'Captin?' Gorbals Wullie's voice, shrill with alarm

called from the wheel. 'Somethin's happening. Oot there, deid aheid!'

'Didn't I bloody WARN you?' I shouted feverishly as we both rushed to the front of the bridge, ignoring the metallic rattle of weapons being snapped to the ready behind us.

Clearly seen against the yellow light from the horizon the sea had begun to boil, perhaps three cables ahead of the *Charon* and at least an hour and a half ahead of schedule.

Trapp stopped gaping long enough to lunge for the voice pipe. 'Stop ENGINE! What's that . . . ? Lissen, Spaghetti 'ead, I don' care if yer DID 'ave a bugger o' a job gettin' it started; you just bloody *stoppit* again – JALDI!'

Slowly the great black silhouette thrust upwards, blowing through the surface with the white water streaming from its pressure hull and the sea between us all leaping and dancing under the excitement of such leviathan prestidigitation.

Trapp turned to me looking sour, having lost a good hour and three-quarters' scheming time thanks to the Soviet Navy's early arrival, though why *he* was so put out I couldn't imagine – well, he must surely have anticipated it? Him knowing them Popovs as well as he claimed, jus' like the back o' . . . ?

I froze. Staring at the long black shape ahead.

'I s'ppose that's yer bloody submarine then, Mister,' Trapp growled somewhat unnecessarily.

'*Is* it?' I muttered.

A whole brand-new fear gripped me while he, too, surveyed her in more detail.

'Christ!' the Captain muttered. Eventually.

But as ever with Trapp's ventures into the world of off-beat commerce, melodramatic events and stupefying disclosures simply had to wait their turn in the crisis queue. I pushed my concern over the submarine aside, on the grounds that I'd most likely be dead before it presented a practical problem.

For a start, though hardly a surprise, it immediately became apparent that Weston never *had* harboured any intention of leaving us free men. The moment the other craft surfaced Hermann, undoubtedly following orders, moved smartly behind us to present the muzzle of his M16 a hand's breadth from Trapp's battered ear. At the same time his oppo stepped into the wheelhouse to offer a similar threat to our predictably petrified key personnel, one Gorbals William.

I had to concede Trapp *was* showing self-restraint. He hardly batted an eyelid. The only sign of resentment he betrayed at being once more threatened on his own bridge – which didn't register with Hermann maybe, but scared the absolute hell out of me – was that the Captain's eyebrows clamped together in even more furious thought.

Trapp Apoplectic was perfectly routine. But Trapp Resigned to His Fate was likely to prove an unpredictable menace to everyone, friend or foe, within striking distance.

Meanwhile the unexpected advancement of the *Spetsnaz* rendezvous time and position had initiated a surge of activity such as the *Charon* had never experienced before – certainly not since Trapp's vulpine layabouts had signed aboard as crew, most of whom had previously conceived of a busy day as perpetrating two muggings, a GBH and a whole rape all in the same twenty-four-hour period.

Taking only small consolation from the fact that the heat was still concentrated on Trapp and Wullie, I leaned dejectedly over the bridge front and tried to decide what to do next. Facing my future squarely it offered a pretty safe bet that, having reached journey's end, Chief Officer

Miller had not only become redundant as mission navigator but held no significance to Weston other than as an undesirable security risk along with everybody else.

Already I could see soldiers taking control in the gloom of the foredeck: the glint of yellow storm light on gun barrels, half a dozen abject figures grovelling on their knees appealing to Allah or Mohammed or whoever . . . standard theological practice for the *Charons*. Apart from the odd virtuoso in profanity – the seemingly rubberoid Choker Bligh, for instance, currently being battered to fulminating submission yet again by half a dozen rifle butts, most of Trapp's gallant lads found instant religion the minute the power base shifted and they weren't the actual ones putting the boot in.

I sighed wearily. It appeared Weston intended to batten our crowd in the foc's'le again.

Which afforded final confirmation of our part in the KGB's grand strategy. Had he intended simply to transfer his men to the submarine, then he wouldn't have given a damn about the whereabouts of the *Charon's* crew. And certainly they would've kept well out of the way, as anxious to see the back of our passengers as I was . . . but concentrating them below like that, the Soviets needed only to drop two or three grenades down the corroded foc's'le ventilators as they finally disembarked to cause utter carnage within the noxious confines of that steel prison.

Then I made out other *Spetsnaz*, still rigged in Green Beret false colours urgently hauling several large containers from the hold and heaving them over the bulwarks to land with a splash alongside. One trooper jerked a lanyard; there rose an explosive hiss of compressed air, whereupon the first inflatable assault boat unfolded alongside.

. . . 'Oh, that's bloody marvellous!' I thought bitterly.

Survival kit like that aboard all the time, yet I'd gone to the trouble of stealing that pathetic Arab craft now slung uselessly in our davits, just in case we'd needed a lifeboat. Chance would have been a bloody fine thing indeed!

I didn't even bother to turn when I caught the measured tread of combat boots climbing the starboard ladder. I knew they had to be Weston's from the way Hermann tensed in anticipation. Trapp seemed to sag then, become even more distant in thought.

A scatter of spray curled over the *Charon*'s bow to carry aft on the rising wind. I heard it hiss across the rusted deckplates, savoured the familiar touch of salt against my face. It felt incredibly precious.

'DO something, Trapp,' I urged silently. 'Get us out of this mess you got us into and I . . . I'll even *like* you. Well, maybe not actually *like* you – but honest to God I promise I'll try very hard to tolerate you . . .'

But even he was beaten this time, I could see that. Suddenly tired and bowed, none of the old aggressive Trapp I used to know.

Chernyshev – and it was Chernyshev speaking, not the brash Weston any more – said correctly: dispassionately, 'I can hardly expect you to believe me, gentlemen, but nevertheless I do regret that my duty to the *Rodina* compels me to offer you poor reward for your efforts.'

I tensed, staring out past the hulking form of Hermann and the hunched apathetic bundle of rags that was Trapp: out to the dim-lit nor'-western horizon again – dammit, there WAS something there. Just a brief white flicker of water bursting below a fast-approaching ship's bow: the barely perceptible darkening of the skyline which indicated upperworks . . . but whatever it was, it would certainly harbour the same intention of killing us as those who were here already – and anyway, it was going to arrive too late even to provide a temporary diversion. Far too bloody late!

I swung, suddenly triggered by helpless rage. 'Just get ON with it, you bastard. At least spare us your apologies on behalf of Mother bloody Russia!'

'Hang on a minnit! Ah mean there's nae RUSH, Mister Miller sir?' Gorbals Wullie's anxious plea carried urgently through the gloom.

'An' YOU shut up, too!' I bellowed, trying to make him feel more secure in the face of familiarity. 'It's got nothing to bloody do with YOU!'

Trapp emitted a long shuddering sigh. Timorous. Incredulous.

'But we 'ad a *contrac*',' he whispered. 'A sacred bond, a contract is, Colonel. I'd keep me mouth shut: cherish the trust you wus generous enough to place in me. Lissen, there's Clause Eight, Para Two f'r a start – The Right o' the Charterer that all matters be deemed "Commercial In Confidence" . . .'

'But he *can't* trust you, Trapp. No one in his right mind could,' I protested, perfectly reasonably I thought, though possibly a little unwisely considering the circumstances. 'Apart from which he's KGB – they don't even trust each other, dammit!'

'Oh Gawd,' Trapp uttered a strangled cry and clutched at his chest before falling against an astonished Hermann. "Ow can you SAY that, Mister – you of all people? That no one can't *trust* me?'

'Trapp?' I said tentatively, suddenly alarmed. 'Trapp, are you all right?'

'It's the cancer,' Wullie explained sagely to the second uncomprehending Soviet trooper with the gun beside him. 'It takes him thon way sometimes.'

He considered the diagnosis a minute, then added, 'Och well: that – an' the thought of gettin' shot wi' a quarter o' a million dollar bank draft in 'is pocket!'

Personally I thought it was a bit bloody quick for cancer to strike, and we all knew the bank draft was a phoney

– even Trapp must have accepted that by then – but nevertheless the Captain *had* turned ashen-faced.

'Me main engine, Colonel!' he blurted as his legs buckled, sending him reeling helplessly towards the wheelhouse, clutching at the battered doorframe for support, 'it's gone an' over-rode its governor: I ain't under command no mo . . . !'

Only there was something a little odd about the way Trapp had begun to change direction.

I saw Weston's eyes widen, first in suspicion then, almost instantly, changing to cold realization as he clawed for his Service pistol, foolishly still in its webbing holster. Not that it mattered – Hermann and the other *Spetsnaz* had also begun to swing with M16s levelled, clearly intending to cut the Captain down and the hell with waiting for orders.

'. . . LOOK OUT, TRAPP!' I screamed, suddenly terrified for him, but as usual he ignored me, already moving rattlesnake fast by then while reaching, for some quite inexplicable reason, up *above* the wheelhouse doorway instead of towards the frame for support.

He didn't look sick any longer, either. Just venomous.

Not that it mattered.

Even as I hurled myself despairingly for Hermann's legs I knew I'd reacted far too slowly.

Certainly too slowly to save Trapp!

Chapter Fourteen

Everybody seemed to be shouting at that moment – warnings, imprecations, Russian, English . . . all except Gorbals Wullie, of course, who just stood there slack-jawed with surprise while generally proving about as useful in our current crisis as a chocolate bloody teapot.

Yet even preoccupied as I was with – somewhat to my own surprise – diving low in best rugger blue style for Hermann's straddled tree-trunk legs, I could still distinguish Trapp's bellow above the general pandemonium.

'Yer CAP!' he seemed to be roaring somewhat obscurely. 'Use yer bloody CAP, man!'

'Cap?' Wullie muttered, beginning to panic. 'Whit's 'e meanin' – mah *cap*?'

Then his ferret face cleared and he snatched the oil-stained cloth cap from his unkempt locks. 'Och, he means mah BONNET, so he does!'

I became temporarily distracted when my shoulder contacted Hermann's calves with agonizing force. Literally bouncing off the bloody man I floundered like a beetle on its back, dazedly trying to refocus while feeling more as though I'd just tried to tackle a concrete lamp standard.

I'd succeeded to some extent, mind you. The giant Russian immediately faltered in his aim of shooting Trapp – beginning to turn on ME instead . . . !

It was all terribly dispiriting. Well I mean, helping Trapp out had been one thing; actual self-sacrifice *per se* went far beyond my original intentions . . . numbly I

registered Gorbals Wullie, now firmly clutching his revolting headgear, suddenly lashing out for the second
Soviet soldier's face with the panic-stricken desperation
of a gutter mongrel: the cap itself flailing viciously to
betray the stainless glint of razorblades catching the glow
from the binnacle – the ones Wullie always kept sewn,
Glasgae hard-man fashion, into the edge of its peak.

A shocked cry from the *Spetsnaz* trooper echoed
through the wheelhouse as the blades slashed deep
through skin, muscle, and into bone itself.

Trapp himself finally snatching a long and oddly cumbersome artifact from concealed clips above the wheelhouse door before whirling to level it at West ...
Cherny ... ?

Suddenly a movement at the head of the starboard
ladder as yet another shadowy figure arrived – Spew ...
Mister SPEW, by God! Amiable and bear-like as ever,
single eye interestedly trying to encompass the bedlam
which met him.

''Allo, everybody,' Mister Spew greeted. ''Scuse my
butting in, but has anywun 'appened ter notice there wus
a submar*ine* jus' over th ... ?'

'Gettim OUT the bloody *WAY*!' Trapp roared in mid-
swing. Meaning Mister Spew.

'Oh, *orl* right, Captin,' Mister Spew said. Thinking
Trapp meant Hermann.

'Awwwww JESUS!' *I* bawled. Thinking solely of Hermann's M16, currently arriving precisely in line with my
still helplessly spreadeagled body.

Obligingly Mister Spew lifted Hermann; M16, grenades and all, as though the Russian Colossus had been a
mere feather mattress, then ambled to the back of the
bridge before obediently dumping the thunderstruck
soldier in a threshing bundle of club-like arms and legs,
clean over the rail to the deck below.

Which shouldn't have been too injurious to any

commando-wise fighting chap under normal circumstances – the height of the bridge rail above main deck level couldn't have been more than a decent pole vault.

Only the point where Mister Spew unloaded his human cargo also happened to be situated directly above the starboard side gangway entry.

I registered the dull *thud* as Hermann the Melon Squisher hit the alleyway itself. Then the rumble of rusted and collapsing deckplating as that particularly fraught area of the *Charon II*'s structure finally succumbed to the inevitable, followed by a long piercing bellow of agony – the only sound I ever heard him utter – as the bulk of Hermann, by then appallingly lacerated during his irresistible passage between scalpel-honed edges of corroded steel, continued clear through and down to the ship's double bottoms a further twenty-odd feet below.

Then a second rather more distant, and very final, *thud*!

. . . whereupon, abruptly, the white teeth of the murdered Arab survivors from the Libyan Komar came strangely to mind. They *must* have been smiling at that particular moment. At least briefly. From the bottom of the sea where Hermann had so ruthlessly sent them.

But there wasn't time to savour even that small taste of accidental triumph. Chernyshev was still dragging *his* pistol from its holster when Gorbals Wullie's shriek of terrified appeal cut across my bizarre reverie.

'CAPTIIIIIN!'

It seemed the second trooper had recovered from his frenzied assault and was now leaning weakly against the wheelhouse door, blood coursing unheeded from slashed features to level his weapon for a second and final time on Wullie.

'Ohhhhhh BUGGER it!' Trapp raged, forced to change

228

tack yet again. 'I ain't *never* goin' ter get to choose me own target!'

The explosion of the ancient elephant gun – the one I'd forgotten he always kept secreted above the wheelhouse door in anticipation of finer contractual points demanding firm resolution – sounded more like a twenty-five-pounder field gun in the confined space.

First and foremost it starfished Wullie's least favourite Russian straight through the flimsy wheelhouse bulkhead and clear over the port wing in gory over-kill.

It also blow-torched most of the desiccated paint from the deckhead; blew the entire door off its hinges like a butterfly's wing taken by a gale; decapitated the top half of the ship's wheel; showered our by then prostrate and hysterically scrabbling Key Personnel with a century-old film of dust and mummified woodworm corpses shaken from every nook and cranny – which, when I came to think about it, didn't actually make Wullie look all *that* much different from normal anyway – and generally left the wheelhouse appearing as if it had been hit by one of Chernyshev's Vipers.

. . . the whole affray couldn't have lasted more than a minute. Mister Spew was still peering curiously over the after rail, trying lugubriously to figure where Hermann had gone; the *Spetsnaz* on the foredeck were still staring uncertainly up at our darkened bridge. Half of Trapp's crew hadn't even stopped whimpering for mercy, and Choker Bligh certainly hadn't tired of holding sulphurous conversation with those Soviets still trying to remodel him with their rifle butts.

Trapp's expression then was terrible to behold. I held my breath as that awesome elephant gun swung ominiously on KGB Colonel Chernyshev . . . But then, it always had been a somewhat amorphous concept – the Captain's sense of justice. He would blithely concede his customers' inevitable attempts to destroy him personally as an intrinsic part of Life's great and exciting gamble: he would even tolerate, if barely, an attack on his profit and loss account – but there were some actions which really choked him: went right against his principles.

'He was just an old man, Korky Tokoglu wus,' Trapp said ever so softly, 'an' he didn't really harm no one – or not excep' in the wallet anyway. He certainly wusn't no soldier or matelot; he didn't make atom bombs an' he never even talked politics, so he wasn't no threat to your precious bloody *Rodina* . . . but you cut 'is throat anyway, Colonel. Just because, to you an' your kind, one old Turkoman's life wusn't important in your grand plan.'

I knew then what he was about to do, and why.

Chernyshev, too, must have guessed what Trapp intended: he *must* have foreseen his own imminent death reflected in Trapp's eyes, yet he didn't try to mask his contempt for us, the patriotically uncommitted; the scum on the surface of Western capitalism. His response was curt, even mocking.

'As Miller said – spare me the sermon, Trapp.'

Obligingly Trapp's finger began to whiten on the trigger.

All my fears flooded back. Either Trapp didn't comprehend or, because he was Trapp, simply didn't care that the moment he avenged his fondly remembered Istanbul adversary he wouldn't simply be executing summary justice: he'd be committing suicide.

On behalf of all of us!

'NO, Trapp!' I shouted urgently.

Hauling myself groggily to my feet I tried desperately to take stock of the situation.

Outboard things had changed only marginally: to seaward, vented ballast was still streaming from the saddle-tanks of that low black submarine less than two cable lengths ahead, while the first faintly seen heads were only now appearing above her sail structure.

Of less immediate concern, the luminescent bow wave of the second fast-approaching vessel still flickered ominously, but a less pressing three miles to the north-west . . . hurriedly I filed the newcomer for future reference: as ever our list of insurmountable Trapp-engineered crises had to be refined to one of priorities.

My mind began to race. Trouble was it had begun to race in neutral – I couldn't think of one damn solution even to our most fundamental predicament: that offered by the submarine.

'Kill him,' I nodded lamely at Chernyshev, 'and his team will wipe us out in thirty seconds flat, Trapp.'

'. . . don't kill him, and we've extended our life expectancy only by minutes, because he's ruthless, untrustworthy, and his orders demand our silence,' the voice of cold reality screamed within me.

I can still see Trapp as he was then, a thunderous conflict of black and white – face black-suffused with the frustration of it, finger still white-drawn against the trigger of that terrible weapon.

I held my breath. Suddenly even those few minutes seemed very precious.

An ominously warm wind curled over the tattered dodger and plucked at my hair. Already the *Charon* had begun to list sluggishly, unstably, to port under the press of the coming storm while, all around us in the half-light, I could see the little whitecaps hissing and starting to fight with each other in their attempts to grow bigger. Even discounting *Spetsnaz* and killer submarines and fast-approaching so-far unidentifieds which may or may not be the Libyan Navy determined to exact retribution, simply as a seaman marooned aboard the nautical equivalent of a lead balloon I'd *still* have felt the hopelessness of our situation.

'Och Jeeze, but what're we goin' tae DO, Mister Miller sir?' Gorbals Wullie whimpered with true British grit.

'Look, *I* don't bloody know, do I?' I flared, totally fed-up with trying to solve the insoluble. 'Ask him – *he's* the bloody Captain!'

Mister Spew, always a few preoccupations behind, chose that particular moment to scratch his cropped skull in bewilderment.

'Why d'yer think,' he speculated, still doggedly pursuing some rationale for Hermann's abrupt disappearance, ''e decided to go down the engineroom so sudden anywa . . . !'

'Ohhhhh, SHURRUP!' Wullie and I screamed with one voice.

Suddenly Trapp relaxed, shrugged philosophically, then eased the pressure on the trigger. Just like that. Cheerfully acknowledging the dictates of common sense.

A concession which disturbed me, personally, more than anything else that had happened so far.

'Looks like it's a stand-off, eh? So you better order your lads ter go then, Colonel,' he said matter-of-factly.

I saw the undisguised relief in Chernyshev's eyes. He bowed shortly. 'You will not regret your decision, Captain,' he said levelly.

And, to his credit, I swear he had his fingers crossed when he told the lie.

But that was hardly the point. I stared at Trapp incredulously. 'Go . . . ? Go where, for crying out loud?'

He jerked his head innocently across the intervening sea towards the black-silhouetted submarine. 'Over to their mates, o' course.'

'But you *can't* let them go, Trapp,' I panicked, knowing what I knew. And what *he* knew – but what Chernyshev still obviously DIDN'T know. 'It's a . . . !'

BOOOOOOOOOOM . . . !

I'd never thought to see West . . . Chernyshev on his

hands and knees like that before, imitating Gorbals Wullie. However, fortunately for them both, Trapp must've allowed the elephant gun to wander slightly before involuntarily squeezing the trigger.

When the cumbersome machine went off it not only drowned the rest of my protest but also blew a huge ragged hole through what was left of the *Charon*'s spindle funnel, caused the remainder to lean even more drunkenly to starboard than before . . . and, quite fortuitously for us, exploded a third Russian – presumably a sniper who'd just that moment wriggled himself unnoticed into position – clean from behind our wretched smokestack and across the engineroom skylight like some hideously disintegrating doll.

Bloody careless! Apart from being dead typical – how Trapp's mistakes invariably seemed to initiate such lethal legacies?

'Oh heck an' *dash* it all,' he muttered, recovering himself with an effort . . . meanwhile slipping a further two cartridges, which looked more like howitzer than shotgun ammunition, into the twin breeches while Chernyshev was still on the deck.

'Lissen, you'll reely 'ave to tell your lads to keep well clear o' me bridge while they're packing up, Colonel. I can't be trusted with nothin' ternight, can I?'

'. . . while *you*, Mister,' he hissed out of the corner of his mouth, 'you just shut UP about that bloody submarine!'

Of course Trapp wasn't completely foolhardy – I've NEVER claimed that . . . !

Not *completely*.

He certainly made damn sure the barrel of that devastating weapon never deviated again from Chernyshev's midships region, particularly when a Soviet sergeant arrived somewhat hesitantly on the bridge to –

presumably – request instructions. It wan't easy to be sure: he and the Colonel spoke only rapid Russian to each other.

'Don't forget,' Trapp had interjected briefly, 'them lads o' yours take only their light weapons – I'm stickin' to the deal because we don't have no choice, remember? I wouldn't feel too relaxed if I thought you still 'ad one o' your Viper launchers handy while we wus sittin' all trusting an' good natured, wavin' goodbye from over 'ere.'

'And myself?' Chernyshev asked grimly. 'What guarantee do I have of release if my men disembark without trouble?'

'The same as we do that you won't order that smart-lookin' boat out there to torpedo us, soon as you pull clear. Mutual trust it's called, Colonel.'

'Hah!' I thought acidly. But what other option *did* we have?

A last snap of commands and the sergeant left the bridge looking understandably angry: a few KGB Special Forces egos had been pricked that night. Trapp leaned comfortably back against the rail keeping the gun pointed uncompromisingly on the Colonel while darting the odd wary glance at the Soviets as they began to disembark, silent and disciplined as ever it seemed, into their violently gyrating boats.

Actually my stomach felt much the same as those inflatables by then – full of wind and gyrating violently. Not only was I trying to identify the steadily closing new arrival as well as sweep the horizon for even more bad news, but also to keep one eye hypnotically cocked as shadowy activity atop the submarine's sail suggested they were taking a leaf out of Chernyshev's manual of military measures.

. . . mounting heavy machine-guns on *their* bridge!

Lord, but Trapp was playing a damn dangerous game. I swallowed, trying to dispel my tension. Bluff, counter-bluff, international skulduggery . . . ? Dear God but he really had landed us in the big league this time. All I could do by then was cling desperately to the hope that, just for once, he might do the right thing in error.

. . . where was that second ship? Still reassuringly distant, but time was getting short – we would still have to cope with whatever threat from *her* when she closed us in the next few minutes.

'Priorities, Miller. Concentrate on the priorities . . . !'

'Two boats already away. Last man in the final boat,' I muttered tightly. Trapp turned to West . . . Chernyshev, and jerked the gun barrel meaningfully.

'Give my love to the *Rodina*,' he said drily. 'Though I can't say it's been nice doing business with you.'

I saw that mocking smile betray itself briefly for the very last time as the Colonel nodded brusquely, then turned for the ladder. It was a dispassionate farewell, in keeping with his manner. He must have realized he'd won; that he would soon be able to complete his mission according to plan.

I watched the last Soviet raft carrying Colonel Chernyshev begin to paddle unsteadily across to that silent black submarine. There was no turning back now. The Captain's greatest ever gamble had passed the point of no return.

The moment they'd left, Trapp grabbed for the engine-room voice pipe

'FULL Ahead! An' if yer ever wants to knot spaghetti again – go like 'ELL, Chief!'

'Course he *might've* gone ter collect 'is personal kit, mightn't 'e, Mister Miller?' Second Officer Spew speculated, still desperately worried about the late Hermann.

'He just *might* have done at that, Mister Spew,' I agreed, giving up the unequal struggle.

. . . the shooting aboard the submarine began before we'd hardly got the *Charon* under way.

Chapter Fifteen

I watched most of it through my binoculars.

The start of World War Three.

... and I *still* say it was all Trapp's fault. Caused entirely by the way he'd interrupted me earlier. When he accidentally triggered that bloody elephant gun and completely sabotaged the point I'd been trying to make.

Anyway, I remember watching the shadowy figures of the first *Spetsnaz* leaping from their crazily tossing inflatable to clamber, not without some difficulty, up and over the rounded saddle tanks of the submarine. Certainly it couldn't have been easy to gain a foothold on that smooth, water-streaming steel while also clinging to a weapon; particularly in view of the fact that no crew member had yet appeared on her decks to assist them.

Yet there *were* men aware of what was happening aboard that sinister warship. I could still see the heads atop the shark-like sail structure quite plainly, leaning over between the machine-gun mounts to gaze down at the commandos struggling unaided to gain her almost awash foredeck ... ?

The second raft bumped alongside: more Soviet Special Forces jumping for a tenuous handhold. They had guts, I conceded that. I wouldn't have fancied attempting to leap from a feather-stable raft across that heaving black sea ... but then, they didn't have a lot of choice, either. Not by then.

I chewed my lip nervously. The first group were hesitating uncertainly, obviously nonplussed by the cold reception from their comrades of the Soviet Navy, then warily beginning to move aft, staring up at the soaring bridge above them.

Yet still no one acknowledged their presence from atop the high sail.

Which, one might have thought, was very, very odd.

. . . but the *Charon* herself was shuddering dementedly by then, turning unsteadily to port under Gorbals Wullie's nervous hand while Chief Bucalosie's bloody *Spatz*, belaboured by a fear-spirited combination of heavy spanners and highly-strung Italian oaths, did everything in its vindictive repertoire to dismantle us rivet by rivet through vibration alone.

A great rolling cloud of choking smoke, thick as a stoker's blanket and bearing the odd spark along with a few vagrant flakes of rust, belched from the shot-away side of our funnel and briefly enveloped the bridge deck. By the time it cleared and I'd rubbed my streaming eyes and grabbed a few lungfuls of blessed Mediterranean air again, the third and final *Spetsnaz* raft carrying Chernyshev himself had bumped violently alongside the submarine.

Then, distantly, I heard a shout from across the water.

A somewhat alarmed shout.

'I'd say,' a voice growled conversationally at my elbow as a slightly sooty Trapp appeared beside me from the gloom, 'they wus about ter introduce themselves to each other, eh Mister?'

'You do realize,' I said heavily – but not at all nastily, I stress: it was far too late for anything like that – 'exactly what you've gone and done. Don't you, Trapp?'

'Delivered 'em to their rendezvous, yer mean? As requested?'

'That's not what I meant, but while we're on the subject, you didn't. You delivered them roughly twelve sea miles and two hours *short* of the rendezvous requested.'

'I told yer you always wus a nit-picker navigashun-wise,' he retorted smoothly.

More shouts – startled, terribly angry shouts now – drifted across the slowly opening gap between our fleeing . . . well, more our asthmatically withdrawing, stern and the submarine.

'Lend us yer binoc'lars,' Trapp asked.

'No,' I said.

KGB Colonel Chernyshev slammed into focus, balancing with difficulty in the heaving raft, head angled back to stare up at the host sub's towering sail.

At that range I could only guess at, rather than see, his expression. It wouldn't have been sardonic any longer. More, well, disbelieving I supposed?

Meanwhile his troopers had begun to scatter in much the same manner as for an impending air attack; urgently pulling back along the spray-spattered foredeck, though precisely to where I couldn't imagine. Neither, it seemed, could they. Eventually I saw one Russian soldier kneel in brave defiance, raise his US-issue M16 – and empty a full magazine at the sailors on the bridge.

The warship's machine-guns returned fire instantly. Her crew's rules of engagement must have been pre-scribed well in advance of the rendezvous: shoot back – and aim to kill the bastards!

I stared hypnotized through the lenses as men began literally to explode under the impact of heavy-calibre rounds from above. All the Soviet *Spetsnaz* were shooting now, but from a hopeless situation . . . bodies spun, were seized as if by some giant wind and flung brokenly overboard from the exposed foredeck.

One final glimpse of Cherny . . . No – WESTON, dammit! He'd always be Weston to me – dragging his issue Colt from its webbing holster and triggering it, recklessly gallant as ever, at those who were destroying his men.

. . . until one submariner ever so deliberately swung his barrel to maximum depression, whereupon the soaring white fountains rippled and danced across the heaving sea instead, to overtake the Colonel's flimsy raft.

And then there was only an awful, operationally-expedient Thing smashed backwards into the Gulf of Sirte.

Which didn't look at all West Point, and certainly not KGB Officers' Academy, smart.

Grimly I lowered the glass. I'd seen it all before, and anyway it seemed more bearable to watch the last of *Charon II*'s no-longer silent soldiers catapulted into death as distant, less real figures. Violently puppeteered little matchstick men.

I'm sure it was then I heard ex-US Special Forces Sergeant Jablonski laughing. Derisive, triumphant . . . cold as a grimace from a frozen corpse. Or maybe it was only my imagination; maybe it *had* been nothing more than the chuckle of the wind in our tattered rigging?

Trapp stirred.

'Christ,' he had the grace to mutter, even he visibly subdued.

I tensed. Something was happening back there . . . the bows of the submarine had begun to swing. She was starting to forge ahead. Waves already exploding angry white against the black broadsiding hull; khaki-clad bodies beginning to wash callously from her foredeck to spiral and revolve in the slowly building eddies from her single screw . . .

Turning to follow in our own pathetic wake. It was the reaction I'd feared.

Now the submarine was hunting US.

Not that I could really blame them. At best they must have assumed that Trapp had sent those Soviet troopers across quite deliberately, in order either to capture or sink them.

Not that explanations mattered right then. It was chillingly clear that with Chernyshev's passing only the source of threat had changed, yet oddly I didn't feel frightened any more, even accepting as I did that she would overtake and kill the *Charon* and all aboard within minutes.

I was much too over-awed by then, can't you see? Having just begun to appreciate the full implications of Trapp's scheming.

'It's only occurred to me now,' I said faintly. 'You've just started the next WAR, Trapp. You do *realize* that, don't you?'

'Who?'

'YOU!'

"No I 'aven't,' he denied petulantly, such trivia as killer submarines and other sundry closing warships instantly dismissed when it came to defending his sacrosanct bloody ego. 'It wusn't *my* fault Cherny-whatsit wus a Russki pongo, a bloody ignorant soldier – didn't even know one end of a boat from the other!'

'You could still have told him. At least I *tried* to.'

'WHY should I?' he returned with saintly logic. 'It wusn't in me contract, wus it?'

'Jesus *Christ*!' I yelled.

'All right, you show me then, Mister! You jus' SHOW me where it says I had ter tell the Colonel that wus an AMERICAN submarine he insisted on boarding . . . !'

Well he *had*, you know. Technically speaking, Trapp had unquestionably engineered hostilities between the Superpowers. It had only been because of the bloody man's inherent conviction that he was an indestructible smart-ass that Russians and Americans had even begun shooting at each other.

I still say that if he'd let me explain to Chernyshev as I'd wanted to, that Russian and American patrol submarines look very much alike through a layman's eyes, and that the one which just happened to have surfaced twelve miles short of his rendezvous had been a US Navy Skipjack class and not a smaller Soviet Foxtrot as he'd probably been briefed to expect – well, very possibly Chernyshev would've realized the game was up there and then, and surrendered.

Or maybe he wouldn't. Only we'll never know that, will we?

Because of bloody Trapp!

But it didn't end there. Oh, no! Yet it could very well have done, without escalating things further. I mean, the firefight aboard the Skipjack probably wouldn't even have counted as being a proper war at that stage. Not really. Not if Trapp had been content to stop being totally bloody-minded then, and at least *tried* to make his peace with the US Navy.

Well, they *might* have let us go? Or then again, maybe they wouldn't. But we'll never know THAT either, will we?

Again because of TRAPP. And what he contrived to do next.

. . . how he *really* managed, with his second attempt, to screw things up enough to start the Third World War.

I remember sparing a few despairing moments to drag my glasses from the ever-nearing submarine and scrutinize the second ship, now very much closer and overtaking both of us with the high flaring bone in her teeth that told me very plainly she had to be another warship.

It was getting very dark by then, almost too dark to . . . ! I stiffened; gripped my binoculars delicately to counterbalance the all-too-sluggish motion of the shuddering *Charon*.

'My God,' I muttered, hardly daring to hope. 'She's *British*, Trapp. An RN frigate!'

'Lemme see!'

Trapp grabbed my precious binoculars and screwed them below fearsomely meeting eyebrows. 'Yer right, Mister,' he said a moment later. 'By Jimminy but you're dead right. F'r once.'

I let it go, too worried to feel insulted. I could see him immediately thinking again, you see – calculating. Looking clever.

'No, Trapp,' I pleaded, sparing an increasingly apprehensive glance astern. The Americans were overtaking us rapidly and no doubt spitting nails by now at Trapp's imagined perfidy. They could colander our tissue-thin plates any minute with those bloody lethal sail machine-guns, never mind waste torpedoes.

'Let me handle this,' I begged. 'At least let's talk it through. Another ham-fisted move could be our las . . . ?'

I stopped. Right away I could *tell* I'd said the wrong thing. His expression had turned from ordinary grumpy to choleric. 'What d'yer mean, Mister – ANOTHER 'am-fisted move?'

'Ah think Mister Miller means . . .'

Gorbals Wullie – who until then had kept his rat trap mouth noticeably shut on account of being scared bloody witless – chose that moment to pipe up in impeccably miscalculated translation of my plea.

'. . . that ye'll turn this fine mess you already caused, intae a complete bluidy crisis, Captin.'

Mister Spew's sombre deliberations also carried from the darkness just then.

'D'yer fink,' he asked, STILL mystified by the now very late Hermann's vertical departure, ''e might've gone off in one o' them likkle rubber *boats* then. An' I just din't *see* 'im go?'

'That wan's no' real,' Gorbals Wullie decreed after due

242

consideration. 'He's prob'bly thinkin' thon wis a reunion party they wis throwin' aboard that sub.'

'THEY'LL BE THROWING MORE THAN A BLOODY PARTY!' I roared, driven far beyond any reasonable definition of sanity.

'I don't see why yer so edgy,' Trapp muttered huffily. 'Not now our own Grey Funnel Line's here to protect us. An' anyway – they *are* Yanks back there, not Ivans. They're reasonable blokes, the Yanks. Lissen, Mister, if there's one thing I *do* understand, it's the Yankee mentality. I knows them fine people like the back o' me . . .'

I was hurling myself prone in anticipation before he'd even completed the sentence.

. . . the very first burst of fire from the pursuing Skipjack chopped most of the *Charon*'s mercifully vacant port bridge wing off clean as a chippie's axe would've done.

Advanced United States weapons technology also trimmed the *Charon*'s already worm-eroded mainmast down to bulwark level, riddled our long-suffering funnel so's it finally did squirt more smoke sideways than upwards, and persuaded even Trapp's black-furious face to a level with mine.

'That's IT!' he roared from the deck. 'That's bloody IT, Mister! This is a British ship, b'God, an' worth a fortune . . . Where's the Ensign. Where's me bloody Red Duster . . .'

I knew for *sure* we were in trouble then. He never hid behind his birthplace Flag unless he was really pushed . . . the bloody tax authorities in Britain had spies everywhere!

More machine-gunning from astern. Shrieks as per usual from the foredeck. The eccentric thunder of the *Spatz* vying with Chief Bucalosie's terrified appeal up the voice pipe, 'We're gonna die thissa time for sure, Capitano: we're alla gonna DIE . . . '

Wearily I crawled over and shoved the plug in it.

Suddenly Trapp scrambled to his feet again. 'The RADIO,' he shouted triumphantly. 'By God I'll show them Yankee Doodles what our Royal Navy's made of.'

Our Royal Navy suddenly?

'Radio?' I muttered dazedly. *Radio* . . . ? Dammit, the wretched old skinflint hadn't even spent money on providing an Aldis lamp, a proper galley stove – *life*jackets! I wriggled round. 'What rad . . . ?'

'Friggit, friggit, 'Er Majesty's Friggit: this is the British Steamship *Charon* calling from two miles fine on yer port bow . . . Mayday, mayday, MAYday! I am being attacked by a hostile submarine wi'out provocation an' in lawful pursuit o' trade . . . '

'Oh dear *God*,' I thought. 'He's using that bloody radio the Russians rigged before we entered Djibela.'

There came a splurge of static, then a slightly uncertain but very British voice.

'Steamship *Charon*, this is Her Majesty's Warship *Tynecastle* . . . We can find no trace of your vessel in the British Register of Ships. Say again your situation. Over!'

'Bloody desperate!' Trapp bellowed. 'I am bein' attacked, Mister, an' I demands protection . . . '

'Thass it. You gie they poofy Navy lads hell, Captin,' Wullie, who hadn't modified his contempt for naval authority one bit since World War Two, encouraged from under the half of the ship's wheel we had left.

Rat . . . *tat* . . . *TAT* . . . *!* More bits of the bloody *Charon* fell around me. They'd launch a torpedo next. It would only require a very small one.

'Lissen,' Trapp was shouting by the time I'd screwed up courage to lift my head again. 'Who's in command there? What's yer rank, Mister . . . Over?'

'Rankine-Forsyth. Lieutenant Commander. Over!'

244

'Lieutenant Commander?' Trapp jeered. 'I got more Lieutenant Commanders aboard 'ere than we've 'ad 'ot dinners . . .'

'That's true,' I snarled bitterly.

'. . . well you look up yer Navy List forsooth, Forsyth. Right at the *top* o' the three-ring list you'll find ME – full Commander Edward Trapp, Royal Navy; medals an' bloody bar . . .'

'*That's* true tae,' Wullie nodded sagely. 'The "bar" bit.'

Crackle . . . splurge . . . the distant British voice held a careful note of respect. 'Affirmative, sir – we are closed up to action stations: please identify the threat, Commander Trapp.'

A sudden horrific thought hit me.

'TRAPP?' I shouted. 'You're not going to . . . ?'

'Surface gunfire from submarine direc'ly astern o' me. An' by God, Mister, if you so much as chips me paint when you opens fire I'll 'ave you court-martialled in the Bloody Tower.'

'What bloody tower's that, then?' Mister Spew asked interestedly, sidetracked into a temporary respite from Hunting Hermann.

There came a momentary hesitation over the ether. Then:

'Sir. My Rules of Engagement . . . ? I still must ask you to positively identify the vessel firing on you. What nationality? I repeat – *what* nationality?'

'NO, Trapp. PLEASE!'

But it was sincerity that counted. The pure ring of truth.

'The last I saw of 'er she wus crawling with RUSSIANS!' Trapp said.

'Oh, Christ!' *I* said.

'Oh, *Christ*!' Lieutenant Commander Rankine-Forsyth, Royal Navy, said.

*

The first British surface-to-surface missile ever to be fired at a United States Navy vessel since the War of Independence – which was almost certainly started by some eighteenth-century ancestor of Trapp's, anyway – struck home forty seconds later.

Chapter Sixteen

Of course it wasn't over then. The next and Third World War hadn't begun just because Trapp had ... well, stretched the truth a little.

I mean, Great Britain and the United States of America were hardly likely to slip into thermo-nuclear gear against each other on account of a small Trapp-contrived confusion at sea, were they?

Lord, no. The Atlantic Alliance was strong enough to survive even Trapp.

... I think?

But the trouble with what Trapp still firmly believed were his inspired strategems was that he never really thought them through; didn't waste time on considering the full consequences of his actions – usually, I concede, because one or other of his customers were trying their apoplectic damnedest by that time to blow him clear out of the bloody water!

Which none the less meant that, once launched, Trapp's machinations did tend to escalate under their own Machiavellian momentum; to steam remorselessly beyond human control.

Added to which, you've also got to remember that Edward Trapp *had* no national loyalties, so felt bound by no rules. Not since those disillusioning days spent as a very young midshipman-child on that sea-tossed raft, with only an ever-diminishing shipmate for company.

No loyalties at all. Other than to profit, and the

over-riding determination to survive even if at the expense of others.

I think I'd worked my way through a few more Chinese boxes between crises. Certainly I'd concluded that the Skipjack's remarkably astute pre-emption of Colonel Chernyshev's rendezvous with his comrades of the Soviet skulduggery fleet hadn't been a result of chance interception at all.

My guess was that US Intelligence had probably learned of the Russian plan to defuse Qaddafi's nuclear ambitions a long time before Trapp ever met Cherny . . . well, Weston as he then purported to be, in Instanbul.

So what would the Pentagon have done? Certainly the last thing they'd have wished was to prevent the Kremlin from pressing ahead with such a welcome and mutually beneficial piece of military surgery. So why not let Ivan go ahead: take all the risks and casualties to his *Spetsnaz* Forces . . . with the potential added bonus of exposure and the subsequent condemnation of Soviet duplicity from the Arab world?

But the Americans, having compromised the Russian plan, must also have learned of the KGB's intention to misinform the world of the identities of the raiders – to fit the United States itself into the political frame, so to speak.

Which was why *they* sent one of their patrol submarines into the Gulf of Sirte two hours ahead of Soviet plans: with the express intention of anticipating Chernyshev's withdrawal . . . and then to heist both his team and their private enterprise contract carrier – meaning Trapp and crowd – as living confirmation that it *had* been the Kremlin, not good old Uncle Sam, who'd initiated the whole deplorable plot against Colonel Brother Qaddafi.

Hell, armed with such indisputable confirmation of

Soviet double-dealing, the CIA might even have been tempted to persuade the world it had been the Russians who'd *really* carried out the Libyan AIR raids as well!

Finally, it explained who had so dramatically torpedoed the Libyan frigate in the nick of time, while we were still Ras al Djibela bound. And why West . . . Chernyshev *had* been genuinely perplexed – it had been the US, not the Soviet Navy, who'd lent that last-minute helping hand to ensure the mission's success.

. . . but the unforeseen snag was that no one, Russian or American, had made any allowance for Trapp's innate ability to dislocate the best laid plans of mice and Super-powers.

Who'd ever have imagined, for instance, that he would actually have conned Chernyshev's group into boarding a United States Navy vessel while still believing it was a Russian? No bloody *wonder* they all started shooting at each other . . . No wonder the Yanks thought Trapp was *attacking* them.

And who would *ever* have imagined that Trapp, even after unwittingly screwing the KGB/CIA's own meticulously prepared intrigues and counter-intrigues like that, could STILL be so egocentric and pig-head contemptuous of common sense that he would actually put two grubby fingers up to a whole 3,500-ton hunter-killer submarine by blithely trying to outrun it?

In the *CHARON* . . . ?

And *then*, when he discovered his bungling ineptitude – which Trapp invariably euphemised as 'jus' a bit o' bad luck' – brought the heavy-calibre wrath of more or less everybody down about his ears . . . well, then he suddenly found it convenient to remember *he* was a Royal Naval officer and gentleman, didn't he? And so contrived to drive a wedge clear through an alliance over two hundred years ol . . . !

'Ohhhhh, LORD!'

It had just struck me – assuming I was right, then didn't there have to be a somewhat disenchanted *Russian* naval presence still cruising out there somewhere?

Waiting impatiently for Comrade Colonel Chernyshev?

. . . who THEY, presumably, still believed was aboard our *Charon*?

'The only thing worries me a bit,' Trapp pondered, leaning comfortably over the after end of our still maniacally vibrating bridge, 'is that when that Forsooth hyphen Forsyth bloke comes aboard – which 'e'll want to do soon as 'e's picked up survivors an' apologized to the Yank skipper, even if jus' ter pay 'is compliments ter a senior Naval officer – 'e might ask to take a peek in our hold, Mister . . .'

I didn't answer. I was still staring dazedly astern at the stricken American submarine, by now stopped dead and listing drunkenly in the water with what was left of her high conning sail vying with what was left of the *Charon II*'s spindle funnel in eccentricity.

There was even smoke coming from both structures, too. In rather similar volumes.

'. . . which might be a bit embarrassin' seein' I *did* sort of, well, imply we wus going about our lawful trade – an' yet here we are, jus' off the coast o' Libya, while we gotta whole hold stuffed ter the deckhead with high explosives an' illegally-acquired Top Secret American weapons . . .'

'He means we're in it tae oor necks still, but even deeper,' Wullie pointed out somewhat confusingly.

'Good! Then I hope the US Navy court-martials you for sabotage and un-American activities as *well* as Rankine-Forsyth hanging you for treason from his highest bloody yardarm!' I snapped unfeelingly. 'Apart from which Chernyshev made you a Commander, didn't he?

Which means you're probably a Commander in the SOVIET Navy as well, now – so the Russians'll probably have something to say abou . . . !'

I stopped. Dead.

. . . the *Russians*?

HMS *Tynecastle* was less than a mile astern now, and creaming to overtake us at an anxious thirty knots.

'The radio, Trapp!' I blurted as The Most Terrifying Thought Of All took root. 'You've got to warn *Tynecastle* off – there has to be a REAL Soviet submarine around here somewhere. And Rankine-For-thingummy won't have any reason to suspect a Red Force threat because, thanks to you, he already believes he's SUNK it!'

'*I* can't do that,' Trapp growled unimpressed. 'It'd be good as admitting I wus in the wrong.'

'Oh, *gosh*!' Wullie reeled dramatically with a shocked hand over his mouth. 'Jist imagine anywan thinkin' THAT, Captin?'

'Anyroad, them Popovs won't dare hang around now they know the game's up,' Trapp promised: a lid-bobbing, unctuous-looking mountain of sheer complacency. 'Take it from me, Mister: I knows th . . . !'

'NOoooooo Tra . . . !'

BOOOOOooooooom!

The Soviet torpedo struck *Tynecastle* somewhere abaft the funnel. It was too dark to see for sure. I only know I stood there with my hands white-gripping the *Charon*'s scarred bridge rail, staring aghast as the low, rakish silhouette of the British frigate slewed crazily off course before coming to a sluggish halt in the water with turbine steam shrieking from her safety valves and long tongues of flame already clawing for the wild Mediterranean night sky.

. . . and that WAS how Trapp caused it.

The start of World War Three.

*

But there wasn't time for recriminations right then. Not that they'd've done any good anyway.

Trapp would never change: Trapp would never admit to the slightest weakness. The words 'Self-criticism', 'Error', 'Sheer bloody stupidity' ... even 'Slight mis-judgement' simply didn't apply to his view of him-self.

He was the complete megalomaniac. He could've given Hitler lessons. To sail with him you either lived with and accepted that knowledge or, more probably, died with it by – the chances were – sheer incompetent accident at that.

. . . which was why I should have thrown that bloody letter away the moment I set eyes on it in Rotterdam.

But I hadn't. So there I was. Marooned as First Mate of a persistently collapsing hulk not that far from a coast full of Libyan zealots all out for our blood – which I'd rather forgotten about seeing we'd been too busy dodging most of the rest of the world in the interim – with a storm rising, and a few square miles of the Gulf of Sirte now strewn with shipwrecked British and American sailors leavened with a not-inconsiderable number of gunshot corpses of Slavic origin notwithstanding the suits they were wearing.

All, basically, our fault.

TRAPP's fault!

Oh ... and with a Russian submarine well within torpedo range, and just thirsting for our blood.

Almost certainly her commander would carry direct orders from the Kremlin to liquidate us as witnesses to the Soviet involvement at Djibela in the event of Chernyshev's having failed to do so.

To say nothing of being keen to kick a few answers out of us first – not only about how Trapp had managed to manoeuvre *him* personally into a place in history as being the submariner who started the next global war, but also how Trapp had contrived to mislay a whole shipload of his army comrades in the interim.

Or maybe he wasn't that curious. Maybe he would simply shoot first, and the hell with a few idiots from the KGB?

We didn't have long to wait before we found out.

Remarkably, it was Second Officer Spew who heard the noise first. A strange, high-pitched singing noise. Getting louder.

'What's that strange, 'igh-pitched singin' noise?' Mister Spew wondered, taking a second stand-easy from Hunting Hermann. '. . . gettin' louder?'

Trapp stirred. He'd been remarkably quiet since the frigate was hit, I have to admit that. Almost subdued. Even when I'd nearly punched him on account of forty years of frustrated rage starting with World War bloody Two, working through Trapp's so-called PEACE, and culminating in the loss of Her Majesty's Warship *Tynecastle.*

'What noise?' the Captain muttered, grumbling out to the wing and peering over while guiltily avoiding looking at the gradually fading flames and smoke from astern.

I trailed over too. The *Charon* had begun to roll sickeningly by then, making progression across the bridge a series of little runs followed immediately by a short clamber uphill. Just for a moment I thought I saw a flash of phosphorescence broad on the beam, but it instantly merged with the rest of the whitecaps and disappeared.

Then the noise faded away.

'Nothin' out there,' Trapp growled irritably.

Anxiously I scanned the dark horizon. Trouble with submarine spotting was that it presented an impossible challenge by definition, but my nerves still insisted I try. And then we had to remember the Libyans, Qaddafi's posse: still undoubtedly searching for us.

Boy, were we in a *mess*? We weren't even heading for the open sea any more . . . Oh, sorry: hadn't I remembered to mention that minor detail?

No . . . ?

Well it just so happened that, ever since Trapp's asthmatic escape under full rudder while Chernyshev's *Spetsnaz* were boarding the Skipjack, *Charon* had been steadily steaming back IN-shore . . . back *towards* Ras al Djibela! While even I hadn't suggested we returned to a reciprocal course for the open sea and freedom quite yet – I didn't feel quite ready at that point, to face the embarrassment of picking our way through Lieutenant Commander Rankine-Forsyth's not-at-all-Jolly Jack Tars any more than Trapp did.

Which was just as well, it turned out.

I saw them coming against a lighter yellow patch of sky.

'Aircraft!' I blurted. 'Green one hundred!'

'Don't be silly,' Trapp snapped irritably. 'Them Russkies wouldn't come in *air*cra . . . !'

The two Libyan MiGs screamed above our remaining foremast at nought feet, hammering us with their downwash; exploding the sky into tattered swirls of superheated avgas . . . 'JESUS!' I yelled.

From nought inches.

'They're turnin' BACK!' Wullie squealed.

'What are?' Mister Spew queried attentively.

'Ohhhhh I'm bloody SICK o' this!' Trapp bellowed.

BROOOOOOOMmmmmm . . . ! Five hundred plus knots. Displaced air a near-solid mallet beating clouds of rust from the reeling *Charon*'s plating, causing the whole ship to shy in terror . . .

. . . and then they were gone! Beating up the holocaust astern, hunting elsewhere for the saboteurs of *wadi* Djibela.

Well, you couldn't really blame Qaddafi's pilots for

being deceived, could you? There was no way any sane invader would be heading BACK towards the place they'd just invaded!

Trapp Really Put Out was a sight most awesome to behold.

I knew he was berserk with rage because he forgot to claim credit for having accidentally outwitted the Libyans. He was too self-absorbed mad even for that.

'Thass *it*!' he raged. 'Thass bloody IT, Mister! I'm fed up wi' people always takin' a narrow view. Always tryin' ter push me around . . .'

'I suppose we *are* thinking about the same people?' I wondered faintly. 'The ones he's just been responsible for blowing up their multi-billion-dinar atomic research plant? The one's who've just lost a billion dollar sub because of him? The ones who've just watched God knows how many million pounds' worth of the Royal Navy's defence budget behave like a diving bell when it wasn't designed as one – I suppose he *is* meaning THEM being the ones taking a narrow view?'

But I didn't say it. There were times with the Captain when silence was not only golden but essential to one's future well being. Even Key Personnel Gorbals Wullie had the half-wit to keep his usually hyper-active mouth firmly shut right then.

'. . . you get down ter that forr'ad hold, Spew,' Trapp snarled viciously, 'an' you bring up as many o' them Viper missile launchers as yer can carry – we'll see 'oo's scared of Ivan bloody submarines, Mister. WE'll see!'

'Oh Lord,' I panicked. 'He's really gone crazy. Now he imagines he's the US Sixth Fleet . . .'

Trapp rushed to the head of the ladder. 'An' give one ter Choker Bligh on yer way back,' he screamed at Spew's obligingly departing figure. 'Choker's always wanted ter massacre a ship's crew legitimate!'

I took a deep breath. 'You really *can't*,' I pointed out as logically as I could, 'expect to take on a major Soviet Mediterranean Fleet hunter-killer – which will almost certainly attack us from under water anyway – with a fucking anti-TANK gun!'

He grinned unexpectedly, temperamentally mercurial as ever.

'Nit-pickin' again, eh Mister?'

'Lord, no,' I said. 'Perish the thought. I'm only making small talk to relieve the boredom.'

'Anyroad, them Russkies've probably hopped it by now,' Trapp added almost disappointedly. Then he caught my eye. 'But I won't say as ter WHY I thinks that,' he added hastily.

. . . .wheeeeEEEEE . . .

Trapp frowned, back to being irritable. 'There's that *bloody* noise again.'

. . . EEEEEeeeeee . . .

It had faded by the time I reached the wing and glanced a little more anxiously down into the black heaving water.

Still nothing.

Hurriedly I swept the horizon again while, below me, the *Spatz* continued its spitting damnedest to disjoin us at the rivet holes while, above our heads, the broomstick funnel oscillated in creaky, leaky angulation. Even the embarrassing confusion astern had faded to a less emotive distance.

A good two minutes passed in contemplation without Trapp upsetting anyone. Even I'd begun to feel some hope for our eventual survival: certainly any Soviet captain intending to kill us would've made his move long before now and, after Trapp's latest misadventure into the world of maritime battle strategy, there wasn't anyone else left to threaten us.

It all seemed a bit of an anti-climax, in a way.

*

Eventually the Captain had stirred.

'I reckon we might as well go about an' head homewards now,' he'd grunted still feeling, I suspected, a little thwarted at not being allowed to be a warship since having remembered we were carrying about as much high explosive as a proper one would anyway.

Mister Spew's shambling silhouette reappeared at the head of the bridge ladder. 'Captin sir? There's somefink I reckon –'

'Look, jus' take 'em BACK,' Trapp smarted, frustration and disappointment now plainly evident. 'There's nothin' happening. It's all bloody over.'

. . . wheeeeEEEEEEE . . . ?

'There's that bloody *noise* again!'

'Mister Miller sir?' Spew persisted, trying me this time and tendering something which didn't look at all like a Viper rocket launcher. More squat. Sort of bulkier, with wires hanging from it. 'I found it in the 'old among all them explosives. There's lots more like it – wiv' the wires an' that.'

. . . EEEEE*EEEEEE* . . . !

'Hang *on* a minute,' I snapped anxiously, frowning down from the wing yet again.

I saw it this time – the unmistakable streak of phosphorescence which was making the noise.

Coming straight *for* me!

'TorPEDOOOooo!' I heard myself yell. 'Starboard BEAM!'

'Hard a port the *wheel*!' Trapp roared, reacting instantly.

Until . . .

'SubmarIIIIINE!' Gorbals *Wullie* shrieked. 'Surfacin' on the PORT BOW!'

'Well . . . Oh, 'ard a STARB'D then!' Trapp mouthed in numbed fury.

'It's got a dead natty clock in it.' Spew insisted, waggling his bloody box right under my already fear-popping eyes.

'TIME BOMB!' I screamed. '. . . on the *BRIDGE*!'

Chapter Seventeen

Trapp and a modern homing torpedo have a great deal in common, when you consider it.

For a start, they're both utterly bent on self-destruction, while taking everyone and everything unfortunate enough to get in the way along with them.

Furthermore, once having embarked upon a specific objective, they are both implacably obstinate, both totally oblivious to any attempts at external control, and both are programmed to think furiously – but, again in both cases, without ever necessarily arriving at a logical conclusion.

The self-targeting, or homing, torpedo does its limited best to cope with the information gathered by its somewhat crude electronic sensors – its basic eyes and ears – by means of a micro-processor brain.

Trapp employed only God knew what.

. . . which was why the Russian torpedo missed us.

Regularly!

Christ – it had been *trying* to sink us for the last ten MINUTES, don't you see? Only we hadn't caught it at it. Just going round and round and round in increasingly frustrated circles, it must have been: each one becoming progressively smaller, yet still missing the *Charon II* every time.

. . . oh, it knew it had been sent by its parent submarine to kill some floating object – the Leningrad micro-chips in its metallic brain had been told to get out there and do just that; that Soviet torpedoes are really only *born* for the sole purpose of sinking ships – preferably ones belonging to NATO but not to be *too* selective – and have very little social justification for whizzing around the ocean otherwise.

It had probably been a fairly clever torpedo as torpedoes go, perfectly well able to anticipate even the *Charon*'s erratic course and somewhat laughable speed . . . but that was where it became limited. Unable to work out a logical solution as to why it still kept *missing* success?

Just like Trapp was. Once he became distracted; once events ceased to conform to his particularly fixed opinions of how they should behave. Things he reckoned he knew like the back o' his 'and?

Though to be fair the Russian scientists had probably never conceived of a target quite like Trapp's *Charon*. They'd foolishly assumed any target vessel would be a reasonably stable structure for a start, with some draft and even a keel so's it wouldn't simply topple over in the middle of some night and sink. So they hadn't told the torpedo that it might, one day, be confronted by a problem which was neither stable nor, for that matter, could possibly even float by any marine architect's yardstick – one which simply squatted waterbeetle-like on the surface of the water so's there was only a few feet of it actually *in* the element it was mis-designed for.

So the Trapp-cloned torpedo had persisted in homing in on us at the minimum depth its inelastic brain had been programmed to expect of a proper ship . . . and because it couldn't extend pure furious thought to embrace logic, had kept whirring clean under our keel. Time and time again.

Mind you . . . it had *still* scared the SHIT out of me!

'Hard a st'bd,' Trapp had commanded to avoid the submarine.

'Mak' up yer bluidy MIND, wull ye?' Wullie screamed

back, having just that second been ordered to go to *port*. To avoid the thoughtless torpedo.

'Well, what d'yer fink then, Mister Miller sir?' Second Officer Spew, undisputed shipboard *doyen* of the *idée fixe*, pursued.

About the time bomb.

I didn't answer right away. I was still hanging perilously over the rickety wing of the bridge trying to keep my legs bent at the knees so's the kick of the explosion wouldn't drive my thigh bones clear up through my diaphragm – which was me being more than optimistic anyway, considering its proximity – and staring hypnotically as the speeding line of bubbles whirred straight under the *Charon*. Right *below* where I was standing.

. . . wheeeeEEEEE . . .

Priorities . . . ? You gotter be *joking*?

. . . EEEEEEeeeee . . .

It reappeared from under the port side . . . then uttered a funny, tired sort of wheeze as its electric motor finally ran out of amps before floating wearily to the surface where it wallowed, no doubt *still* thinking furiously – in Russian, I suppose – about precisely WHY it had been a failure.

Which, judging by his black-incensed complexion, was exactly what Trapp appeared to be doing as well right then. Only in your basic colourful Anglo-Saxon.

'Golly, it's even got an *alarm* clock,' Mister Spew said delightedly. Then his brows met in the middle. 'Funny. It's set ter ring in about ten minnits, Mist –'

'Everybody DOWWWWWWN!' I roared, snatching the malignant package and throwing it as far from the side of the ship as I could. Fortunately Spew had found it in time, but there was no point in taking chances . . . !

BOOOOOOoooooom . . . !

I stood there numbly, with amatol-tainted water dripping from me and splaying into a widening pool on the deck. Its anti-handling device must have triggered instantly with the impact of the demolition charge hitting the surface. Only Spew's God – who must have been particularly tolerant out of sheer necessity – and the man who'd actually put the bomb together could have explained why that particular one had possessed a less sensitive mercury switch than most.

But I should've suspected. I should have realized Chernyshev had left far too docilely not to have left something aboard to ensure our certain liquidation. I mean – a hold full of high explosive, compliments of the KGB . . . ? Yet Trapp, with his profit-blinkered brain, his pocket-calculator myopia, had been pleased as a cat with two tails over pulling off a deal for its acquis*ition*?

'Did you say there were more of those clock things down there, Spew?' I asked, ever so calmly.

'Lots, Mister Miller,' he reassured me, genuinely anxious that I shouldn't be too upset over having spoilt one. 'An' don't worry, they're all workin' lively. I could 'ear 'em tickin'.'

Nobody said anything for a few moments. Most noticeably, Trapp.

Through the by then practically demolished wheelhouse I watched as the second black submarine nosed silently, vengefully, towards us.

She *was* Russian. Soviet Foxtrot diesel-electric patrol class; small enough to operate undetected inside the shallow waters bounded by Qaddafi's Line of Death, and nasty enough to ensure the accuracy of that description. Already I could make out figures of armed sailors swarming through hatches on to her long foredeck, preparing to board and finally put the seal to Comrade Colonel Chernyshev's operational orders.

It was a curious irony, typically Trapp-like of course, that in a world of at least semi-educated torpedoes and ballistic nuclear missiles and space flight to the Moon, his beloved *Charon* should obdurately remain such an anachronism that the only way man's military ingenuity could contrive to destroy her and the utter incompetents who sailed her, was by clambering over our crumbling bulwarks and doing a cutlass-to-throat job.

I felt the scarred deck throbbing violently beneath us as Bucalosie flung the last of his hysterical Latin temperament along with a few hammers and wrenches at the bloody *Spatz* to encourage it to go even faster than its diabolical Prussian designers had planned.

'Even steaming flat out we've got fifteen minutes at most before she overtakes us,' I snarled at Trapp. Then I shrugged. 'But what the hell: it's not important.'

'Why isn't it?' Trapp perked up hopefully, clutching at any straw.

'Because the bloody BOMBS'll go off in *ten*!'

'Er . . . mair like aboot eight, now,' Wullie corrected anxiously.

'We could go an' . . .' Trapp saw the look in Wullie's eye. 'I could order *Spew* ter go an' ditch the rest?'

'We'll all get blown to hell the moment he touches 'em,' I dismissed flatly. 'Luck and sheer bloody stupidity seldom combine more than once.'

'No' usually onyway,' Wullie modified, glancing pointedly at his Captain.

I took a deep breath.

'We don't have any choice. You've *got* to abandon, Trapp; before we all go down – up – with her. Then . . . ?' I waved my hands uncertainly. 'I dunno: just hope the Russians can't find us in the dark, I suppose.'

'Abandon, Mister?' he spluttered, beginning to jump up and down. 'ABANDON me precious *Jewel*: me Queen o' the Seas?'

The last remaining door to the wheelhouse creaked tiredly, listed, then fell off with a crash.

Seven minutes left . . . I glanced nervously astern. The

submarine was catching up faster than I'd anticipated.

'You could always steal another one. Maybe even one that floats properly next time?' I tempted hopefully.

'NEVER, Mister!' Trapp roared. 'D'you 'ear? Never will I give up me ship. Never while there's a puff o' steam lef' in 'er boile . . . !'

There echoed a massive BANG from somewhere down below. Then a giant tearing of long-past-fatigued metal and splintering of wood followed instantly by a pandemonium of appeals and operationally expedient prayer from the foredeck.

The old *Charon* began to slew wearily to starboard as she lost way for the very last time, then simply lay listing and dead in the water.

'Mah Goad but they bombs've gone OFF,' Wullie bawled. 'Ah could hae telt ye Russian clocks wis bluidy useless: aye goin' fast . . .'

Steam began to shriek from *Charon II*'s spindle funnel as it slowly, ever so majestically, keeled over to collapse in a thunderous cloud of rust clear through the engine-room skylight. Chief Engineer Bucalosie shot on deck like a pitch-black cork from a particularly dirty bottle and shook his cartoon-enormous tattooed fist at the bridge.

'Amma sicka fed uppa, Capitano!' the Chief screamed. 'Your bloddy engine – SHE issa finito . . . ! AMMA bloddy finito! Thissa bloddy ship – SHE issa finit . . . !'

. . . we had, maybe, five minutes left?

'ABANDOOOOOOOON *SHIP*!' Trapp roared.

Having finally learned something. Even *if* only from a rather stupid torpedo.

Chapter Eighteen

You've probably guessed the rest already. How, after all that had happened, we finally escaped the clutches of the Russian bear.

Even survived the Third World War, come to that.

By accident, of course. Though Trapp will always boast it was his sheer mastery of the craft of deception which made the impossible possible.

I remember the last minutes of the *Charon II* only as a nightmare approaching the level of the loss of Trapp's first *Charon* a long war before.

Even as we tumbled down the collapsing bridge ladder we were met with a panic-stricken tide of humanity on the boat deck. One half of the crew were babbling and scrabbling to clamber *into* the multi-coloured Arab *caique* I'd had the blessed inspiration to pick up from Djibela, while the other half were babbling and scrabbling to climb OUT of it – largely on account of the fact that no one had thought to *launch* the bloody thing first, and there didn't seem a lot of point just sitting in a boat still suspended from the davits while waiting for the bloody ship to blow up!

Bosun Bligh was the only one doing a seaman's job. Standing there brandishing his beloved marlin spike and trying to hold them off like he'd seen them do on *SOS Titanic*.

'Get BACK, yer scurvy dogs!' he was roaring, happy as a pig in muck which, on reflection, was a very good analogy. 'GEBBACK yer * * * * * * * * * * DOGS!'

'Oh, do shut *UP*,' Trapp growled irritably, poking Choker forcibly amidships with the tiller bar.

'. . . go ON, then! Get on with wot yer paid for, Mister,' he snarled at me. 'Launch number one lifeboat hif you please.'

Number ONE lifeboat?

. . . maybe four minutes left. And the Russian hit squad already tensed to jump aboard as soon as the submarine nosed ever so carefully against the *Charon*'s port side.

'Stand-by to swing out – *star*board side!'

I said.

We'd barely pulled clear when the old *Charon II* blew up.

Roughly half a century later than she should've done, if her previous owners had had any sense.

Loaded down to the gun'les with that nauseous crew, with Trapp staring, uncharacteristically silent, over his shoulder and Gorbals Wullie curled up on the bottom-boards with his fingers in his ears, there had been only the urgent thump of crude oars in thole pins as most of 'em sweated for the first time in their misbegotten lives while mesmerically watching the slender silhouetted periscope standard of the Russian boat slide in behind, and hard against, the forlorn and listing hulk.

We all heard the staccato yammer of the Kalashnikov PPKs spraying her upperworks just to make sure the boarding would be unopposed . . . then it happened.

A great, eerie flash in the sea. Bluish-white. With long luminous fingers darting out below the surface. Then a sort of pause as if nothing was taking place at all – and then a sudden contraction of the sea all around the sad old relic . . . and a giant rolling, soaring blister of yellow fire sweeping up towards the frightened sky with white water sucking up behind it and the first roar of the

266

explosion scampering towards us across the intervening waves.

'Jesus!' someone said quietly.

That was all.

But even for men such as those, the murder of a ship was a time for silent reflection.

... then the Soviet Foxtrot blew up with an even greater detonation as all her thinking torpedoes became utterly confused and decided that, when in doubt, panic.

... and then there was nothing. No submarine.

No *Charon*.

Only rusted bits and pieces still raising little white splashes all around us.

And half of a very old ship's wheel which fell from heaven to float right alongside the *caique*.

Silently I reached out and handed it to Trapp who took it carefully, then just sat hugging it, all hunched up in the sternsheets.

I looked away.

He was crying.

Epilogue

A British submarine picked us up in the end. Thanks to Trapp it was to prove a busy night for submarines in the Gulf of Sirte. British, American, almost certainly more Russians with, probably, an Israeli boat or two and maybe the odd Egyptian and Syrian watching rather dumbfoundedly from the wings.

There were no Libyan warships around. Colonel Qaddafi had probably decided against insisting on his Line of Death for the night. Especially now he didn't have any nuclear prospects to back it up.

The British submarine captain was very tense, and her crew stayed closed up in War Condition Red all night. He wasn't very pleased with Trapp either at first, because there hadn't been a World War going before Trapp visited Libya, but of course he didn't really know the full facts about Trapp's and our involvement.

But by the time Trapp had finished explaining them, and modifying them just a little bit in the telling – and who else was left alive to dispute Trapp's Truth . . . ? Well, the captain seemed a bit more amenable. Even called Trapp 'sir' once or twice and let him use the officers' wardroom and gave him a blanket to put round his shoulders and a mug of Royal Navy rum to clasp in his horny lying hand.

Gorbals Wullie got to stay with Trapp, being his batman and Key Personnel, which pleased Wullie no end even though the Captain did insist on his leaving his cap with the razor blades in it in the charge of the submarine's master-at-arms.

He let me use the wardroom, too. Being one of Trapp's ship's officers and still Naval Reserve to boot.

He didn't let Mister Spew use it, officer or not. One had to draw a limit on hospitality . . . but Mister Spew didn't mind. He spent a deeply absorbed night in the senior rates' mess trying to figure for once an' for all exactly what *did* happen to Hermann.

Choker Bligh was carried, foaming at the mouth, to be locked firmly in the heads – the junior seamen's toilet compartment – where *he* spent the first half of an absorbed night unscrewing every valve he could find, tryin' ter sink the fuckin' boat!

After that, the rest of Trapp's appalling crew were locked in the forr'ad torpedo room under heavily armed guard, Royal Naval hospitality or not.

The submarine carried the latest British homing torpedo, the Tigerfish: a very educated missile, much cleverer than the Russians.

It was quite awesome, when you consider it. That just one torpedo had a greater capacity for using its brain than the whole of Trapp's crowd put together.

And the Third World War that Trapp had started . . . ?

No, I KNOW you didn't hear much about it. That Moscow and New York and London are still on the map – but I never said it was a *long* war, did I?

It was largely over by morning, fortunately. Oh sure, the hot lines had been melting between the Superpowers like mad for a bit while they all sat with fingers on their thermo-nuclear buttons – which must have miffed Colonel Qaddafi no end seeing he didn't have one to look forward to pressing any more. But eventually they'd agreed that everybody had lost one major fleet unit thanks to Trapp: the American sunk by the British, the

Brit by the Russians . . . and the Russian as much by accident as by Trapp's design.

So they called World War Three a draw before EVERY-body wanted in on it.

. . . and all the torpedoes got told to go back to just *thinking* about the future.

And Trapp himself. And Gorbals Wullie?

Well, the cancer must've got to Trapp eventually, which almost certainly meant that Wullie would have died soon after too, of a broken heart. I'll probably never know for sure. But he DID swear to me that time in Brindisi that he *had* incurable cancer, didn't he? I mean, I wouldn't have gone with him to Ras al Djibela if he hadn't put moral pressure on me by telling me that.

Mind you, he looked suspiciously bloody healthy all the same. The last time I saw him as the submarine landed him and Wullie ashore covertly in the Lebanon, being the one place in the world where it was unlikely they could enforce all the arrest warrants Interpol had forwarded on Trapp.

I was never quite sure why the British Government took that politically risky chance for him. I think it was because someone high up in the Ministry of Defence told the submarine captain to get rid of him *anywhere*, the more dangerous the better, just in case he decided to rejoin the Royal Navy and turn it all into an internashnul business enterprise.

But they hadn't known about the cancer, of course.

So Captain Edward Trapp is dead, and there's an end to him. And hopefully, in the fullness of time, to my nightmares.

Good sailing, Trapp! And you too, Gorbals Wullie. Voyaging for ever and together in the hands of Charon across those Satanic Stygian waters already so familiar to you.

God help me, I loved you both . . .

I got a letter the other day. Grubby as anything. And still sticky with jam.
  It said:

deer mister miller: if you
reely want ter make a lot
o money

ring Singapore 7389

I smiled softly. Wistfully. And put it in a drawer.
  I think I'll have another look at it soon.
  . . . now I've finished telling you about Trapp.